Zeru Zeru Girl

Barbara Kerr

In loving memory of Peter Jason Davis who deeply felt the injustice and suffering of so many people and animals in the world.

O, I have suffered
With those that I saw suffer!"
> --William Shakespeare
> Miranda from *The Tempest*,
> Act I, Scene 2

The Swahili phrase *zeru zeru* translates to "ghost people" and in Tanzania refers to one of every fourteen hundred citizens with albinism. The phrase is both descriptive and prophetic, as much a metaphor for the white skin resulting from the condition's absence of melanin as it is a reflection of societal treatment. From the beginning of their lives, people with albinism are insulted, mocked, harassed, and isolated. When they are killed in this part of the world, their bodies are often never recovered. Like ghosts, they disappear.

> --Soraya Matos, "The Ghost People of Tanzania,"
> *Orion Magazine*

Table of Contents

PART ONE

1

Arusha, Tanzania, 1985

Lost in thought, Samuel climbed three flights of stairs to unlock the door to his and Lily's one-bedroom apartment. He paused a moment at the door to arrange a smile on his face. No use in getting Lily upset. She was good at reading his moods, maybe even his thoughts, though just considering this possibility made him shudder. He had been thinking obsessively for the past few weeks about what to do to protect their baby girl.

He hesitated in the doorway. Lily was not there to greet him with the Annika in her arms. There were no smells of dinner, which Lily had never failed to have ready at the end of his long hours at the Kibo Palace Hotel. He heard only the sounds that drifted up from the swarm of tuk-tuks, motorbikes, and the occasional auto in the street three stories below. As he closed the door behind him and slid the bolts on both locks, the clicks echoed in the silent apartment. His smile was replaced by tight lips and a clenched jaw.

Samuel stood still, moving only his eyes. He had learned to do this as a boy, hunting the lion with the men of his village. He took in the kitchen area--a wooden table and two chairs, a hot plate on the counter. Three baby bottles stood in neat alignment on the drying rack near the sink. He glanced at the sparsely furnished living room. At the line of bright pillows arranged to dress up the rescued sofa. The plush toy elephant rested on a pink and yellow blanket folded neatly at one end. A framed photograph and a lamp on an end table. Everything was as usual, clean and tidy, the way Lily kept it.

He was momentarily reassured by the smells of baby lotion and cleaning fluid, but his thoughts raced, searching for the meaning of the undisturbed silence. One leg quivered as he held his muscles taut, ready. Something wasn't right. He had thought there would be more time to make a decision. More time to make a convincing plea to Lily. More time to keep his family safe.

A muffled cry made him open his eyes wide. He turned his head toward the bedroom. Taking two silent strides into the kitchen, he opened a drawer and lifted out the sharp knife Lily used for cutting up a chicken. Another brief cry floated from the bedroom.

"Lily! Where are you?" His lips and mouth were dry, his voice hoarse.

"I'm here," Lily said, letting out a high-pitched squeal. Like a young zebra, he thought, caught in the jaws of the lion.

He pulled the closet door open, the knife held ready above his head. Lily and Annika were on the floor half-hidden beneath the clothes. The baby's skin glowed in the dim light, as white as the bleached cloths Samuel had spread on tables that day in the hotel dining room, as white as the snow they could sometimes glimpse at the top of Mt. Kilimanjaro. The chubby-cheeked child looked up at him, a smile forming on her face with tears still visible in her violet-blue eyes. "Ba," she cried, lifting her hands in the air so he would pick her up.

Samuel placed the knife on the floor and took the child into his arms, hugging her close to his chest.

He helped Lily stand up. "Lily! Are you hurt? Sick? Is Annika sick?"

"No, no. But they are coming, Sam. They are coming!" Panting for breath, she grasped his arms. Her eyes shone with crazed determination. "They must not find our baby, Samuel. We must leave here. They will come in the night. Or when you are at work. We must leave here now."

"Please be calm, my love. Tell me what has happened." As he pulled Lily close to him and the baby, he felt Lily soften a little. "Don't worry now, my love. Everything will be okay. I will keep you safe." He kissed Lily on one smooth, bronze cheek. "Tell me what has frightened you so."

Lily tipped her chin back to look her husband in the eye. "Everything is not okay. Cannot be okay. You must listen to me now, Samuel." She paused and closed her eyes for a few seconds. Then her words came in a rush. "Cousin Latifa came in secret to tell me. She was here only two minutes. Her husband has betrayed us! His mind is only on money."

"Rafiki." Samuel's brow furrowed in a frown. Anger flooded every muscle of his body.

"Our Annika is valuable to him," said Lily. Will make him very rich. Or very lucky," she added, bringing one hand up to cover her trembling lips.

Samuel murmured, "I've never really trusted him." How had Rafiki afforded a new motorbike and a leather jacket? And a new set of cooking pots for Latifa?

Samuel shook his head as Lily looked away. He would not re-open that argument now. He knew Lily had not wanted to believe anything bad about her cousin's husband.

Lily gently placed her hand on Samuel's cheek. "Please, Sam. Please listen to me. Latifa said Rafiki went to see a healer--a witch doctor--just outside the city. And then she overheard him talking to some bad men to do ... terrible things. Please! They will come. This is true. I know it is true."

The baby was bumping her forehead into Samuel's and giggling. He gently bumped heads a few times and then kissed the woolly blond hairs on Annika's head, marveling for the thousandth time that this fair, precious child was their flesh and blood. He hadn't known he could love so deeply. That he could feel so connected to another human being. *They will not touch one hair of your head, my little beauty. I will keep you safe.*

He got Lily to sit down next to him on the sagging sofa and handed the plush white elephant to Annika, who nestled between them. He had purchased the toy at the hotel gift shop the day after she was born ten months ago. It had become her favorite, a comfort as she drank her bottle of milk before going to sleep.

Everything was happening so quickly. Drums pounded in Sam's ears. He pressed both hands over his eyes for several seconds.

"Be calm now and listen to me, please, my love." He took a deep breath and exhaled. "During these past weeks, I've been talking to a guest at the hotel, a doctor from England. He asked me about the politicians in our country and about their beliefs in buying luck and wealth from our witch doctors. I've told him what is true. That many in our villages, and our cities too, believe in the old medicine, in the lies. And I ... I told him about Annika."

"You told him? Why would you tell a stranger about her?" Lily stared at him with her mouth open in disbelief.

Annika crawled onto Samuel's lap and clapped her hands. Samuel and Lily laughed and clapped their hands too. They were rewarded with a chortle and a wide smile on their daughter's face.

Samuel took another deep breath. "Please, Lily. Let me explain." Lily would not meet his eyes. "Some time ago, the doctor showed me an article in his newspaper about the *zeru zeru* here. It was a shocking piece on the mutilation and murder of these children from a village just a few miles outside Arusha. White children." He paused and glanced at his wife. "Like Annika."

Lily put her hands up to her ears. "No! You must not speak aloud of these things. You will bring us bad luck. Very bad luck."

At that moment, he felt vomit rising from his stomach. He swallowed the sour bile.

"The doctor is European, but he knows all about this special kind of whiteness." Samuel placed his hand on Annika's head. He tried to smile at her as she sucked on an ear of the toy elephant.

Lily brought her hands down from her ears. She didn't look at him, but Samuel knew she was listening.

"The doctor said that in his country--in England--it is not dangerous to be so white like Annika. And Lily . . . he may be able to help us." He wanted to say more, but he feared Lily's reaction.

In the next moment, Lily's words jumped out of her throat, harsh and loud, startling them both. "How? How can he help? Just tell me, Sam, why would a white man help us?"

Samuel hesitated, blinking his eyes several times. "He thinks--" Again, Samuel heard the drums pounding in his ears. He took a deep breath and continued. "He thinks he can get Annika on a flight to England with you as her nurse." He steeled himself to listen to his wife's reply.

"Her nurse?" Lily scoffed in a way that sounded like a water buffalo's snort. "What nonsense is this, Samuel? Listen to yourself. England? What would we do in England? Shall we visit the queen? Drink tea at the palace? And where would you be?"

"I will follow--later."

"Later?" She stared at him, a fierce light burning in her eyes.

"I have to get a visa first, but--"

"A visa? And what about me?" Lily's voice was high and tight, as if she were being strangled.

"The doctor can get you a special ticket on an NGO classification. For an emergency, he said. He understands the danger here for our daughter. He may be able to arrange a ticket. If we agree."

Lily folded both arms over her chest, hugging her shoulders. "What are you saying? Leave our home? Our families? That is not possible. No. No. No."

"In England, no one cares about another white face. They have a scientific way to explain this kind of whiteness, and everyone believes it. Our daughter can live a normal life without fear. Listen, Lily, Annika can even go to school, have a future."

"No. No. We cannot leave our country and . . . everything. How would we live among the white people? They do not even see us."

"That's not true, Lily. I talk to such people every day at the hotel. They are like any people. Some are kind and generous. Some are rude and selfish. I am not afraid of them."

Lily looked into her husband's eyes. Her voice was calmer now, but her dark eyes flashed as she spoke. "You are not afraid. You are a man. But how can I, an African woman, hold up her head in such a place? I cannot do this, Samuel."

Annika had tired of the elephant and was fussing. Lily stood and lifted her from Samuel's arms, positioning her on one hip. She began to sway back and forth to a rhythm known to all mothers for soothing babies.

"But you know that what cousin Latifa said is true," Samuel said. "They will come for our daughter. Sooner or later. I cannot even think about what that means, but I know it's pure evil."

He would not tell Lily of the pictures in the article that Dr. Oliver had shown him. Images of small children found lifeless, their limbs severed with machetes. Their mutilated bodies ransacked for their magical organs and left lying on dark stains of their blood. Samuel had not wanted to look at the images, but when he did, he could not help staring at the children's white hair and skin, thinking about their innocence.

Lily paused her swaying for a moment and looked at her husband, her eyes wide. "I have an idea. Listen, Samuel. We can go away! We can escape from these monsters. Perhaps Dar es Salaam. Or the lake island we have heard about to the north. Annika would be safe there."

Samuel heard the mixture of hope and desperation in her voice. Everything inside his body was shaking like a volcano about to erupt. He willed himself to speak calmly. "We could go to another town, another city, but we can't keep Annika hidden forever. This problem will follow us wherever we go in this country. Many people believe this nonsense about their bones, their fingers, their hair. Lily, you know what happens."

He turned his eyes away from her and bowed his head. He had not wanted to speak so harshly to his wife. He had not wanted to remember the images from the newspaper.

Annika had found the bright yellow beads around Lily's neck and was putting them in her mouth. "No, no, my sweet babe. I will get you something good to eat." Lily took a few quick steps and stood behind the kitchen counter. Samuel knew she was thinking about what he had said.

"Tell me more about this white doctor," Lily said with a dark frown.

"Oliver. His name is Dr. Oliver. He is a doctor for babies and children in London, and he has been here in Africa for two months to treat children." Lily was humming to Annika as she fixed dinner. Samuel added, "He is a good man, Lily." He glanced at her to gauge her reaction.

Lily tipped her head to one side as she looked at him. "You don't know this man. How do you trust him so easily?"

Samuel picked up the toy elephant from the floor and held it. "Dr. Oliver has requested to sit always in my section at breakfast and dinner. He asked me many questions about our life here. Not just about safari tours and Big Five animals like most European guests. And he told me a lot about what it's like in England. About great stone castles and blankets of snow in the winter on all the houses and fields. He has been patient when I have been most busy taking care of other guests. And always generous."

Samuel paused, trying to read Lily's expression. Why had he put off speaking to her for all these weeks? What if it was too late? *Why can't I just make a decision like a man?*

"He and his wife are leaving soon to return to England. He can take you and Annika with him. They'll help us find a place to live. He will help me find a job."

Lily was shaking her head. "This sounds like a nice story. A story for little children. A story that cannot be true." She stared at him from the kitchen. "Real people cannot enter a storybook, Sam."

A sharp knock sounded on the front door of the apartment.

Samuel stood, his eyes wide as he looked at his wife and child. She looked back at him and put her hand up to her mouth.

His shoulders tightened. He motioned for Lily to take Annika into the bedroom and followed her in. The knock sounded again. Lily whimpered softly as she sat beneath the clothes, clutching Annika against her chest.

He closed the closet door and picked up the knife from the floor where he had dropped it earlier.

Moving silently to the front door, he gripped the worn handle of the knife behind his back. His breaths came fast and shallow as he stood alert, one ear pressed to the door. Surely Rafiki would not come so boldly to take his daughter . . .

He waited. Beads of sweat dripped into his eyes. No more knocks came, but he heard the rustle of paper. And then footsteps heading down the hall to the stairs.

When a few minutes had passed in silence, he cracked open the door. Then he opened it a little wider. He grabbed an envelope from the floor, shut the door, and slid the bolts on the locks. He rested his forehead against the doorframe for a few seconds, trying to calm his breathing.

"It's okay. You can come out," he called to Lily. "It is just a letter. From Dr. Oliver, I think."

Without a word or a look at her husband, Lily walked to the kitchen, with Annika perched on her hip. She began pulling leftovers out of their small fridge.

Samuel tore open the envelope, imprinted with the name of the Kibo Palace Hotel, and looked at the neatly printed words in English. He gave silent thanks to his teachers at the School of St. Jude and read:

Our flight leaves at 10:00 on Friday morning. If you have made your decision, I will meet you outside the hotel entrance at 6:30 that morning. All necessary arrangements are in place. It is for the best, my friend. --Oliver Canfield, M.D.

While Lily heated some stew on the hotplate, Samuel read her the doctor's note. She said nothing. She was still silent as they sat down to eat. Holding Annika on her lap, she spooned mashed peas and yams into the child's eager mouth, smiling at her, encouraging her.

Samuel waited for Lily to say something as he pushed the stew around on his plate. Lily was a woman who could think for herself. He couldn't hurry her. Her silence, he decided, was a good sign. In his mind's eye, he could almost see her sorting what she had heard into buckets of truths and lies, measuring the weight of each. He loved her for that. He knew that she might still decide that this opportunity was a lie. But he also knew that her animal instinct to keep their child safe would win out. The deep instinct of a lioness with her cub would throw the buckets of truths and lies into confusion.

"This Friday?" Lily scoffed. "That is not possible." She kept her eyes focused on Annika, her chin raised, and her mouth set in defiance.

"But it's a chance, Lily, a chance for Annika. We can't live like this, afraid every minute for our child. I'm working, worrying about you both, all the day long. Sometimes, I think I'll go crazy worrying. A crazy man in a crazy world," he mumbled as he ran his hand over his closely cropped head.

For one moment Samuel considered dropping to his knees in front of her. He would beg her to save his child. But when he looked up, he saw his own fear and desperation mirrored in Lily's eyes. No longer defiant or stubborn. No longer weighing the buckets of truths and lies. He knew what to say now. "Annika is not safe here. We must do this to save her life."

Lily placed a final spoonful of food into Annika's mouth, then wiped her daughter's chin. She was sobbing quietly. "But how do you know we'll be safe with this man? If Rafiki, one of our own family, can betray us, anyone--especially a white man--can do the same."

Tears shone on Lily's cheeks. Samuel got up from his seat, pulled his chair next to hers and placed his arm around her shoulders.

"Lily, I love you and Annika with everything that's in me. It's my duty to keep my family safe. I trust this man to help us."

She leaned her head against his chest in wordless submission. Tears dampened her husband's shirt.

* * *

Two days later, the taxi, a rusted, mustard yellow Toyota of indeterminate age, beeped again in the stillness of the early morning.

"Why, Sam? You must come to the airport with us." Lily's eyes pleaded with her husband even as she raised her chin like a recalcitrant child.

"Lily, I must show up at work. They will be expecting me. Come, we'll ride together to the hotel. We'll meet the doctor there. The taxi is waiting."

Annika began fussing, and Lily's attention turned to the child. She looked around the apartment to be sure she had packed everything she and the baby would need for the journey. Bottles and baby formula, a blanket and sweaters, diapers and creme. Before walking out the door, she picked up a framed photo of herself and Samuel. In the picture, she was holding Annika, a tiny bundle swaddled in a soft blanket. The photo had been taken by the kind nurse at the Mount Meru Hospital just after Annika was born ten months ago. Lily slipped it into a side pocket of the diaper bag that was already full to overflowing.

The taxi smelled of cigarette smoke and sweat. Samuel saw Lily's eyes fill with tears as they pulled into the road, but she managed to hold them back. The time for crying was done.

She turned her head toward Samuel, who held Annika and the beloved toy elephant. She watched as he kissed the tiny heart-shaped birthmark—the only bit of color on Annika's body—at the nape of her neck. Annika patted her father's face, her transparent violet-blue eyes looking directly into the deep brown of his, her expression serious as if asking a question.

"What will you tell people?" Lily asked. "You must not give cousin Latifa away."

"No, no. I wouldn't do that. I'll say you've gone away with Annika to get her eyes fixed. That's partly true anyway."

A few minutes later, they were at the Kibo Palace Hotel, where Samuel had worked six days a week for the past three years. He helped Lily out of the car and placed Annika into her arms. He saw the doctor was already waiting there with his wife. Oliver Canfield, a tall, slim man in his fifties, wore an unwrinkled tan suit with a starched white shirt and blue striped tie. His neatly brushed graying hair and trimmed beard gave him a look of authority. He and his wife were waiting with their baggage among the white columns that graced the hotel entrance. A shuttle van stood in the driveway.

"I'm Oliver Canfield, and it is my pleasure to meet you and your daughter," the doctor said to Lily in crisp British English. "I am sorry we meet under such circumstances, but you are doing the brave thing for the sake of your daughter." He smiled at her and Annika.

Lily tried to smile back as she studied his face. She wondered if he were hiding something behind his beard. Or if white men somehow smiled differently.

"And this is my wife, Charlotte Canfield."

Lily turned to her, a petite, blondish woman, perhaps ten or more years younger than her husband. She was thin with an angular face. She wore a floral print dress with a short cotton jacket and white, heeled shoes.

"Hello," Lily managed to say.

"Pleased to meet you." Charlotte nodded her head and gave a small, tight-lipped smile. She glanced at Annika but said nothing.

Samuel helped place Lily's battered suitcase in the back of the shuttle and then came around to hug his wife and daughter. "I will come as soon as I can," he whispered. "Be safe, my darlings." He felt his throat closing up and was unable to say another word. He blinked his eyes several times as he pulled the van's door shut. Standing outside the hotel entrance, he watched as the people he loved most in the world disappeared into morning traffic.

Surely, he had done the right thing, the brave thing? He was remembering the time when he was eleven, when a lion had killed a man of their village during the night. It was Samuel who had found the old uncle partially eaten in the early morning. Samuel's father had allowed his son to go with the party of men to hunt that lion. Samuel had been full of pride to accompany them. A few hours later, when the lion was brought down a mile or so from the village, it was wounded but still alive. Blood seeped from its stomach and spread into a dark red stain beneath the animal, a fascinating and indelible image for eleven-year-old Samuel.

Samuel watched as his father sliced through the beast's tawny hide at its neck with a machete. He wanted to cry out, even to save the big animal. He heard his father then, speaking to him in a low tone that no one else could hear. "*Lisilo budi hutendwa*"--whatever should be done has to be done.

Samuel put away the memory. Now he must hurry to change into his uniform—a short white jacket trimmed with an orange and black African print and a round hat in matching fabric that sat atop his head. He swallowed hard and silently repeated his father's words, *Lisilo budi hutendwa.*

2

Kilimanjaro International Airport, Tanzania, 1985

Lily shifted in the molded plastic chair at the Kilimanjaro Airport, awaiting the plane. Was it too late to change her mind? Could she just stand up and walk out the big glass doors at the entrance to the terminal? She imagined running with Annika across the expanse of parking lots toward the road.

Annika slept, her head nestled against Lily's breast, her tiny pink mouth open just enough to show the first two white teeth that had recently erupted, a source of great joy to Samuel and Lily.

Lily needed to pee, but she didn't want to awaken Annika. Or hand her over to Dr. Canfield and his wife while she went to the ladies' room, only a few steps from where they sat in the waiting area. She doubted that there could be a bathroom on an airplane, but then, what did people do for so many hours in the air?

She did not think she could ask Mrs. Canfield, who sat silently across from her sipping tea from a paper cup. The woman seemed almost as nervous as Lily, reaching down to fiddle with a tote bag at her feet and then leafing absently through a magazine. In the van, on the way to the airport, she had looked at Annika and said, "She is a beautiful child. Please tell me her name again."

"Annika. It was my mother's name," Lily added to be polite. She wasn't sure the doctor's wife understood what she said. She had little opportunity to use English now.

"Annika," Mrs. Canfield repeated. She didn't ask any further questions, and Lily had remained silent as well.

Lily was sure the woman was avoiding eye contact with her. She was used to that. When she was single and worked as a housekeeper at the hotel, she had discovered that most white people behaved as if she were invisible. She was the ghost who changed the linens on their beds, scrubbed green gel toothpaste from their sinks, and pulled hair from their shower drains.

Dr. Canfield held the *Arusha Times* spread out in front of him, blocking his face from view. He seemed uncomfortable in the plastic chair, putting one foot on the other knee, then spreading both legs in front of him before pulling the other leg up. His neatly trimmed beard and mustache were visible only when he turned to a new page. He didn't look in Lily's direction either. Perhaps he was just absorbed in the stories about his own country.

Lily studied Annika's face, drinking in the smooth, perfect features with a deep thirst and a fierce sense of ownership. When Annika was born, Lily had vehemently rejected the superstitions, the ignorant warnings, and the ancient stories about children like Annika. A young nurse's aide, present at the birth, had gasped audibly and then covered a scream. The doctor had ordered her from the room.

"Children like her are often taken by ghosts right after they are born," her cousin Latifa had whispered to Lily as she sat in the hospital bed after delivery. "They say it is for the best."

"No ghosts have stolen my child, and I will fight any who try," Lily had told Latifa. "Do not speak to me of such things. That is just ignorance."

Thank God, Sam had not been so stupid to mistrust his wife by suspecting her of sleeping with a white man. It seemed that everyone knew a story of someone in a nearby village or town whose husband had left his wife after the birth of such a freakish child. A white man! Lily couldn't even imagine such a thing.

Relatives and friends learned not to say anything about Annika in Lily's presence, but she knew that a few had managed to stoke fear in Samuel's heart. He didn't talk about it with her, but she knew it caused him great pain and worry.

Glancing again at the door of the ladies' room, Lily tried to think of what to do. She must pee before boarding the plane. Looking down at Annika's delicate features, she watched the sleeping child's eyes moving back and forth under her eyelids, which were thickly fringed with fine white lashes.

Then, without warning, Annika's eyes flew open, and she began to scream, a sound of terror, Lily thought. A scream she had not heard in all these months since Annika's birth. Could evil dreams visit such a small child? She stood up, hugging her daughter's body close to hers, but still, the child screamed.

"I will check her diaper," she said to the doctor and his wife. She saw them glance at each other. Had they read her thoughts?

"Of course," Dr. Canfield said. "But the plane will be boarding in ten minutes."

In the ladies' room, Lily was able to quiet the baby. She sang *La La Mtoto,* a familiar lullaby in Swahili as she paced the green-tiled floor in front of the two stalls and a sink. She managed to change Annika's diaper and then dandle her on her lap inside a stall as she relieved herself. Was it too late to back out? Could she just return home? Panic tightened her throat, and for a moment, she felt that she couldn't breathe. Perhaps she could call Samuel at work. He would come to the airport. Together, they would figure out a way to keep Annika safe. They would move far away. A secret from everyone.

Annika smiled and patted her mother's face with both hands. Lily smiled back, admiring the dimples on her chubby face. When she left the stall and washed her hands in cold water at the sink, a chill ran through her. In the mirror, she observed herself, an unmistakably black, African woman holding a white, light-eyed child who had been born from her womb. These were truths she could not escape.

She spoke aloud to Annika. "We will go, my darling, my love. We will go to this cold place with a white queen and begin a new life. I will keep you safe and warm. May God help us."

* * *

Dr. Canfield and his wife stood outside the ladies' room as Lily and Annika emerged.

"It's time to board," the doctor said. "Remember, you must let my wife carry Annika when we give our tickets to the attendant. Please remain quiet. I will explain everything."

Lily's heart sped up. How could she put her child into this stranger's arms? "But she would not like to be away from me."

"Charlotte must hold her now," he repeated. Then, in a softer voice, "Just till we get settled on the plane. And remember, if anyone asks you, you are the baby's nurse."

Lily bit her lip. She knew already what she was supposed to say and do. Samuel had explained it all to her last evening as she packed the warmest clothes she could for herself and Annika.

As they walked toward the gate, the doctor's wife placed a cool hand on Lily's arm. "Here, let me take her now." Seeing Lily hesitate, Charlotte tightened her lips and added, "That will be safer."

Reluctantly, Lily allowed her to take Annika from her arms. As Charlotte awkwardly lifted the baby, Lily was surprised to see her turn to Annika with a wide, toothy smile. Annika stared at Charlotte's white face, then back at Lily. The corners of her mouth turned down. Lily smiled at her, trying to make the handoff smooth, trying to assure her child.

A slim young woman, looking sharp and official in a red uniform, stood at the gate. "I must see your passports," she said, looking at Dr. Canfield.

Annika held her arms out to Lily, frightened and insistent, an expression of terror on her face. Charlotte Canfield smiled her toothy smile again and made some strange clucking noises to get her attention. The baby ignored her and let out a howl as she leaned her body toward her mother.

"I will hold her now," Lily said, trying to keep alarm from her voice.

Dr. Canfield was talking to the airline representative at the gate. "Yes, these are our passports. Our daughter is not yet a year old. Here is her birth certificate. The baby's nurse is to accompany us on special permission."

The young woman looked blankly at him. "I'm sorry, sir. I cannot allow your nurse to travel without a passport. I will have to call security."

Lily looked around the huge terminal at the crowds of people waiting in the seats or standing in lines beneath the neon lights that blinked now and then. She was helpless, a ghost standing alone next to her frightened child, unable to comfort her. The foreign smell of jet fuel reached her nostrils and made her dizzy. She thought she might scream as she watched Annika wriggle and cry in the white woman's arms.

Lily pulled the toy elephant from the diaper bag and held it out to Annika to calm her. "Please, let me hold her for just a minute," Lily pleaded.

"I must hold her now," Charlotte told her in a harsh whisper as she turned the child away from Lily. Then she gave an order, still turning her back to Lily. "Get her bottle out of the bag."

Lily's mouth fell open. "No. I cannot do this. I cannot---"

Two security guards in khaki uniforms approached.

"You'll have to come with us, madam," one man said to Lily, placing one hand on her arm. "You must come to the security office."

"But my child. She--"

Dr. Canfield broke in then. "Please, I am a doctor. This woman is our baby's nurse. We have an NGO special pass for the flight."

"I'm not a nurse! This is my child," Lily screamed.

Dr. Canfield spoke softly to one of the security guards. Then he turned to Lily. "I'm sorry, Lily. You will need to go with these men to the security office. They will help straighten everything out. Everything will be fine."

The guards took Lily by the arms as Annika screamed and reached for her. Dr. Canfield took the child from his wife then and called out to Lily, "We will take good care of her until this gets sorted out. Don't worry." Charlotte did not turn to look at Lily.

Lily's body shook with sobs as she looked back to see Annika reaching toward her from the arms of Dr. Canfield as they disappeared into the boarding tunnel. She struggled to free her arms from the officers' hands and kicked at their shins. She would have bitten them if she could have reached them. As they pulled her away from her precious child, the being she loved more than life, her body collapsed and became as limp as a ragdoll, even as she continued screaming and sobbing. Lily could hear Annika's screams long after the guards dragged her toward the airport security office.

* * *

When Samuel arrived at the airport, still dressed in his hotel work uniform, Lily was no longer sobbing, no longer talking to the officer behind the desk. She sat staring at her empty hands.

"Your wife has been in a hysterical state, sir. A doctor has given her a sedative."

Samuel looked at his wife. "Lily? Are you all right, my love?"

Her eyes turned in his direction, like a robot being switched on. Her glassy eyes showed no recognition.

"What have you done to her? What kind of sedative?" He looked at the officer sitting behind a cluttered desk and then at the two guards who stood near the door.

"She tried to board an international flight without a passport," said the officer. "Take her home. She will be okay." His tone was dismissive.

Samuel kneeled next to Lily's chair. "Come, Lily, we must leave here."

She let herself be pulled gently to her feet.

"We'll go home now," Samuel said.

Outside the airport, they waited for a taxi. Samuel held Lily with one arm around her waist. "Talk to me, my love," he whispered. "Talk to me, please."

Lily said nothing. Her eyes were red rimmed but dry. When the taxi arrived, Samuel opened the door for her, and they both got in.

Lily calmly studied her husband's face as if looking at a stranger. Then she turned her head to look out the window. "You knew," she said in a flat, emotionless voice as she watched a jet plane climb into the sky.

Samuel sobbed in response and reached out to take her hand. Neither one spoke for the rest of the ride. *Lisilo budi hutendwa* . . .

3

Southern California, 1989

The first thing Alex noticed was that it didn't smell like a doctor's office. Sitting on a large soft chair in the windowless waiting room with her legs dangling halfway to the floor, she became curious about the distinctive scent coming from a shallow bowl on a lamp table. A pile of children's picture books was neatly stacked on a lower shelf of the table. With a little help from her mother, Zara, she slipped down off the chair and walked across the room to breathe in the scent from the bowl.

"Those are leaves from a eucalyptus tree," her mother told her. "They are like the leaves that koalas eat. Remember seeing them at the zoo?"

Alex knew she would not forget this smell, which felt strange to her nose and somehow slightly menacing. She would tuck that scent into the neat compartments of her mind (she thought of them as drawers, like her own neatly organized socks and underwear drawers), in the one containing smells that interested her and could take her back to places she had been--the smell of a freshly peeled orange that her grandmother shared with her on a beach picnic, the nose-wrinkling stink of pelican guano coming off the rocks of the jetty near the ocean pier, and the dusty odor of the pavement after a rare southern California rain when she got to stomp in actual puddles on their driveway.

"But why are the leaves here? Is the smell a medicine? Does the doctor want us to smell them?"

Her mother smiled. "No, darling. It's just to make the room smell pleasant. Do you like it?"

Alex didn't have time to answer as a door opened, and a tall, bearded man smiled down at them. "Zara, so good to see you--it's been a long time. And this must be Alex." He smiled. "I'm Dr. Espinoza. Please come in."

Inside, bright sunlight poured through large windows on one side of the room. Alex looked out to see several palm trees happily waving their wide, green arms in the breeze. There were no eucalyptus leaves here, no smells to savor or reject. Until she sensed a faint odor of a perfume or perhaps a man's aftershave like her dad's. For a second, she thought the light people might appear to her, but the moment passed. After a glance around at what seemed to be a sort of living room (nothing like the all-white examining room at her pediatrician's office), Alex was happy to look out at the whitecaps being whipped up by the wind on the great Pacific Ocean. That's what her dad called it when they took walks along the strand. She thought about the ocean smell now, a mixture of the fish, seaweed, and salt, her dad had said.

"How old are you, Alex?" Dr. Espinoza asked after she and her mom had settled into their seats on a small couch.

"Four, but I'll be five on my birthday." She knew this grown-up did not need her to hold up four fingers as she had observed other children do when asked this question by adults.

"And when is that?" he asked.

"June second." She paused for a second and then added, "It's the day I was adopted. My real name is Alex, but my mom and dad call me Lexy."

"I see," he answered, his thick eyebrows raised in two half circles above his eyes. "I understand that your mom and dad have told you about how you came to live with them and be their daughter."

"But they don't know everything about it. They were very surprised when a doctor who lives far away across the ocean--a different ocean, not this one--" Alex pointed in the direction of the windows--"called them up on the telephone and told them about me. Then they flew across that ocean to pick me up."

"I see," he said, looking into her eyes. "And do you know, Alex, why your mom has brought you here today?"

Alex looked over at Zara, who sat with her hands clasped tightly together on her lap. "She wonders about my dreams."

"Ahh, and why is that? Can you tell me about the dreams?"

Alex watched the doctor closely, waiting for him to glance up at her mother, but he kept his eyes on hers. She could tell that he was wondering about the color of her eyes, not exactly blue, not exactly purple. People-- strangers even--had made comments about them when she rode in the cart at the supermarket.

"Sometimes," she said drawing the word out, "I see the light people."

"I'm not sure I understand," he said. "Could you tell me more?"

"I call them the light people because I can see right through them. They are no color."

"Ah, do you mean like the pictures we can sometimes see in the sky on a cloudy day--the way the clouds look like faces or animals?"

Alex stared at him in silence. She focused on the hair that surrounded his mouth and moved as he spoke. The doctor reminded her of one of the light people. That made her wary. But it couldn't actually be him, she knew that. She bit her lip and looked out at the ocean.

"Please, Lexy," her mother prompted. "Can you perhaps tell the doctor about the elephant dreams?"

Alex pulled open another drawer inside her mind. The tiny plush elephant lived there. She knew because she visited with it often when she was alone in the dark at night. Its name was not known to her, but she had decided to call it Sam. Sam was a great friend, but sometimes he made her feel sad that she couldn't hold him in her arms. And she had to be careful when she was with Sam. If she opened the drawer right next to Sam's by mistake, she could feel strange hands holding her so tightly that she couldn't move, and she could feel the vibrating sound of desperate screams.

"I don't remember anymore," she said. "Maybe the clouds are covering the dreams now."

"But, Lexy," her mother said softly, "we agreed that you could tell Dr. Espinoza about your dreams. Perhaps he can make them go away."

"Go away?" she repeated in a flat voice, searching her mother's face. She was surprised that "going away" was what her mother seemed to intend all along. There must be something wrong with seeing the light people. Perhaps they made her mother sad or angry. Grown-ups didn't always tell children what they were really thinking. Alex trusted her mom, but she couldn't make her understand about the light people. She didn't want the dreams to go away. Rather, she wanted to enter the dreams, like Alice who followed that rabbit down into the hole. She wanted to find out more about the light people. She knew they were important somehow, but she couldn't explain why.

Dr. Espinoza spoke again, keeping his voice gentle. "Is it a very big elephant, Alex? Is it scary? Can you tell me more about it?"

She would not tell him. She knew now that she would never tell him--or anyone, ever again. No one could see inside her mind, she already knew that. She would keep all the drawers tightly closed.

"I think that elephant must be very big, but it's gone now," she said to dismiss the topic. "Like the clouds when the wind comes."

Dr. Espinoza asked her a few more questions about her preschool and about her friends and what she liked to play. About going down the big slide with her friend Mike at the park. She told him how they laughed when she was the first to be brave enough to try it. She told him about the puzzles she did with her dad, and about making chapatis with her mom. No more was said about the dreams.

"Would it be okay if I talk privately to your mom for just a few minutes, Alex? You could sit in the waiting room and perhaps look at the children's books on the shelf under the table?"

Alex agreed. Once back in the waiting room, she chose a book from the shelf, but she kept it closed on her lap and just sat quietly until her mother emerged from the doctor's office a few minutes later.

Riding down the elevator, Alex held her mom's hand and looked up at her.

"I didn't want to talk to him, Mommy." The smell of eucalyptus leaves was still strong in her nose. She welcomed the familiar scent of her mama, a mixture of cumin and the flowery perfume she dabbed on her wrists each morning.

Her mother knelt next to her and put her arms around her right there in the elevator. "That's okay, my sweet Alex. You did great. I love you. Don't worry. We won't be going back to see Dr. Espinoza."

4

Southern California, 1993

While Coach Mack gave instructions to Alex's third-grade class on the school playground, she looked out toward the sea, which was visible at some distance. On this autumn morning, the cobalt blue expanse of the Pacific Ocean looked alive as white caps rose and fell in the brisk wind, like a code written in disappearing ink. Alex knew there were no secret messages to be found in the watery script, but a weird feeling of anticipation had come over her. Not an entirely unfamiliar feeling. Not a comfortable one. There was something about the sea though that calmed her.

She turned her eyes away from the flashing white caps to focus on Coach Mack's face as he spoke.

"Pretend the finish line is way past the tape at the other end of the field," he was saying. "Don't let up and don't slow down. Keep your head up and keep those heels kicking your butt. Run through that finish line as if you could go on forever."

Several students giggled at the Coach's casual use of "butt."

His words are true, Alex thought. *They make good sense. Dad would say the same thing.*

"We'll run heats--six of you at a time," the Coach was saying, "and then the winners of each heat will race in a final runoff."

Earlier that morning, Alex's dad, Paul, had tightened the braided lanyard that held her thick glasses in place. Her eyes were weak, so she wore the glasses not only for reading and other schoolwork but also when she wanted to ride a bike or run around the track with her dad on Saturday mornings. Now, she reached up to straighten the glasses and make sure they sat securely on her ears.

When all the students had raced, Alex and the other finalists made themselves ready at the starting line. She measured herself against her new classmates and determined that she was the second tallest and the only girl among the six in the final runoff. Grant Johnson, blond and blue-eyed and considered by many of the girls to be the cutest boy in the third grade, was the tallest. The idea that he was cute had confused her, though she didn't question the girls about it. She had observed him carefully and only found him rather rude and not all that smart. Cuteness was a quality she attributed to babies and puppies, not to a mere eight-year-old boy.

She placed her feet just behind the yellow plastic tape that marked the starting line. Closing her eyes for a moment, she imagined herself taking off like a pelican-- sudden and fast--when it dove into the sea for a fish.

When Coach Mack counted down to one, she flew out in front of the boys and held the lead until she saw another yellow tape ahead. Sensing the thump of footsteps close behind her, she raised her chin and kicked hard against the grassy surface. Her glasses slipped from her face, but she kept running, pushing her legs to help her fly, moving without slowing well past the tape.

"Alex is first! Grant second, and Jason third," the Coach's assistant called. Alex slowed then, reached for her glasses dangling under her chin, and replaced them on her face.

Taking several deep breaths, she walked back toward the finish line. Immediately, she could see that Grant was not happy. "She's just a white nigger," he said loud enough for her to hear. A couple of the boys barely covered their laughter with their hands.

"Or maybe a vampire," another boy said. "No wonder she doesn't wear shorts for gym. She's afraid of melting in the sunlight." They made no attempt to hide their laughter.

Alex, confused and hurt by their words, looked out at the sea again as she walked back toward the starting line. Then she stopped and turned to look directly at Grant. She spoke softly and directly to him. "You almost beat me. But I know how to run." She paused, still staring at the boy. "And I know how to win." The small group of boys went quiet and stared after her as she headed back to join the rest of the class.

* * *

At dinner that evening, Alex sat silent as her mom served her favorite meal, a spicy *murgh makhana*, with garlic naan and mango chutney.

"My sweet girl is thinking," her dad said, smiling at her. "Things going well at your new school?"

She smiled back. "It's okay. But I have a question," she said as she watched her mom spoon the hot chicken and lentils on her plate.

"We love your questions," said her mom. "Questions will make you very wise."

"What is —" She hesitated, a quizzical expression on her face, "a 'white nigger'?" She looked from one parent to the other.

She watched as her mom and dad exchanged a glance in a nano-second of silence.

Her dad spoke first. "Can you tell me, Lexy, where you heard these words?"

Her mom's face had clouded over with concern as she placed a piece of warm naan on each dinner plate.

"Well, I beat Grant Johnson in a race during gym class today," said Alex. "He said I was a 'white nigger.' I didn't argue with him because I don't know what that means."

"I see," her dad said and then paused for a couple of moments. "I'm sorry you had to hear that. First, I believe Grant was embarrassed to be beaten by a girl, especially in front of his friends. But that doesn't excuse him. 'White nigger' is a bit of hateful speech. 'Nigger' is a word that some ignorant people use to refer to black people, black like your friends Kyra and Whitney. 'Black' is many different shades of brown and black. The word "nigger" is full of hate. No one should use that word. Ever."

"But my skin is not black like Kyra and Whitney. It's whiter than anyone's. Whiter than Mom's, whiter even than yours, Dad." She held her bare arms out in front of them.

"You have beautiful skin, my sweet Alex," her mom said. She took her seat at the table. "But now you are old enough to learn more about your skin color. It is all a matter of genetics."

"I remember what you've told me, Mom, about genes and chromosomes and why Veronica and her little sister look so much alike but also different," said Alex, taking a forkful of her mother's excellent meal."

"Yes, my darling. Each of us is unique. You have an excellent memory, and it never ceases to amaze me. But I think I must now explain to you a little more about your genetics. Although there are other people who have the same light skin and hair and eyes that you do, that combination is considered quite rare. It's called albinism. You are absolutely normal in all other ways, but you lack something called melanin that gives most people and animals their coloring. Unfortunately, it is also what makes your eyes weak--though happily you have glasses to help with that."

"But why did I get albinism?" Alex looked from her mom to her dad. When neither answered right away, she felt like she did the time she was carrying her boogie board out of the ocean and a giant wave arose and knocked her over from behind.

"Lexy-pie," said her dad, "we don't have all the answers that you might want, but we will tell you what we know. There is nothing bad about having albinism. You are a beautiful girl, and you will be a beautiful woman someday. And we love you."

Alex put her fork down and pushed the plate away from her. What did this mean? Why hadn't she known this earlier? Why hadn't anyone told her?

"The traits of albinism--including your poor eyesight--would have been passed to you from the woman who gave birth to you--your biological mother as well as your father," her mom added.

Alex held back tears. But her voice shook when she spoke again. "You told me that a doctor from England called you to tell you about me--and that you decided to adopt me. Right?"

She saw them look at each other again.

"Was that doctor my father? Did he want to give me away?"

"No, no, he is not your father," Dad said. "He was only looking for good parents who would care for you and love you."

"We didn't learn any details about where you were born or who your parents were," said Mom. "We assumed that because he was a children's doctor that someone must have asked for his help in making sure you had a good home. Perhaps your parents were unable to take care of you. There must have been a good reason that they gave you up. We just don't know."

"Gave me up? But why? Is there something wrong with me? Did my parents not want me because I have--albinism?"

"Of course not, Lexy," said Dad.

He looks like he might cry, Alex thought. She had never seen such a sad and serious look on his face.

"When we heard about you," he said, "we were so excited to bring you to America to live with us." He paused a moment to take a breath. "But we couldn't follow the usual rules about adoption--rules that require certain papers. So, we didn't ask a lot of questions. We just fell in love with you and brought you back home to be our daughter. We were more than thrilled."

"I am truly sorry that we don't know more," Mom said. "But what is important to remember--and we know you remember everything," she said with a wide smile, "is that we love you now and always--just as you are."

"I love you too," Alex said, her voice trembling. "But I still don't understand why Grant called me a white nigger."

"Come, let us sit on the couch together," said Mom. "We all need a group hug, I think. And we will figure it out together."

Later, when Alex was lying in bed before falling asleep, the light people appeared in the darkness. The man with the beard and mustache. The woman with cold hands. Another woman who would not stop screaming. And the little elephant, Sam, whose secret presence in her life had made him the recipient of all her fears and questions. When the vision disappeared, she lay thinking, wondering what had happened to her real mother and father. Did they not want her? Had something happened to them? Where were they now? How would she ever know for sure why they had given her away?

She did not want to hurt her mom and dad by speaking of it any longer. She would not bring the topic up again. Instead, she would share her questions and her fears with Sam, her dear elephant and constant friend.

I'm only eight, Sam, but one day, we will find them, and then we will understand.

5

Addis Ababa, Ethiopia, 1991

A long line of red and yellow buses rumbled up the road toward the refugee camp in Addis Ababa. It was only an hour after sunrise. Seth, who was accompanying his youngest sister to the latrines, stopped to watch a cloud of dust rise from the battered vehicles as they climbed toward the camp.

"It must be happening today," he whispered aloud to Lala. "Today we will go to Jerusalem." At four years old, Lala was too young to understand what that meant, but ten-year-old Seth repeated it for her anyway. "Jerusalem, Lala! Today we will begin a new life in Jerusalem!"

Then, silently, he spoke to his father. *My Abba, this is the day you waited for all your years. How many times did you tell me of your dream to go to the Promised Land? But how can we leave you alone in this land that is not even our home?* He blinked away tears. "Hurry, Lala. We must get back quickly to Mama. I'll wait here for you."

Hoisting his sister onto his back a few minutes later, Seth hurried to the tent that had sheltered them for the past nine months since their trek had brought them through the desert from their rural village. Six-year-old Deborah met them at the tent entrance.

"Mama says we must pack up right away. We are all going to the airport!"

Inside, Seth found his mother and grandmother folding clothes and blankets and sorting them into piles.

"Seth!" his mother said. "Go to the administration tent and listen for what we must do."

Seth stood as tall as his ten years would allow him. "There are many buses, Mama--they are coming up the road--I've seen them. Finally, they will let us go!"

Hazir paused and looked at her small son. "Perhaps. If it is His will, we will go to the Promised Land." She paused and then spoke more softly, her lower lip trembling. "You must be the man of our family now, my son. Go find out what we must do to leave this place."

He paused a moment to look more closely at his mother, her belly swollen with another child. Seth was hoping for a brother this time. He knew that was what his father had hoped for as well. Seth rubbed his eyes. "Yes," he said, "I'm going now, Mama."

As he ran through the labyrinth of dirt pathways among the tents, Seth looked up at a huge airplane flying low overhead. Even after all these months in the camp, he loved listening to the jets taking off or landing at the nearby airport. Sometimes, when he lay awake at night, he tried to imagine who was in them and where they might be going. They must be people from far-off lands who wore fine clothes, jewelry, and shoes. He had heard that such people had pipes inside their houses that carried water, and that they cooked their food by turning knobs or pushing buttons on a machine.

Jet planes were just one part of this new, strange world, so far from the humble home he had known in his village. Could it really be that he and his family would soon rise into the sky on such a huge metal machine? The sacred texts written so long ago on goatskins said nothing about jets. He could remember only a mention of eagles' wings, though he had long wondered whether anyone could possibly be lifted up on a bird's wings. For a brief moment, he thought he would ask Abba about that. Then, with a stab of pain in his stomach, he remembered, and he felt ashamed that his excitement had caused him to forget. They had buried his father only three days earlier.

When he returned from the administration tent, quite out of breath, he told his mother and grandmother Bibi that they could stop their packing, for there would be no room on the plane for their clothes or any other possessions. Instead, they must put on whatever clothes they could and walk immediately to the lot where the buses were parked, ready to take them all to the airport. The planes would have enough room only for people, no baggage.

"We must stay together," he told them, repeating what he was told at the administration tent, "so no one gets lost."

As he spoke, he was surprised to see all of them--his mother, his grandmother, his sisters--looking at him as if they were waiting for him to give them further instructions, as if he were a grown man. He drew in a breath and held it. How could he possibly step into his father's shoes? He wanted to run, to hide his grief from everyone. At that moment, he remembered the warmth of his father's hand on his head as he whispered a blessing for his only son.

"On the way to the buses, we will stop at the place where Abba is buried. We are not coming back, and we must say good-bye." It was his first order as the man of the family.

* * *

In the early afternoon, Seth stood quietly with his family among thousands of other people standing in long lines on the tarmac of the airport in Addis Ababa. Many of them had dressed for this journey in garments made from the white cloth woven and carried with them from their rural villages. Before they had left their homes and made the long journey here to Addis Ababa, every man, woman, and child wore clothes made of this same white cloth each year on Sigd, an ancient festival of exile and redemption in Ethiopia. Together, they prayed, as many generations had done for years beyond memory, that they would, at last, be delivered to the land from which their ancestors had come. Until the nineteenth century, his people had been convinced that they were the only Jews left on Earth.

The black Jews of Ethiopia had lived their lives in this foreign land for over two thousand years. Seth's forefathers, perhaps descendants of a tribe that came through Egypt and Sudan, had fought to remain Jewish, even when their community was crushed five hundred years earlier by a Christian ruler. Living under the restrictive laws, the Jews took the only jobs they were allowed. They became excellent pottery makers, weavers, and blacksmiths. And they became known as "Falaches," landless wanderers, who developed their own strict rules of conduct to keep themselves independent of those who did not believe as they did. Until the late nineteenth century when a French professor was sent to investigate reports of these black Jews, the Ethiopian community had only a single Torah written on goatskin in the Ge'ez language. They observed the Sabbath and other holidays they knew from the Torah, but they had no knowledge of Jews the world over who observed the Passover Seder, Hannukah, or Purim, holy days that had been added to the calendar and celebrated since the writing of that goatskin Torah.

Even to Seth, the great crowds of people now waiting at the airport seemed strangely hushed and calm, perhaps in awe of this anticipated deliverance to the Promised Land, perhaps because they had been warned that their emergency flight to Jerusalem must remain a secret from those who would harm them. Most had crossed the perilous desert less than a year ago as drought, famine, and war threatened them in their homelands. And many of them had lost family members and friends on that journey. Now new threats of violence were rumored as rebel forces gathered outside the city. Faith and desperation lay thick upon them as they awaited the planes that would take them to safety. Only later would they learn that they were part of a secret airlift that would rescue over 14,000 Ethiopian Jews in a period of thirty-six hours. It was called Operation Solomon, and the existence of a community of Black Jews from Ethiopia would henceforth be known over the entire Earth.

Seth watched in awe as several giant jet planes touched down on the runway. He sensed that his life was about to change. He promised himself, as he stood amid the silent crowd of fellow refugees, that he would do everything he could to fulfill his father's hopes and faith in him. He would make his father proud.

6

Operation Solomon, 1991

All the seats on the Israeli military jet had been removed. In their place, over a thousand men, women, and children, most of whom had never flown in an airplane, sat hushed in family groups on the floor. Mothers who had carried babies and small children in slings on their backs during the long wait at the airport had abandoned all evidence of their lives in Ethiopia to make room for more people on the plane. The men kept track of their families as they made their way through the press of the crowd to see them safely seated together. Only religious elders had been exempted from the no-baggage rule. They protected their ancient, sacred text, carefully wrapped in red cloth, never putting it down during the several hours of flight.

Some on the plane believed that the city of Jerusalem would shine with gold and that all hardships would vanish in such a sacred place. Most believed that God was to be praised for bringing them on this journey to the Holy Land. None, however, understood that the four-hour flight above the Earth would take them through time as well as space and that their lives were about to change in profound ways as they entered the twentieth century, soon to be the twenty-first.

Young men who were Israeli Defense Force soldiers and wore casual civilian clothes for this rescue mission, walked among the passengers making sure that everyone had a place to sit. For many of the travelers, these men were the first white Jews they had ever encountered.

Among them was Benjamin Bendler, a young medical doctor who had made aliyah to Israel from America a year earlier and was now fulfilling his obligation to the military. The doctor stopped beside Seth and his family. Seth stared up at him, awed and curious. He examined the soldier's clothes--a white tee shirt, jeans, sneakers, and a white baseball cap. Another soldier had summoned Benjamin on his walkie-talkie.

"This woman might be in labor, Ben. The family doesn't speak any Hebrew. Except the kid there--I think he knows enough to be helpful."

Seth and his sisters sat near his mother, who was leaning against the side wall of the plane. Her belly was large, her face was contorted in pain, and her breaths were shallow. His grandmother sat beside her, holding her hand and weeping softly.

Benjamin knelt beside the family. Seeing the worried look on the boy's face, he put his hand on his shoulder. "I'm called Benjamin. What's your name, son?"

"Seth Melaku."

"And is this your mom, Seth?"

"Yes." His large brown eyes were focused on Benjamin's as if pleading with him to make everything all right.

Benjamin called out to another soldier. "Will you clear some space for us here? Maybe get these little ones busy somewhere else? Except for the boy--I might need him."

He turned back to Seth and asked, "And your dad--is he on the plane?"

"Abba died last week," the boy whispered, looking away, his chin trembling.

Benjamin gently lifted the woman's wrist to check her pulse.

"I'm so sorry, Seth. I lost my dad when I was about your age. I know you must be feeling sad. Let's do what we can to help your mom right now. Will you help me talk to her?"

Seth nodded. "She is Hazir. She has a baby in her belly." His words, spoken in Hebrew, were halting but clear.

Benjamin used a stethoscope, moving it around on Hazir's belly. "This baby may be born very soon. Please tell your mom, Seth, that I am trained to help. I'm a doctor, and I can help her. Do you understand?"

Seth spoke to his mother, who opened her eyes wide to look at him and then at Benjamin. She nodded her head, her mouth twisted in a grimace.

Benjamin called on the communications device to ask for an emergency medical kit and blankets. When another soldier arrived with supplies, Seth helped convinced his mom to stretch out on blankets they had spread on the floor. Her moaning scared him. He could do nothing to help her. As the doctor opened the emergency kit and pulled on a pair of gloves, Seth spoke silently to his Abba. *Where are you, my father? How can I take care of Mama without you? Why did you have to leave us?*

"Everything is going to be okay, Seth," said Benjamin. "Your mom will be fine. You've been a great help."

Hazir groaned then, and Seth's eyes grew wide. Benjamin looked at his watch. "Now I need you to go look after your sisters. They might be frightened, and they'll need their big brother. Your mom will be fine. I promise. I'll come to talk with you when we have any news."

* * *

Only thirty minutes later, and not quite an hour into the flight, Hazir gave birth to a baby boy. Dark-skinned like his mother and three siblings, with sparkling brown eyes and a good set of lungs. She smiled through tears and named him Kofi, "born on Friday." It was May 24, 1991, and the baby, her spotless new lamb, was about to enter his strange, new homeland thanks to God, Operation Solomon, and a young IDF soldier named Benjamin.

When Hazir and her baby were comfortably resting and being taken care of by other women on the plane, Benjamin went to find Seth and his sisters. He announced the news, which Seth conveyed to Deborah and Lala. Smiles all around. Seth breathed a sigh of relief. He and his sisters would not be orphans.

During the rest of the flight, Benjamin checked on the children when he could, entertaining them with his one and only magic trick--pulling a shekel out from behind one of their ears. The girls, shy at first, laughed gleefully and indicated that they wanted him to continue. Seth, older and wiser, studied the soldier. Could he grow up to be like him in the Promised Land?

When the pilot announced that the airplane had entered the airspace above Israel, word spread among the passengers, and they began to clap and sing. A short time later, the plane landed at Ben Gurion Airport.

Seth stood at the top of the steps that had been rolled to the doorway. He would be the first of the Operation Solomon refugees to step onto the Holy Land. Benjamin followed him carrying Lala down the stairs and waited with the children while a medical team boarded the plane, explaining to Seth that they would take his mother and the baby to a hospital for a day or two to be sure they were all right. Benjamin assured the boy that the children and their grandmother would be taken to an apartment and cared for. Hazir and the new baby would join them there in a few days.

Seth watched as the religious clerics from his community carried the holy Torah, protecting it from the late afternoon sun with a cloth parasol. He watched as several of his countrymen knelt to kiss the holy ground. Many more people in blue or white caps were on the tarmac to help the new arrivals move toward the buildings where some would be reunited with loved ones who had emigrated sometime earlier. Someone handed him a small Israeli flag, a blue, six-pointed star on a white background. He knew he would not forget this day.

A few minutes later, he watched as his mother was carried down the narrow stairs, followed by two soldiers who were carrying a portable incubator where his brother lay asleep. His grandmother followed.

"Mama, you are okay?" Seth said standing beside his mother, who lay on a gurney. At that moment, he wanted to be in her arms again like a baby, feeling her warmth, feeling safe. He stood up straight and squared his shoulders. Of course, that time was long gone. He could take care of himself now.

"Don't worry, Mama. We're finally here in the land that Abba has so often told us about. And now, I will be the man of the house and help you."

"I'm depending on it, my son. We will make a new and wonderful life here just as your father dreamed." Tears rolled down her face.

7

Jerusalem, Israel, 1999

Seth wore his recently issued dress uniform with both pride and trepidation as he headed home for his first visit since beginning his mandatory service in the Israeli Defense Forces. Like all the young men and women who had recently completed high school, he had to endure basic training. To his surprise, he had liked the training and the discipline of the army. He pushed himself hard, learned to work with a team, and enjoyed being active in the outdoors all day long.

The past few weeks had changed him, he thought. He felt respected by the officers and his peers. He had a new sense of confidence in his abilities. He recalled now the excitement of a field exercise when he had silently made his way, crawling through the scrub-thorn bushes of the desert to surprise the training commander. Afterward, Commander Leib spoke in front of the entire squad, claiming that he had never had a soldier sneak up on him successfully in that exercise.

"You, Private Melaku, have an outstanding future ahead of you in the IDF."

Seth knew it was not a story to tell his mother. She would not like to hear it--not only because she wanted him home. She constantly reminded him that his father would not have joined the IDF, that he was a man of peace and patience.

He knocked at the door of his mother's apartment. Deborah and Lala both ran to open the door, with eight-year-old Kofi not far behind.

"Come see, Mama!" Deborah called out to Hazir. "The IDF has turned Seth into a handsome soldier. All the girls will be after him."

"But his ears are still sticking out like handles on a soup pot," added Lala with a giggle.

Seth laughed, throwing his head back so far that his sisters could see his mouthful of white teeth. "You will have to respect me now, you two. No insults allowed."

"Where is your gun?" Kofi asked as he hugged his brother's legs.

"No gun today. I've come home to celebrate your birthday--happy birthday, little man." He placed his hand on Kofi's dark, close-cropped curls.

Hazir appeared in the dim hallway to greet her son. She was drying her hands on a dishtowel. Seth studied her plump face, her eyes looked puffy as if she had been crying.

"Girls, leave him be. Go help your grandmother in the kitchen," she said shooing them with the towel. "Kofi, go wash your hands. Dinner will be ready soon."

Seth grinned broadly and kissed her on both cheeks. "I am back for a visit, Mama. Wearing my A uniform. Do you like it?" He made a mock-heroic pose as if he were on an action-adventure movie poster.

Hazir did not smile. She studied her son from head to toe, her face as stern as any military commander he had met so far. "They have given you these clothes to wear? These boots?"

"Yes, Mama. We all get the same." He reached out to hug her as she burst into sobs.

"This is not our way, my son. I'm sorry, but I cannot accept this. Fighting. Killing. And besides, I need your help. I can't do this alone."

"Come, sit down, Mama. You are upset. We've talked about this many times. I am just fulfilling the law of mandatory service--an opportunity to help keep all of us safe." He paused and smiled at his mother. "I have some news that you will find helpful."

They moved down the narrow hallway to the room that served as living room and dining room, as well as a bedroom for Kofi. In a few moments, they were joined by Deborah and Lala, who were helping their grandmother navigate with an aluminum walker.

Seth kissed his grandmother's cheek and hugged her. "I love you, Bibi," he said in the language of their homeland as she knew very little Hebrew. His grandmother held his hand and beamed a smile at him. Seth had begun learning Hebrew at the age of ten while in the refugee camp at Addis Ababa. After a few months at school in Israel, he was determined to speak only Hebrew and for a long time had refused to speak Amharic even to his mother and grandmother. The eight years since then had softened him and increased his empathy and gratitude for both women, widows who worked hard not only to take care of their family but to fulfill the vision of their husbands and their forefathers in a strange land.

"How long can you stay?" Lala asked, pulling on his arm.

"I must be back tomorrow evening to talk to my commander," Seth said, with a glance at his mother. But I didn't want to miss celebrating Kofi's birthday."

"Will you come with me to the community center to see me dance?" asked Deborah. "It's tomorrow afternoon. We share our folk dances with the Palestinians, and they share theirs with us."

"You will be dancing? Wow, I'd like to see that."

"I have a good friend there, her name is Nouf. She is Palestinian and loves dancing as much as I do."

"I would like to see you dance and to meet your friend, too."

"Do you like being a soldier?" Lala asked.

"Actually, I do. I'm learning a lot and training to become a good soldier. With the others, I will help to keep us safe here in Israel."

A few minutes later, they all sat together at the small kitchen table. Seth's mouth watered as several scents reached him at once. The aroma of this food always took him back to his childhood, to memories of coming in from a long day of shepherding to a hot dinner that Hazir had cooked over a fire. Now, in the middle of the table, she had placed a huge plate of *tibs*, sauteed meat chunks in a spicy sauce, and a platter of *shiro be kebbe*, a legume stew, and an Ethiopian favorite.

After Bibi gave a short blessing, everyone tore off a large piece of freshly made *ingera* flatbread and tore it into smaller pieces to scoop up the meat and vegetables. "How is the catering business, Mama? Are you getting a lot of weddings?"

"We are managing. Bibi is still able to help in the kitchen, and Deborah has been doing much of what you were doing to get business. But it's not the same without you. I don't know what we will do. I'm in doubt every day that we can be successful."

"Mama," Deborah spoke up, "we are doing fine. Even Lala has been helping. And we have one funeral and two weddings scheduled before the end of the month."

"Hush, child. You don't know everything." Hazir looked at Seth. "We still owe a lot of money for the investment we made in materials and supplies. Those men are asking for their money every week, and I have to keep giving them excuses."

"So--I have some good news, Mama," Seth said. "I can help now with money. We can talk about it after we eat."

As they ate, all the family--even Bibi--told Kofi again about the day he was born eight years ago 9,000 meters up in the air. About Addis Ababa, about the giant airplane without seats, about landing at Ben Gurion airport where people kissed the holy ground in gratitude. Lala always remembered Dr. Benjamin's magic trick that involved pulling a shekel out of her ear, although now that she was twelve, she recognized that there was no real magic. Seth liked to tell how he translated for his pregnant mother and the soldiers who helped her. Bibi praised Hazir's courage in delivering a baby thousands of meters above the Earth.

As they were finishing dinner, the doorbell rang. A colorful bouquet of spring flowers set among a couple of olive branches had arrived. Every year on this date, Dr. Benjamin Bendler either brought or sent flowers to Hazir. It had become an important part of Kofi's birthday ritual and a poignant reminder for all of them of the day they left Ethiopia and Abba behind. In addition to the flowers, there was a gift for Kofi.

"Can I open it now, Mama?" As soon as she nodded, he tore off the paper to find a new soccer ball, and even better, an athletic shirt with "HARAZI" across the shoulders--Kofi's favorite player. He ran out of the room to try it on and returned exalting.

"I have a little gift for you as well," Seth said. "Come here, little brother." It was a set of binoculars, which Seth had purchased on the base.

"Cool!" Kofi said, putting the glasses up to his eyes. "Are these like the ones you use in the army? I want to go outside and try them out!"

As his sister and grandmother cleared the dishes, Seth turned to his mother. "Let me tell you some news, Mama. You will no longer have to worry about money."

She smiled. "What is this mysterious news, my son? I see that you are still a dreamer. I'll always worry--but I love you for trying always to make things better."

"My Sergeant Commander, Mama, he's a really good guy. He thinks I'll make a fine soldier, and I've told him how things are here at home--how I am needed. He took me to the bank to talk to someone in the collections department to try to work out a solution for us where we would make small payments to get rid of our debt. But the next day, he sat me down to tell me that our entire debt is paid off!"

Hazir pressed her lips together in a tight line. "They are giving you money? Have you not told him how hard we have worked all these years supporting our family? We do not accept anyone's charity. It's you that we need, Seth, not this government's money."

"No. Not the government's money. Sergeant Commander told me that someone--I don't know who--has offered to pay this debt so that we can begin fresh. You will keep all the profits from the business now, no debts to repay." Seth looked at his mother with wide eyes as he made a plea for her to understand. "The army training is such an opportunity for me--and for us, Mama. I will be able to get a good-paying job with this experience behind me. I will be respected like any other Israeli citizen--not just a black immigrant, not just a Falache." Seth watched his mother carefully to gauge her reaction to his words.

Hazir looked at her son. She saw his determination, his sense of responsibility, and his desire to belong to this country as his father had long envisioned. She saw, too, the little boy who lost his father at the age of ten, who had done his best to be the man of the family since then though he was but a child. It was time to let go, she knew that. He was eighteen, and it was his time to become a man, to live his own life. Slowly, she nodded her head at him.

"My son, I know I have not said it often, but I am so proud of you. And I am certain that your father would be proud of you as well. You dare to make difficult choices. You have integrity. And you have compassion for others." She sighed deeply. "Tell your Sergeant that we will accept the money to pay off the debts."

Seth hugged her. "Thank you, Mama. I hope that I'll continue to make you proud."

"Go now," she said, pushing him away with a laugh. "Find Kofi and kick that new football around for a while. Though he is only eight, he knows already that his brother is a hero."

8

Jerusalem, 1999

Seth tried to look relaxed as he waited with his fellow recruits, the young men who he had learned to call brothers over the past two months of basic training in the Israeli Defense Forces. Today, they would be formally sworn in. Despite the crowds and the heat here at the Western Wall, he couldn't help comparing this civilized scene to what they had been living through since being inducted. Over many weeks, the recruits had learned what it meant to obey orders as they practiced shooting and cleaning rifles, crawling under barbed wire obstacles, and hiking with fifty pounds of equipment through the long night. For most of the men, spending probably ninety percent of their time outdoors, separated from their families, and feeling constant physical and emotional stress, the experience had been radical. Seth, who had been born into a family of shepherds and lived much of his youth outdoors, took to the training easily. He had, in fact, excelled.

Jeremy, his best friend in D-1 Squad, another "lone" soldier without family support in Israel, (Jeremy's family had emigrated to Belgium when he was five) reached up to adjust Seth's newly bestowed beret to just the right angle.

"The hat suits you, Private. You look every inch the heroic soldier today." Jeremy smiled and adjusted his own beret as well. "Will any of your family be here?"

"No--my mother and my sisters wouldn't even consider walking into such a crowd. Anyway, my mother doesn't think much of me serving in the military," he added in a low voice. "Are your parents here?"

"In the end, they couldn't make the trip, but they promise to come when we graduate from our specialty training. Have you told your mother your plans?"

"No way, man. I have to walk softly," Seth said with a grin. "I'll have to visit her and have a talk. She will not take it well, even though all our debts have been paid off."

"I understand. Perhaps if you--"

Their conversation was interrupted as their Sergeant Commander gave orders to get into formation. Seth listened with attention as a hymn was sung and verses of the Psalms were read over the public address system. He wanted to cement the memory of what was happening in this place on this day, so far from his childhood home.

A bass voice boomed over the loudspeakers. "Commanders, the people of Israel are entrusting to us their most beloved possession of all: their finest sons."

Seth raised his chin a little and squared his shoulders as he focused on his Sergeant Commander standing at attention in front of the squad. Only twenty years old himself, the man had the impressive responsibility to mold these young men--mere boys, really--into fierce, loyal soldiers. Seth judged that the Sergeant Commander had done a good job. He had inspired him and all the squad members to see themselves as a part of the lifeblood of Israel, standing in a line with heroes and leaders of the country's embattled history. He had taken the squad to Mount Herzl National Cemetery where they viewed the graves of many veterans and heroes of modern Israel.

Seth listened with awe to a story about a an IDF soldier in the Six Day War of 1967. Even with thirty bullets in his body, he kept going until the final bullet got him in the head.

The voice from the loudspeakers then addressed the recruits. "Combat Soldiers, the path you have chosen is not an easy one, but it is filled with gratification, action, and glory with unparalleled self-sacrifice. Today you are becoming part of a glorious chain of generations."

Seth felt his throat tighten. For a moment, his father was there with him, his eyes glinting with excitement as he talked about the hope of one day going to Jerusalem, the Promised Land, which had been the fervent hope, too, of many generations of Ethiopian Jews before him.

What might his father think of him today wearing his beret and preparing to swear to defend this country with his life? His father had been a man of faith and peace. But how could he not be proud of his son protecting the people of the Israel? *I'm good at this, Abba. And I will make you proud.*

Each recruit was called to come to the platform at the front to shake the Commander's hand. Each was given a rifle from a rack of weapons before saluting and rejoining his squad. Then they were asked to rise for the swearing in. The crowd grew quiet as the young men recited together.

"I swear on my honor to dedicate all my strength and even to give my life for the protection of the homeland and the freedom of Israel. I swear!"

9

Near Arusha, Tanzania, 2010

Kaj crouched barefoot in front of his grandfather's hut and stared at the skinny rooster strutting in the dust, searching for insects and crumbs. The animal seemed to be enjoying itself. Maybe not thinking like a person, but smart enough to find enough food to stay alive and walk around as if it owned the place, its dusty black and gold tail feathers announcing its place in its limited world.

Kaj studied the jerky movements of the bird, which was oblivious to its imminent fate. In his mind's eye, Kaj saw himself stepping around the random junk and garbage in the yard, scanning for overlooked scraps in hopes of finding a bit of sweet potato or a half-eaten corncob. What did being alive mean to such a creature? What was the magic that made this scraggly, yellow-legged animal have "life?" Wasn't it every bit as alive as Kaj himself? What gave him, a human being, the right to end its life?

He frowned and picked at his toenails. His mind was full of thoughts and questions that had no answers. He had left the St. Cecelia's Orphanage and School almost five years ago at the age of eleven with a basic knowledge of reading and writing and some arithmetic. But his appetite for knowledge had been whetted, his imagination ignited. He knew there was a great salty ocean a few days' walk from his village, a place he had vowed to himself to visit someday. He knew there were many villages, cities, and countries outside of Tanzania. But was the Earth really round like his teacher's globe? Could it actually be spinning and hurling itself through space when he couldn't feel that movement at all? Sometimes, at night, as he lay on his pallet in the hut he shared with his mother, he thought he could sense it, that spinning, when he closed his eyes and let the darkness carry him through a wide-open sky.

When he had told Sister Angelica that he would not be returning to school, she had asked him questions in her gentle voice.

"Is it your grandfather who says you must leave school, Boniface?

"No-- Yes. I must help him gather the herbs and learn more about the medicines."

"And your mother--she agrees with your grandfather?"

Kaj looked away and then turned his eyes toward the floor. He knew Sister Angelica was waiting for an answer. "My mother, she is sick, I think."

"Is it the same as your father was?" she asked in a whisper.

"She is tired. I must help her."

"Would you like me to visit with her and see how she is doing?"

Kaj looked up sharply. "No, no, she would be afraid."

Sister Angelica sighed. "All right, Boniface. Maybe another time. But I hope you will come to St. Cecelia's to see us when you can. Would you like to borrow this book with the maps for a little while? I know you would take good care of it."

Kaj smiled.

"I am so sorry, my child. You are a good student. You have a genuine thirst for knowledge."

Kaj treasured those words. He still thought about them and the way Sister Angelica had looked at him, a look of pity he realized now.

If only he could have continued. If only he could read the books he had seen neatly lined up between heavy stone bookends shaped like the front and back of an elephant on his teacher's desk. He would not be here contemplating the life of an ugly bird in this miserable yard. He would be among the people who knew the answers. People who made their own decisions and their own money.

Inside the hut, his grandfather was talking to the man who had traveled from Arusha, seeking help for-- what? For potency in his lovemaking? For some problem with his bowels? For a spell of revenge on an enemy perhaps? He might be a politician seeking good luck, though Kaj knew little about why politicians needed luck. He knew only that the man seemed desperate when he had met him at the rutted road below the village and led him the half kilometer or so to his grandfather's isolated hut. Kaj had studied the man's black car, covered with a layer of pale dust, but a recent model with dark tinted windows, well cared for.

"You can leave it here. No one will touch it," he told the man.

"You will take me to the healer?" the man asked in a gruff voice, glancing in all directions before glaring at Kaj.

Kaj grunted in reply as he examined the man--a large head as smooth as a chicken's egg, an old scar that stretched from his eyebrow to his chin on one side of his face, a comfortably round belly under his neat tan suit, his feet in polished leather shoes, a glimmer of a gold watch on his left wrist. "This way, sir," he said remembering what his grandfather had taught him. He had to show special respect for customers who traveled from the city to see the Babu.

The day was warm and promised to be even warmer. Kaj rolled up the sleeves of the patterned red and yellow shirt he always wore to meet his grandfather's city clients. They walked the dusty trail in silence for almost ten minutes. "Can we rest a bit?" the man asked, obviously out of breath and wiping his face with a large white handkerchief. Kaj noticed that the man kept looking around as if expecting a lion to spring out from behind a rock.

"Here is some shade just up ahead. We will stop there," Kaj said.

In the semi-shade of a twisted acacia tree, the man sat down on a rock. "Do you go to school?" he asked Kaj, sounding more friendly now.

"Not anymore. I can read though." Kaj held his head up, his chin out.

"That's good. That's good. If you can read, you can teach yourself anything." Again, the man wiped beads of sweat from his bald head.

Kaj looked at him in silence. What did this man, a city man with a big car, fine clothes, and shiny shoes want from his grandfather, a man who could not read more than a few words, a man who wore ragged clothing picked out of the sisters' charity box and was paid for his healing by the local community in chickens and millet?

"Okay, I'm ready to go." The man took a deep breath and exhaled as he pulled himself up from the rock.

"It's not so far now. My Babu will be waiting for you."

They did not speak again, but Kaj kept turning over what the man had said about teaching himself as he led him toward his grandfather's hut, isolated some distance from their small village. It was a new thought, and he wanted to remember the words and think about them later.

When he had ushered the man to the door of the hut, he returned to the yard and released the latch on the rooster's cage to let him enjoy a final meal. At first, he could not stop thinking about this man with his sleek black car and his polished shoes, both now covered in dust.

Then his thoughts turned to the bird. And to what he was expected to do. One twist of the rooster's neck or one stroke with the machete and it would no longer breathe or eat or strut. For a moment, he felt himself a god with power over that creature, power to decide life or death. He quickly pulled back from that thought, knowing that the good Sisters would admonish him for comparing himself to God. But where would the bird's "life" go? And why should he, not yet a man, have the power to make it disappear? Some part of him knew that the very ability to ask these questions somehow set him apart from the feathered creature. The bird was not capable of thinking about anything. At the same time, it was obvious that it wanted to go on living, scrounging for anything edible in the dust and dirt. He sensed that life itself was of value to the rooster. But why?

"Kaj! It is time. Now!" his grandfather called from inside the hut.

Kaj stood quickly and made a soft clucking sound as he held out some dried corn to the bird. It strutted toward him, confident and bold, happy to be offered a feast. It was almost too easy. Kaj shut his eyes for a moment as he grabbed the creature by the neck.

In another minute, he used the machete to chop off the head. He held the warm body of the bird upside down. A sharp metallic smell entered his nostrils as he let the blood, dark and warm, drip into a battered tin bowl that he would take into his grandfather and his visitor, the man who wore a spotless tan suit and a shiny watch.

He didn't understand it all yet, but he knew the visitor would pay the Babu well for the magic he had wrung from this silly bird. The blood might be smeared on the man's skin or added to a soup of herbs and bark. He would drink it and go home satisfied that he had obtained what he so desperately sought. The Babu would add the man's money to a leather pouch he kept under his pillow.

When Kaj had delivered the bowl that held the bird's life, he hurried outside far from the hut and threw up what was left of the tea and *uji* his mother had prepared for his breakfast. He wished he had a cup of water to rinse his mouth, but he simply wiped his face on his sleeve and went to meet the man from the city as he emerged from the darkened hut.

"You will need to walk carefully now until your eyes can take in the light," he told the man. "You can hold onto me if you wish." The man put one large hand on Kaj's shoulder and let himself be guided.

"Your Babu--he is a good healer?" the man asked in a shaky voice.

"He helps many many people." After a pause, he added, "He is much respected."

Once the man's eyes adjusted to the bright sunlight, he walked without Kaj's guidance, but he was clearly exhausted. Kaj slowed his pace. When they reached the car, Kaj pulled a rag from the pocket of his shirt and bent to wipe the dust from the man's shoes.

The man seemed stunned, dizzy perhaps. Kaj saw that sweat streaked his face and was rolling down his neck to the shirt beneath his jacket. He helped him into the car. The man pulled a 5000-shilling note from his pocket and handed it to Kaj. "For you," he said as he started the car. His eyes remained averted as if he did not want to acknowledge the boy's kindness. But then he rolled down the window and looked directly into the boy's eyes.

"You keep reading, boy. Hear? You could be like me." He laughed loudly.

Kaj nodded. "Yes, sir. Thank you, sir," he managed to whisper.

He watched the man turn his big car around on the narrow road and drive off toward the highway. He put the note inside his pocket and tucked the rag in on top of it.

It was a beginning.

10

As the heavy door clicked shut behind her, Alex took a deep breath and tried to smile. Alfredo Garcia was seated at a table in the middle of the windowless room. A loose-fitting red jumpsuit hung on his slight frame as it would on a scarecrow. His dark hair was shaved close to his head, and his cuffed hands lay in his lap. He glanced up at her but quickly lowered his eyes to the table.

She set her satchel down on the gray tiled floor next to her and pulled out a yellow legal pad and a pen. "Hello, Mr. Garcia. I'm Alex Carter, with the Innocence Project. We believe you are innocent, and we want to free you from prison."

"Innocent, huh? Why?" he asked, his dark eyes still on the table.

She noted his accent. He was born in Honduras, she remembered. But his hostile tone threw her off. She decided to keep her expression neutral. "Mr. Garcia, we don't have much time, so I'd like to ask you a few questions."

"I already heard every question, lady. Already been to trial two times."

"I know that the legal system has been so disappointing--so brutal for you. But we've studied your court transcripts and the police reports, and we've found errors. We also know that someone else--a serial killer--has recently confessed to this crime. Are you aware of that?"

Garcia looked up and stared. "What are you?"

Alex tipped her head to one side. "I'm a law student in Chicago, volunteering with the Innocence Project. We help people like you who have been unjustly accused and found guilty. I thought you knew--"

"I mean, what are you--like a white nigger or a vampire or something?"

The question hit Alex like a gob of spit in her face. Was he putting her down because of her skin color or because she was a woman? She wanted to reach over the table to slap him. Instead, she drew a deep breath and looked directly into his eyes. "Naturally, you're curious," Mr. Garcia, "and I'll tell you what I am, but if I'm going to help you, I need you to answer some questions."

"Yeah. Okay." He sat back as far as the metal chair would allow.

"I have a condition called albinism. Have you ever seen a white rabbit with reddish eyes?"

"A rabbit? Nah. No rabbits where I lived," he smirked.

"Well, I can't explain it all to you now, but please just take my word for it. I am a regular person, no more, no less, and how I look has nothing to do with what I'm here for." She glanced around at the gray-painted cinder blocks. A shiver slithered up her spine like a snake.

"Our time is short. We can help you Mr. Garcia. Another man has confessed to this crime, and you should no longer be on death row."

"I heard all that before. Plenty of times. And I'm still here in this fucking hole. Ten years! Don't waste your time, lady. I didn't hurt that kid. That's all I can tell you."

"I understand, but I want to ask you a few questions about your case to help us with some things that we aren't sure about. I'd like to start by asking you if you have anything you want to say that might help us. Or any questions you want to ask me?"

He stared at her, and for a moment she thought he wasn't going to answer. Then he said, "Yeah. I got a question. You believe in God?"

Alex suppressed her desire to look at her watch. Was he really thinking about God right now? Is this what Professor Wright meant about taking the measure of the man?

"Well," she began, "I know from talking with your mother that you were brought up Catholic. I'm not a Catholic, so my ideas about God may be quite different from yours."

"You talked to my mother?" Garcia's eyebrows lifted slightly.

"I did." Alex paused. "I was raised by a father who was the son of a Lutheran minister and a mother who was raised in India as a Hindu." She saw a spark of interest in his eyes.

"Did they believe that you burn in hellfire if you weren't good in your life?"

Alex met his gaze. She answered him in a soft voice. "No, Mr. Garcia. They don't believe that and neither do I. But I'm afraid that I'm not the best person to talk to about religion. I can tell you though, that your mother firmly believes that you are 'innocent as a lamb,' she said, and that she will see you in heaven one day."

"Yeah," he said as he turned his eyes toward the ceiling. Alex saw him clench his jaw.

"I'd like to ask about your friends--the ones who were also charged with this crime. Mr. Rivera and Mr. Nelson," Alex read from her notepad. "Did you get to talk with them at the police station when they brought you in?"

"Nah. They kept us apart. Ain't my friends anyways. They lied about me."

"Why would they do that?"

"Cash. Big-time cash. What else?" One corner of his mouth went up in a crooked smile.

"Cash from who? How do you know this?"

Garcia just shook his head.

"Please, Mr. Garcia, just help me understand. You went to the police in the first place to tell them about the murder--about finding the dead child--in hopes of getting the reward, right?"

"Yeah," he said closing his eyes and nodding slightly. "Yeah. Some fucking reward."

"But you testified that the police pressured you into saying that you committed the crime. Can you tell me what they said to you to make you confess?"

His reaction was immediate and startling. "That's fucking bullshit!" He tried to stand. The chains on his ankles clinked as he fell back down into his chair. His voice was shaky now. "Listen, lady, no one will ever make me say that. I never confessed to no one, nowhere, never. Not then, not now. Never." Alex looked up from her notes. Her eyebrows, as white as her hair, were drawn together in a frown.

"Are you saying that the police lied about your admission of guilt? That the detective lied--under oath--at your trial?"

He looked at her in silence for several seconds. "Yeah, lady, the nice white policeman lied."

"Can you tell me about him--let's see, Detective Boyle? What can you remember about what you told him or what he said to you? I know it's been a long time--"

"No problem. I remember every word. He said, 'You fucking piece of garbage, I'm gonna make sure you burn in hell.'"

Then, to Alex's amazement, a single tear rolled down Garcia's face. His lips trembled like a four-year-old trying to be brave.

"Please, don't do this to me," he whispered. She had to lean closer to hear him. "I'm gonna die now. I know it. I can't do this again. Please, just let me be. Let me die in peace."

"But Mr. Garcia. We can help--"

"Guard!" he called out in a loud voice. "I'm done here."

Alex watched as Officer Schneider entered, jangling his keys as he walked. He grabbed the prisoner by the arm and pulled him to a standing position. The ankle cuffs caused Garcia to shuffle in short steps toward the door.

Alex had the distinct sensation of falling, like the time she had slipped off the hiking path in the Sierras and slid some way down the hill before being saved by a downed tree. What if this man, who she really believed to be innocent, was put to death because of her failure to ask the right questions? She had the fleeting thought that everything she had worked for was slipping away. And so was this man's life.

***

Outside the prison, Alex took in a breath of frigid air and gave a long sigh. A thick layer of clouds had moved in overhead, and she was glad of her down coat. Somewhere in the world, sunlight was warming the Earth and the people who lived there, but right now, her world was cold, illuminated only by an oblique gray light that pervaded the entire landscape.

She checked her phone and found a message from Quincy: *Got us bargain tickets on a flight to Boston for Thanksgiving. And I've made dinner reservations for Saturday, ma cherie!*

And that was another problem she had to solve and was putting off. Quin seemed to assume that she was taking part in the Innocence Project just to add it to her resume. That it didn't really matter. And that she was wasting her time. Had she been naive to think she could make a difference in this legal morass? Isn't this what she had come to law school for?

Quin--Quincy Huntington III--having grown up with a father who was a prestigious Boston attorney, probably knew a great deal more about this world than she did. But what if Alfredo Garcia, who was now approaching the very real possibility of his death, really was innocent? And what if she could help exonerate him? Surely that mattered. She wouldn't give him up on him now when they were so close to the finish line.

But Quin, she realized now, as she drove away from the bleak prison, would never spend time with someone like Alfredo Garcia, never hold out a hand to rescue someone like him. The thought startled her. Maybe she had been hiding that realization from herself? She wanted the power to slow time down. Time to figure out how to free Mr. Garcia before the execution date. Time, too, to figure out whether she wanted to have Quin in her life.

Snow flurries started within minutes after she got on the interstate. She had faith in her Subaru but slowed down and pulled into the far-right lane as the snow started falling in earnest. Her thoughts were in a whirl, much like the large, wet snowflakes wildly hitting her windshield, and she knew she'd have to pay close attention to her driving. She pressed a radio button for a classical music station. YoYo Ma playing music from *The Mission*, perfect. Alex let the somber, almost ethereal tones run through her body, calming her nerves. The thought of Alfredo Garcia's execution, set for the end of November, loomed large, however.

11

Chicago, 2009

Alex slept restlessly for a few hours and finally threw back the down quilt and got out of bed around 4:30 am to review the thick file of information that she and her team had gathered about Alfredo Garcia. She was determined to find something that they might have missed, something that would give her a way forward.

Still groggy, she filled the grinder with beans, replaced the top, and pressed down in three short bursts, followed by a longer one for several seconds. This morning she would skip her preferred chai tea for a strong cup of java. The smell of freshly ground coffee beans always made her think of her father. He and her mother would still be sound asleep in their home in Southern California. For a moment she wished she were there in the kitchen making coffee for her dad and a cup of chai for her mom.

They would sit down with her and listen closely as she filled them in on the details of the Garcia case. While her father was the more emotionally expressive of the two, both could be relied upon to think logically and rationally. Neither was a lawyer, but both were trained scientists. They knew how to sift facts and ferret out overlooked details. They had taught her to approach problems in the same way.

After pulling a fleece robe over her pajamas and finding a pair of wool socks, Alex listened for the kettle and then poured boiling water over the finely ground coffee in her favorite mug, a gift from many years ago. It had been decorated with a photograph of herself as a child hugging her albino cat, Nacho, on the day they adopted him from a shelter. It had taken her some years to realize that her mother had been softening the shocking discovery of herself as a person with albinism.

Sitting at the small wooden desk in the corner of her studio apartment, she gave herself time to savor the coffee and think. What she needed now was a good long run to clear her mind, to meld the facts with her personal observations. But it was still dark outside, not to mention that yesterday's snowfall was now turning to ice. She took another sip of hot coffee. No run this morning.

She pulled the legal pad she had taken notes on at the prison from her satchel. Closing her eyes for a few seconds, she imagined herself laying out the pieces of what she knew about this tragic story for her parents like a jigsaw puzzle. They would not, in any case, be quick to judge. But she'd have to tell them what led to this man being tried and convicted of the rape and gruesome murder of ten-year-old Maria Morales.

Alfredo Garcia was eighteen years old when he showed up at the police station in Ciceroe, a few miles south of Chicago to report finding the body of a child in an overgrown field behind an abandoned factory near the river. He had gone to the site with his buddies, Ric Rivera and Tommy Nelson just after sunset to meet up with a kid from the city who could sell them good weed and sometimes interesting pills. As Garcia made his way through the trash behind the old building, he felt something soft under his right foot. It was the arm of a child attached to a mostly naked body, hidden in the tall weeds. When he looked down, he stepped back with a loud Spanish curse. A little girl, light-skinned, probably Hispanic, her head thrown back, her eyes open, lay as if looking up at the darkening sky.

Neither Rivera nor Nelson agreed with his idea to go to the police station. They warned him against trusting the cops, but he couldn't just leave her there. His mother had put the fear of God into him, and though he wasn't sure he believed in God, he was sure that if there was one, He would certainly be watching him at this moment. He took off his jacket and placed it over as much of the small body as he could. He couldn't help thinking about his sisters. How vulnerable girls were.

The three of them didn't hang around to wait for the dealer. Garcia went home. Then, after a mostly sleepless night, he went alone to the police station the following morning, frightened to go, but more frightened not to.

After a short interview, during which he told Detectives Kelly and Brown about finding the body, he directed them to the site from the back seat of their cruiser. They went into action then and mostly ignored him, though they told him he'd have to come back with them to the station for questioning. He listened to Detective Kelly make calls to bring in investigation teams. Within a half hour, the empty field was as busy as an ant hill. He turned his head, desperately wishing he had a joint or even just a Marlboro. He didn't look when a team of gloved and masked EMTs transferred the body to a black plastic bag. He didn't claim the jacket he had placed over the child.

According to the court transcripts, the next day, when his buddies had been brought to the station for questioning and when Garcia was questioned alone for hours by detectives Kelly and Brown, he admitted that he was indeed guilty of raping and murdering the child, a confession that even now he vehemently denied making. He became one of many men on death row who maintained that they were innocent.

Alex tapped her pen on the desk. She believed Garcia. Why? What was it about anyone that made her trust or deny her trust? She had read over his testimony several times, and her gut told her he was telling the truth. But she needed something more concrete to be able to convince anyone else and especially a judge. What advice would her parents give her if she told them all the details? She could imagine the horror on their faces and their worry about their only child. But she could also imagine her mother's voice telling her, "You must have missed something. Keep looking."

She began all over again by reviewing the known facts of the case, this time as if she were sitting on a jury listening to the prosecuting attorney. Garcia had had two trials, both resulting in the death penalty.

Garcia's last words to her at the prison echoed in her ears: "I never confessed to no one."

In a burst of energy, she spread out the papers from the folder on the floor. She skimmed through the trial transcripts until she found Detective Boyle's testimony at both trials. Under oath, he said that on Sunday, January 31, 1999, he had received a call from Detectives Brown and Kelly, had interviewed Alberto Garcia at length and reported that Alberto Garcia had confessed to the rape and murder of Maria Morales.

Alex placed the two testimonies next to each other. Word for word, Detective Boyle had sworn to this fact. She wrote his words at the top of a clean sheet of paper on her legal pad. Under it, she listed two other names: Detective Art Kelly and Detective Lou Brown. Within an hour, she had learned that Detectives Kelly and Brown were no longer available. Kelly had been shot and killed investigating a domestic violence complaint six years ago. Not long after, Detective Brown divorced and moved on his own to Montana or Idaho, according to his colleagues. No one had heard from him, and no one had any information about how to find him.

But the supervising detective, Dennis Boyle, had retired from the Chicago Police Department around ten years ago, soon after the brutal child murder. Looking at a list of seventeen Dennis Boyles in the Chicago area, Alex began with five addresses that were in the far southwest side, an area known for its Irish culture and pubs. The first few calls were unsuccessful. On the fifth call, a woman's voice answered.

"Hello?"

"Hello, Mrs. Boyle?"

"There is no Mrs. Boyle anymore. I'm Mr. Boyle's nurse."

"My name is Alex Carter, I'm a law student in Chicago working with the Innocence Project, and I'm looking for Detective Dennis Boyle. It's extremely important that I speak with him."

The nurse hesitated. "I'll have to ask his daughter. Give me your name again and your number. I'll get back to you."

Twenty minutes later, the phone rang. It was the nurse. Boyle's daughter had agreed to a brief visit, but only when she could be present. Would tomorrow around 11:00 am work? Alex made sure of the address and thanked the woman. She felt her heart speed up. Now all she had to do was prepare her questions. First, she messaged Jason Donorovich, a member of her Innocence Project team, asking him to go with her to visit Detective Boyle.

12

Southwest Chicago, 2009

The next morning, Alex and Jason drove to Detective Boyle's home on the southwest side of Chicago.

"This guy Boyle was a senior detective," Jason said, looking through his notes and sipping a latte from a paper cup. "With a long career and a solid reputation. Do you really think he lied? Under oath? That's a little hard to swallow."

"That's exactly what I think, Jason. Look, we know that the serial murderer who recently confessed to the crime is already serving a life sentence in an Illinois prison. Why would he lie now? Do serial killers think about how they can help some stranger who has been wrongly accused? And if you had heard Garcia proclaiming his innocence, I'm sure you would agree with me."

Jason glanced at her. "I believe you, Alex. I trust your judgment. I'm just lining up the facts here."

"Oh, I get it. Hunches and beliefs are not enough. But I have a gut feeling that this Detective Boyle has some piece of information that will help us prove Garcia's innocence. That's what this interview is about. It's like Professor Wright says--we've got to take the measure of the man by looking into his eyes and listening to his voice."

The morning sun was turning the snow and ice to slush. Alex found a place to park on the narrow street near Detective Boyle's home. She noted a wheelchair ramp leading to a side door as they walked up several steps to the front door.

A woman in her late forties, tastefully dressed in black woolen pants, a cream-colored silk blouse, and a herringbone jacket opened the door. She didn't smile. "I'm Janet Boyle, Detective Boyle's daughter. I'm not sure exactly why, but my father has agreed to talk to you. But he is very ill and not doing well. You must keep this interview short. Is that understood?"

Alex and Jason nodded as the woman turned away.

Her heels clicked as she led them down a dark hallway to a small living room that smelled of candle wax and lemon air freshener. Flowered drapes had been pulled shut over the windows, presumably against the cold. A round table in one corner of the room held two framed portraits on a crocheted doily. One was of a gray-haired woman with a lovely smile, a rosary draped over one corner of the picture. The other was of a young man in military uniform, a serious expression on his face. A line of flickering votive candles lit the faces in the frames. A triangular wood and glass case holding an American flag stood behind the portraits, and a polished wooden cross with a crucified Christ hung above the table.

The only other light in the dim room came from a floor lamp that stood next to a leather recliner, where a fragile-looking man was dozing, a colorful afghan covering his legs.

Janet Boyle invited Alex and Jason to sit on the sofa across from the recliner. "I know it's a little stuffy in here, but Dad is often cold," she said standing behind his chair. "Dad, these are the people I told you were coming. They want to talk to you." She put a hand on his shoulder.

Dennis Boyle opened his eyes and took a few seconds to focus. "Sorry. I seem to keep falling asleep even sitting up straight in this chair."

"He tires easily. You must keep it short," Janet warned again.

"Yes, of course," Alex answered. She turned to the old man. "We're sorry to bother you, Detective, but we have a few questions about an old case of yours. I'm Alex Carter, and this is Jason Donorovich. We're volunteers with the Innocence Project."

"I know all about that," Boyle said with a wave of his hand. "I've read about your so-called project. You take the side of criminals."

"Actually, we're on the side of truth, Detective Boyle," Jason broke in.

"Yeah, yeah, truth. You're young--but you'll learn by the time you're my age that truth is complicated." He waved a hand in front of him. "Go ahead. Ask your questions."

"I'll make this as brief as I can, Detective," said Alex. "Do you remember Alfredo Garcia--"

"That's why you're here, is it?" He looked from Jason to Alex, who were waiting for him to say more.

Boyle started coughing. His whole body shook under the blanket as the cough turned into what sounded like a painful fit. His eyes watered as he bent forward trying to calm his lungs. His daughter handed him a handkerchief and patted his back.

"You need to rest now, Dad. I'll see your guests out."

"No, no. It's okay, Janet," said Boyle, reaching for a glass of water from a side table. His hand shook as he took a sip. "Let me talk. Garcia was found guilty of kidnapping a child. Using her for his own ugly reasons . . . And then killing her."

His daughter spoke before he could say any more. "That's enough!" She looked at Alex, fire in her eyes. "What right do you have to come here bringing up some old case that has long been closed? And what does my dad have to do with it anyway?"

"Just a couple more questions--please," said Alex.

"Can't you see--that my dad . . . doesn't have much time left? Have you no decency?" Janet stood over her father, her voice rising, close to tears.

"Wait," said Detective Boyle. "I want to talk, Janet. I have to talk." He took another sip of water and handed the glass to her as the others watched him. Boyle's grayish skin and rheumy eyes indicated that he was approaching death, but his mind was evidently quite clear.

He leaned forward in his chair. "Yeah, like Janet indicated--I'm dying. Stage IV lung cancer. But I'm aware of the news. I know that Alfredo Garcia is scheduled to be executed soon. I assume that's why you're here."

"Yes, Detective," Alex said softly. "The execution is scheduled for November 30th. Alfredo Garcia will die unless we can prove his innocence."

Janet was silent now. Tears ran down her face. Boyle reached up for her hand and held on to it.

"So go ahead--ask your questions. I'm ready."

Alex and Jason looked at each other. "I'll record," said Jason scrambling to get out the voice recorder.

After a few moments, he nodded at Alex to begin.

"Detective Boyle, were you the Senior Detective along with Detectives Kelly and Brown regarding

Alfredo Garcia, who was accused of the rape and murder of Maria Morales?"

"I was. Good men--Kelly and Brown. Both gone now."

"And are you aware that Mr. Garcia has maintained his innocence over the past ten years and that a serial murderer recently confessed to the crime?"

"I am aware."

"Please," said Janet. "Please . . ." She was sobbing.

"Detective Boyle, I want to ask you about what you swore under oath at the trials of Alfredo Garcia. According to trial transcripts, you testified that Detectives Kelly and Brown notified you by telephone on January 31, 1999, that Alfredo Garcia had just confessed to the rape and murder of Maria Morales."

"Yes, ma'am. That is true," he answered in a weak but audible voice.

"I happened to notice that January 31ˢᵗ was also the day of Super Bowl XXXIII. Did you watch the game that day, Detective?"

He hesitated only a moment. "Yes, I did. The Broncos defeated the Falcons, 34-19." He looked up at Alex with a surprised expression. "You've done your homework, young lady. You would make a fine detective. So--I assume you already know that I was watching that game in Cabo San Lucas on vacation with my wife, Elaine? I remember it well."

"And the cell phone reception there in Mexico-- was it acceptable, Detective Boyle? Did you receive a call from Detectives Kelly and Brown on that Sunday?"

"No, my phone wouldn't work in Cabo, ever. No reception. I never got a call from them. Not that day, not any day." His voice shook.

"So, you lied under oath--twice," Alex said softly.

He looked up at his daughter. "I'm sorry you have to hear this, Janet." He paused and looked directly at Alex. "Yes. I lied under oath, God forgive me. I thought--I was convinced-- that fellow did those terrible things to an innocent child. But I was wrong." He hung his head in silence. Alex waited.

"When I read recently that a known serial killer confessed to that tragic crime, I knew it was true. I knew Garcia had to be innocent. I've made my confession to the Church, but Father Riley encouraged me to let someone know what I had done. I want to try to make amends before I go." Tears shone in his eyes.

"Dad--"

"That's my wife and my son over there," he said pointing to the table. "They've already gone to the Father. I'd like to think I'll be joining them soon."

Janet wept softly. Boyle patted her hand.

"Thank you, Detective," said Alex. I'm sorry for the pain you must be suffering, but you've done the right thing. And I believe your confession will save the life of an innocent man."

* * *

Alex and Jason emerged into bright sunshine and fresh air outside.

"That place was giving me the creeps," Jason said. "Like a funeral parlor."

"Thank you for doing the recording," said Alex.

They climbed into the Subaru. Most of the snow had melted from the pavement.

"I have to ask," Jason said, "how in the world did you know about the Super Bowl? I never would have pegged you for a football fanatic."

Alex laughed. "Far from it. I consider the game to be the very definition of gratuitous violence."

"Then how--?"

She hesitated. "I have this weird kind of memory--I can remember things, things I am sometimes barely aware of at the time they're happening. I must have picked up the Super Bowl stats from somewhere, and the date just clicked for me when I was reviewing the transcripts. Then I checked with the department to see if Boyle had been on duty that Sunday and found out that he was on vacation in Mexico."

"So, do you have like a photographic memory? That must come in handy for studying."

"Something like that. But it can be really annoying. Sometimes I have to question what I really remember. I can be flooded with information--you know, overload."

Jason was fiddling with his phone. He started to replay the recording, then stopped. "In any case--it was clever, Alex. Well done. I'll message the recording to you. This is the piece we need to convince the judge. I'm sure of it."

"I hope so. I do hope so," she answered. But she was already far away in her mind, thinking now of the framed photos of Boyle's wife and son in that dimly lighted room. And Boyle's hope to be reunited with them in heaven. What, she wondered, did he think would happen to him when he died if he hadn't confessed? Hellfire and brimstone? That's what he had wished for Garcia when he had been convinced of his guilt. Clearly, he hoped to be forgiven by his God and reunited with loved ones. That's what he was thinking about as he faced his last days, his mortality.

She thought back to Garcia's question about the afterlife. Heaven and hell loomed large for him too when death was near. She was fascinated that it was Detective Boyle's religious beliefs--no doubt instilled in him from early childhood--that had made him fear the possibility of an eternity in hell enough to make him reveal this long-held secret, for surely he had known that he lied all along. But what had taken him so long?

13

Chicago, 2009

A week later, after spending a few hours in the law library, Alex pulled off her woolen gloves and loosened the scarf around her neck before opening a mailbox in the lobby of her apartment building. She was shivering despite a quilted down jacket and lambswool-lined Uggs, which, she was sure, had only just managed to keep her toes from frostbite in the November weather. She smiled to find a letter from her mother, addressed in the familiar handwriting that carried a touch of India. And there was another letter, a business-sized envelope with the CAPE logo and a New York City return address. She felt her stomach tighten. I'm just gathering information, she told herself. No need to think about this yet. Nevertheless, a rocket of possibility was launched in her brain. It could be nothing, but what if it was something more?

She had promised to meet Quin for dinner at seven, but the thought of going out again into the cold was daunting, and she considered canceling. She suspected that he wanted to talk about their relationship. Her mind went blank whenever that topic came up. What exactly was she avoiding? She could feel Quin's vision of the future stalking her every time they were together lately, although perhaps she was only imagining it. Both had been busy with studying, and Alex had been spending a lot of time with the Innocence Project. She had avoided thinking about him. Quin, too, had been busier than usual--focused on writing a lengthy article for law review about something to do with international business. If only she had more time to think. Theworld was spinning so fast . . .

The space heater in her studio apartment was not quite a roaring fireplace, but it helped to thaw out her fingers and toes as she sipped a cup of chai tea. She reluctantly texted Quin to confirm dinner and looked at the two unopened envelopes on her desk. She chose to open the one from CAPE headquarters first.

When the Innocence Project team met in late August, Alex had noticed an information flyer pinned up on a bulletin board outside Professor Wright's office. CAPE, Caring for All People of the Earth, was a non-profit human rights organization looking to hire an attorney for research and policy development in their New York headquarters. The announcement specified requirements including excellent communication skills, fluency in at least one other language, and a strong interest in human rights and humanitarian law. Later, after exploring the CAPE website with increasing curiosity, she had taken the time to fill out the online application, not quite knowing why she did so. A backup plan? It was a long shot anyway. She would likely be judged and eliminated as an inexperienced lawyer. In any case, competition for the position would be strong. Nevertheless, she completed the application, pushed submit, and then more or less forgot about it. That had been months ago.

What if, she asked herself, even as she tried to tamp down her expectations, what if? She opened the envelope carelessly as if to prove to herself that the letter was of little consequence.

> Dear Ms. Carter,
>
> It is our pleasure to invite you to an interview for the position of Researcher at CAPE headquarters in New York City. We have been impressed with your credentials and application. We would very much like to speak with you in person and learn more about you and your goals.
>
> We understand that you must be busy with your studies and exams at this time, but would it be at all possible to visit with us on November 27, the Friday after Thanksgiving?

There were more details, but Alex found that she was unable to focus on them. It was just an interview, after all. But if a magic portal to another world had opened there in her tiny apartment, she couldn't have been more surprised or intrigued. Or more filled with anxiety. It was as if she suddenly discovered a secret trail that branched off from the rocky pathway up the mountain to discover a sun-filled meadow where there were purple lupines, a silvery brook with tiny blue fish, and a clear view of the green valley she had left far below. She got up from her chair, still holding on to the letter, enjoying the moment of excitement, the possibility of stepping into a future that could be so different. Of course, it was just a fantasy.

She looked out the window to watch the last rays of the sun reflected in the windows of the buildings across from hers. It wasn't yet five o'clock. Darkness would soon close in, and the temperature outside would be dropping even further. But for a few lovely minutes, she was in that meadow, enjoying the sunshine, the wildflowers, and the big-picture view of just how far she had come. She smiled as she observed herself in such an altered state. Amazed that a few lines typed by a stranger almost a thousand miles away at some time in the past could so strongly affect her here in the present moment.

She took another sip of the milky tea. The smell of cardamom, cinnamon, and cloves relaxed her into an old comfort, and she took up her mother's letter. It was dated four days earlier. It was not good news:

My darling Alex,

We knew when we all decided that Nacho would remain here at home when you left for law school, that he was already nearing the end of his most beautiful life. When you saw him on your last visit home in the summer, I know you sensed how darkness was closing in on him though he was happy to have you home, delighted to have you hold him in your arms once again.

I am sorry to tell you that now he is gone-- but so glad to tell you that it was a peaceful end for Nacho. We found him curled on your pillow as if he were only asleep. I don't think he was in any pain. Sixteen years is quite old for a cat, and we can all take comfort in having had him this long. He loved you very much, and you had the privilege of loving this beautiful creature throughout your childhood and through your growing-up years.

Your dad and I felt that a letter was better than a phone call or a text, as receiving news of such a loss is, I believe, a private matter--which is not to say that we don't share your grief.

We have buried him under the jacaranda tree in the backyard as you wanted. It is not yet in bloom, but the purple flowers that will appear in the spring will now always remind us of Nacho. I am here when you want to talk.
Love, Mom

Her father had added a note at the bottom:

Hey, Lexy. When I was about seven and my cat died, I asked my father if cats went to heaven--if I'd ever see Cricket again. He told me that no one really knew what awaits us after death, but that we already had a kind of heaven in being able to remember all the love and good times we shared with Cricket, that heaven was possible in our minds at any moment we wanted to remember.

He also reminded me of the words I had often heard in a popular song when I was about your age (but borrowed from Ecclesiastes) -- *to everything there is a season, and a time to every purpose under the heaven.*

I've always thought that he was very wise to speak to me, a seven-year-old, in this way, and his words have sustained me through many losses since that time. I pass his words on to you to give you comfort now and for the many losses that life inevitably brings. Know that Nacho is at peace beneath the jacaranda.

We love you very much, my sweet daughter. And we are so proud of you.
Love, Dad

Alex looked down at her watch with tears in her eyes. Nacho had been at the center of her childhood world. *A time for every purpose under heaven.* Her dad used to sing that song quietly as he worked on some project or was repairing something in the garage. She whispered a few words of goodbye and imagined holding Nacho in her arms for a few moments before showering, dressing for the arctic weather once again, and heading out to meet Quin.

14

Chicago, 2009

Alex and Quin stepped out of the elevator and entered the Signature Room at the 95th, a chic restaurant ninety-five stories above the Chicago cityscape and surrounded by floor-to-ceiling windows. They had left the frigid November evening behind at ground level and found themselves in a warm, dimly lighted space that smelled of expensive perfumes and sauteed garlic. An uncountable number of lights twinkled from far below. Headlights and taillights danced like fireflies on Lake Shore Drive bordering the lake.

When the hostess seated them at a table next to the wall of glass windows, Alex couldn't stop looking down at the fanciful geometry of skyscraper rooftops close by, enjoying the dizzying perspective. For a couple of minutes, she stepped effortlessly into another world, a different reality. Like the way she sometimes secretly entered the visions where she saw the light people.

Alex was both excited and hesitant about sharing her news, and she was hoping to find the courage to tell him about the upcoming interview with CAPE in New York as well. But tonight, Quin had made clear, was to be a celebration. They had both received offers from the Washington D.C. law firms where they had interned during the past summer--he at perhaps the city's most prestigious corporate law firm, and Alex at a highly-respected boutique firm. Quin, she suspected, was already thinking ahead to graduation and to moving in together in D.C. after graduation. And perhaps more? She didn't want to think about that.

"I didn't realize--I would have worn something a bit more glamorous or elegant or something. How do you even know about this place?"

"My parents brought me here when I made law review last year," Quin said. "They always seem to know the best places," he added with a wry grin. He and Alex had discussed the pros and cons of being only children. They agreed that they were both grateful and sometimes a bit smothered by their parents' hopes for them. "Anyway, I thought you'd like it."

"Of course, I do! It just seems a little--over the top--sorry for the pun--just to celebrate our job offers." She laughed. Quin didn't even smile.

A waiter filled their water goblets and told them that their waitress would be with them shortly.

When they had given him their drink orders, white wine for Alex, a scotch and soda for Quin, he leaned slightly over the table to look into Alex's eyes. "We could make this into more of a celebration."

"Hey! We're moving!" She had just realized that the floor beneath her was moving ever so slightly. The whole restaurant was revolving high above the city in a counterclockwise direction, the wall of windows slowly revealing pieces of the metropolis below, like a giant 3-D puzzle. If only time could be slowed down in this same way, she thought. She would have time to think, time to keep Quin from going too fast, from racing headlong into the future.

"Well, I have something I want to tell you--something, in fact, to celebrate," Alex said as she picked up her water glass.

"Really? I'm all ears."

The waiter appeared carrying their drinks on a small tray and set them on the starched white tablecloth.

"First--a toast to our future," Quin said, holding up his glass to clink with Alex's. "We've come a long way with a lot of hard work, and we're about to reap our rewards. Here's to a great future together."

"To the future!" Alex said before taking a large gulp of cool wine from the delicate stem glass."

"You were saying that you had something to tell me?" Quin raised one eyebrow to punctuate his question.

"I've been waiting to talk to you. I just found out this morning that the Governor has granted Alberto Garcia a stay of execution. I'm so excited, Quin. I could just float away. This means we have more time--enough time, I think--to build our argument to convince the judge of his innocence." She could feel her eyes filling with tears and blinked them back.

"I see. Well, congratulations. A job well done." He raised his glass again and sipped. "Now you'll have more time for other things--for your review article, I mean, and more time to spend with me." He smiled as if to soften the egoism of that remark, but Alex knew he meant it.

"Professor Wright called me as soon as he heard. Our whole team is super excited. Just think, Quin. We could actually save this man's life."

Glassware and silverware gleamed in the candlelight as they and the table between them continued to flow slowly backward, or at least that's how Alex perceived it from her position at the table. At that moment, she had a clear memory of trying to peddle backward on her bicycle as an eight-year-old, wondering why it couldn't be done. She shook her head in a quick movement to shake off the memory."

"Alex, I'm happy for you, I really am. But I have to say that I hope this will be the end of your work on that project. It takes so much of your time, and there's really no payoff for doing this stuff. No one in D.C. will care."

The waitress appeared at their table. She apologized for the wait, expertly described the house specials, and took their orders. Alex sipped her wine and noticed that Quin's glass was nearly empty. Then she called out to the waitress, who had turned to leave. "Excuse me please--I wonder, would it be possible to hold off a while longer on putting in our order?"

"Of course. How about I wait twenty minutes or so?"

"And I'll have another of these," Quin said, not even bothering to look at the waitress.

When the waitress left, Quin squinted his eyes at Alex, an expression she had come to understand as disagreement. "What in the world was that about? Aren't you hungry?"

I'm holding back time. I need to back up.

"There's something else I need to tell you, Quin."

"Uh-oh."

"I received a letter today from CAPE."

"CAPE? That do-gooder, bleeding-heart non-profit?" Quin was almost spitting the words.

"Caring for All People of the Earth. They've invited me for an interview," Alex said in a neutral voice.

"You're not serious, Alex."

"Well, let's just say I'm--curious. CAPE does a lot of good. Their human rights investigations and their reports have resulted in important policy changes and--"

"But what about the job offer in D.C.? Are you even considering turning that down?"

The waitress appeared to replace Quin's drink and remove his empty glass.

He took a long swig of his Scotch. Alex turned her head to look out the glass wall. She could see the Centennial Ferris wheel on Navy Pier, a tiny bright thing that took people on rides round and round and deposited them back where they started thirteen minutes later. She and Quin had ridden it once. It was during the spring when they were first-year law students. They were "just friends" then, having met in a class on ethics. Quin had a girlfriend, another law student who was a year ahead of him. The relationship had fallen apart when she graduated and headed for Los Angeles to work in a large corporate law firm. Alex had commiserated, and she and Quin had become friends.

Then, during this past summer, they both had internships at D.C. law firms. They met for dinner several times, excited to share notes about their real-world experiences. And now? Now Alex was afraid that he was envisioning--no, planning--a comfortable urban lifestyle for them as a couple in Washington D.C., making incredible salaries, and climbing the proverbial ladder.

"I know I'm fortunate to be asked back to that position. But I'm just not sure, and---"

"Alex, please, just listen to me." He reached across the table to take her hand. "I had hoped," he said in a hoarse voice, "to ask you to marry me. My parents are planning a small party to introduce you to friends over the Thanksgiving holiday. Please tell me I'm wrong in thinking your answer is 'no.'"

"Oh, Quin." A few tears spilled over despite her best attempt to hold them back. "I don't want to hurt you, Quin."

"But you are hurting me," he said in a loud voice. He pulled his hand away. "You can't do this to me." He picked up his drink and took a long sip.

Alex took a deep breath. "I'm going to get up and take the elevator down and go home now, Quin. I'm not sure where my path is leading, but I mean to find out what is around the next corner." She paused and then quietly added, "I won't be going with you for Thanksgiving. I'm so sorry."

She stood up, gathered her coat, hat, and gloves, and entered the elevator.

15

Mevo Dotan, West Bank, Palestine, 2005

On an early morning in June, Seth stood alert in the already sweltering heat at the edge of the Mevo Dotan settlement in the West Bank. He was intent on keeping a watchful eye on a restless crowd that included both Israeli settlers and a small group of Palestinians from the nearby town of Ya'bad.

Seth's IDF squad had been sent to the settlement by their base commander. Their mission was to prevent an escalation of emotions that had erupted after a group of Palestinian teenagers allegedly threw rocks at the Israeli Army soldiers. This situation was not entirely uncommon since Mevo Dotan, an Israeli-occupied settlement within the borders of the West Bank, was considered illegal by much of the international community. Its very existence was a major source of resentment for the Palestinian population of Ya-bad, who claimed that the territory now occupied by the settlers had been stolen from them.

Seth surveyed the restless crowd as he listened to the raised voices of settlement leaders and representatives from the Palestinian town dispute the situation. Both groups were hurling insults, tempers were high. In his heart, he wasn't entirely sympathetic to the Israelis, to whom he had sworn allegiance. In Ethiopia, his own people, the *Beth Israel*, had a history of being marginalized and taunted as *Falashes*—exiles without a home. His father had reminded him often of that history even as he focused on the future--on the hope that one day they would live in the Promised Land. Now Seth was in that land, but he couldn't let himself forget what it had felt like to be numbered among the outsiders. *Am I disloyal if I have sympathy for these people who have lived here on this soil for many years? Like my ancestors?*

Seth saw the flash of metal a second before he looked down at the girl's face. What he saw paralyzed him for a moment. Surely he knew this face. Who was she? She looked about sixteen. Slight of build and a full head shorter than his six-foot-plus frame. As if he had entered a slow-motion video or a nightmare, he felt time slowing up as the girl drew a screwdriver from her skirt pocket, raised it above her head in both hands, and then stabbed it hard into his right forearm. Though he felt no pain at that moment, his mind registered that blood was quickly dripping from his arm.

He snapped back into reality with a surge of adrenaline. "Whoa, whoa, slow down, girl," he whispered as he tried to grab hold of her wrists. Her stabbing only became fiercer and more frenzied as she raised her arms again and stabbed at Seth's hands and then at his torso. He backed away, one hand clasped over the wound on his forearm. Then he turned and ran toward the settlement.

"That's for Galib!" the girl cried out, her whirling arms slowing now. Tears ran down her face and mixed with the sweat that was dripping from under her headscarf. "My brother is a martyr. I will never forget him, she screamed." She turned and ran but in the opposite direction.

Seth didn't know anyone named Galib, and he hadn't killed anyone during his five years of service with the IDF. *She's got to be crazy*, he thought.

And then he knew. She was Nouf. A friend of his sister, Deborah. Nouf and his sister had become friends several years ago when they had participated in a folk-dance program to bring the Israeli and Palestinian communities together by sharing traditions and cultures. Seth had met her once when his sister introduced them at the community center.

On a recent visit home, Deborah had told him that Nouf had lost her brother, a Palestinian soldier, in a border fight with the IDF. Her friend's grief, she said, was deep and full of rage.

* * *

The next morning, Seth appeared at the Commander's office as ordered. The officer glanced at Seth's bandaged arm and hands but said nothing.

"At ease, soldier. Take a seat."

The Commander had seen hundreds of young men and women come and go as they fulfilled their military service. Each one, he had learned, brought their personalities and experiences to the task. Some broke under the discipline and demands of training, and some thrived, but he had long ago given up predicting who would or would not be successful. He thought nothing could surprise him anymore, but this incident didn't make sense. He thought he knew this soldier well and was puzzled.

"Okay, soldier, I want you to listen to something from the news that has come across my desk. He picked up a paper from his desk and read in a gravelly voice.

Channel 2 news reported that yesterday morning, an elite Maglan combat unit was sent to the Mevo Dotan settlement on the West Bank to quell an altercation between Israeli settlers and a group of Palestinians from Ya-bad. While there, an unidentified soldier was attacked by a young woman with a screwdriver. Eyewitnesses reported that the soldier ran from the woman. When questioned about the incident after the fact, the soldier told his officers, "I was without a gun. I panicked. I didn't know what to do, so I ran."

The assailant, sixteen-year-old Nouf Zaid, a resident of Ya-bad, was shot by another soldier as she ran. She received treatment on site from IDF medics and was taken to Hadera hospital. Her condition is unknown at this time.

Seth kept his expression neutral as he listened, his eyes focused straight ahead of him at a framed Israeli flag on the wall behind the Commander, well aware that his life could be about to change radically. He wished desperately for a glass of water.

As the Commander finished reading the short article, he leaned back, tossed the paper onto his desk, and looked at Seth.

"I'm hoping that you have a damned good explanation for this, soldier. Here's my question. How does a young man who distinguished himself in basic training, who was chosen from more than 200 competitors to train and earn a place on this elite reconnaissance team, and who proved himself an expert in Krav Maga skills--how does this outstanding soldier not only get stabbed by a sixteen-year-old girl but panic and run away from her?"

Seth thought then of the girl who must be lying in a hospital bed perhaps in great pain. And full of grief, he imagined. How could he answer this man, this man for whom aggressive action was the answer to most problems? But hadn't he proved himself a man and a soldier among his colleagues? He couldn't help thinking of his father at this moment. A peaceful man whose great wish was for his son to become a scholar, to study the ways of their God.

The phone on the Commander's desk buzzed, and he picked up. Seth began searching his mind for how to answer the man's question. But in a matter of seconds, the Commander hung up the phone. He was silent for almost a minute as he pushed papers around on his desk. Then he spoke to Seth again. "The girl--your attacker-- died in the hospital from her gunshot wounds not even an hour ago. This complicates things, I'm afraid."

16

Tel Aviv, Israel, 2005

Seth paced outside the emergency room entrance to the Rabin Medical Center in Tel Aviv, uncertain about whether he wanted to go inside. He had traveled from Jerusalem by train and then a short way by bus. No longer wearing a uniform, no longer living according to a strict daily schedule, he had been sliding into a world of shadows, a place where he was no longer sure of himself, a place that had dark corners that he didn't want to examine.

Perhaps coming here to Tel Aviv was a mistake after all. He could still turn around and go home, he told himself. Benjamin had sounded happy to hear from him on the telephone and had invited him to meet him for lunch. Seth was surprised to learn that he already knew about his discharge from the IDF.

The memory of that incident was still on a loop in his head as he thought about how the base Commander had humiliated him for having run from his sixteen-year-old attacker. Seth could not explain, would not defend his actions. Though Nouf had died at the hands of a fellow soldier, he was the one responsible. When the men in his unit spoke up for him, a committee had given Seth the choice of resigning with an honorable discharge or remaining an IDF soldier but with a demotion, a token appeasement to the girl's family and the local Palestinian population.

Benjamin's shift in the ER would be finished at noon. Seth entered the medical center and stood in a short line at the reception desk. A young woman looked up at him with a smile.

"How can I help you?"

"Can you tell me where to find Benjamin Bendler? I'm meeting him here."

"You must be Seth. Dr. Bendler asked me to tell you that he will be finished in just a few minutes. He'll meet you in the hospital courtyard--just through those doors over there."

The day was warm and the air clear, a sharp contrast to his mood, Seth realized. The atmosphere seemed lighter within the greenery of the courtyard, and he thought he might even detect a faint trace of sea air. Taking a seat in the shade of an old olive tree on a concrete bench, a gift from someone to honor a family member according to a small bronze plaque, he was surprised to feel some small measure of calm, as if the bench and the tree in that place and at that time were meant for him. He closed his eyes, enjoying the stillness.

"Seth, my friend!" Benjamin appeared in front of him wearing blue scrubs and sneakers.

Seth stood up, and the two men greeted each other with a back-slapping hug. "Here, let us sit down for a few minutes in this garden." Benjamin said. "I hope it's okay with you if Natalie joins us for lunch. She was able to take a long break from her work at the embassy and really wants to see you too."

"Of course. I'd love to see her. I was just thinking how peaceful it feels here," Seth said looking up at the small, gray-green leaves filtering bits of sunlight through them.

"I'm glad you like it," said Benjamin. "This garden is my home away from home--I sit here whenever I have a break from seeing patients. Trees are something like friends to me This one above us is a strong, mature tree, probably planted when this hospital was built back in the 30s. But did you know that olive trees can live for more than a thousand years? For many people--including both Palestinians and Israelis--they are symbols of peace and abundance."

"I recognize them. I see them all over this country. We had olive trees in Ethiopia as well, growing wild on the hills where I helped watch over the sheep as a boy."

"Some of these trees have been observing us humans and our struggles over who owns the land for hundreds of years. I am convinced that trees have their own wisdom-- and that they're waiting for us to realize we are all just people. And that we'd all be better off if we can learn to get along." Ben sighed.

"Can I ask you a personal question, Ben?"

"Anything."

"Why did you leave the IDF? I mean, you could have stayed on as a doctor and worked for the army, right?"

"When I made *aliyah* from the United States, I was obligated to serve in the army for eighteen months. I was happy to do that because I was excited to start a new life in Israel after I lost my mother to cancer. But I didn't want to be limited by staying in the military. Natalie, too, wanted very much to be part of the gathering of Jews from all over the Earth, and she had applied to work at the American Embassy here in Tel Aviv.

"I get it," said Seth. "You have lots of different patients here--not just soldiers."

Benjamin stood up. "C'mon. Let's walk to the restaurant--not far from here. And there's a tree I want to show you on the way."

The tree, located in the middle of a sidewalk next to the street, rose high above the nearby apartment buildings and businesses. Seth was puzzled to see a few people were picking up leaves that had fallen from the smooth-trunked tree.

"They gather them for the aroma," Ben explained. This is a lemon-scented eucalyptus, kind of a famous tree in this city. The thing I love about this tree--apart from its lovely scent--is its history. It was brought here in the nineteenth century from Australia at a time when early settlers were planting trees everywhere. Somehow, having survived so long here, it is now considered an Israeli tree and beloved by all. What I cannot understand is why we can't apply that same sense of inclusion and affection to people."

"Are you still working with Peace Now?" Seth asked, remembering a brief conversation he had with Benjamin when he last saw him a few months ago.

"I am," Ben said, picking up a large lemon-scented leaf and handing it to Seth. "We're not exactly popular, but I remain hopeful about bringing people together--even here among Israelis and Palestinians. I enjoyed my time in the IDF, but now I use my medical skills for a wider group of people who are very much in need of help. I think it may be the way for me to do the most good I can in the world."

After greeting Natalie at Grains and Greens, the three sat down to fresh salads and crusty bread with olive oil and balsamic vinegar. Natalie asked about Seth's family and showed pictures of their children. Then she asked, "So what will you do with your life now, Seth--after leaving the Army, I mean?"

Even as Natalie was asking the question, Seth realized that his sister Deborah must have talked with Ben and Natalie. It was, in fact, her suggestion that he travel here to visit Benjamin. She must have told them about the guilt he was feeling over Nouf, about the empty pit in his stomach because of leaving the IDF, even if it had been his choice. His sister had been right though. These were good people who cared about him and his family. He would listen to them as he always had.

"I'm not sure what comes next," Seth said. "I would like to take courses at the university--maybe finish my degree, but I also need a job. My sisters now help my mother with catering our Ethiopian specialties, and I have to start looking for a way to support myself."

"I have a possibility for you to think about," said Natalie. "The embassy is taking applications now for part-time security guard. With your background in the IDF, you would qualify. And you could attend classes part-time as well here at the university in Tel Aviv."

"The American Embassy would hire me?"

"You're an Israeli citizen, you are qualified, and you would pass the background check. Ben and I would vouch for your character." She smiled, pleased with her idea. "We need good people like you on our staff."

Ben looked at his watch. When they all got up to go, he put his arm around Seth's shoulders. "I hope you'll come to see us again soon, Seth. With the kids and their activities, we don't get to Jerusalem often these days."

"You have given me much to think about, and I thank you--both of you," he said before they all headed in different directions.

On the train home, he pulled a folded leaf out of his pocket and put it up to his nose. The scent of lemon filled his senses and made him reach for some long-ago memory that he couldn't quite capture. But after today, it would always be the memory of his friends who had helped him when he needed a new direction. He thought about Ben's words--about hoping that he was doing good in the world. When Seth was ten years old, he was inspired by the heroic IDF soldier who took care of them on the jet plane. Now Ben's words about peace went straight to his heart. His father, he thought at that moment, would approve if he were still alive. He would again follow in his friend's footsteps to discover for himself how to do good in the world.

17

Near Arusha, Tanzania, 2011

Kaj washed his face and hands and put on the collared shirt he kept clean to meet the occasional city client. Today, Mr. M was expected, and his Babu had told him that it was a very important appointment. He must not be late in meeting the client out on the road.

He was looking forward to seeing Mr. M., who was always friendly to him. The big city man had visited on several occasions during the past year or so, and he had been generous with both his advice and a tip when Kaj walked him back to his car.

"If you want to be rich like me, you must know more about the world," he told Kaj. "And you must be strong. Then you will know how to put money in your pockets." He had laughed, but the boy took seriously every word the man spoke.

Kaj had explained to Mr. M that he couldn't go to school any longer but that he had learned to read and was sometimes able to borrow a book from the Sisters' school at St. Cecelia's Orphanage. He told Mr. M how he was helping his mother sell her baskets and beaded bracelets, though he didn't mention that lately his mother had grown weaker and could not do as much as before. Mr. M rubbed his bald head and smiled in a way that made Kaj feel he could one day be like him. He, too, would drive a shiny black car, wear a gold watch, and have important work to do in the city.

Kaj stood at the dusty roadside for only a few minutes when Mr. M's car pulled up. He was surprised to see a passenger in the car this time.

"This is my assistant. You can call him Tom," said Mr. M. Tom nodded his head but his facial expression did not change. He was short and somewhat stout with gray, bristly hair, like a wild boar, Kaj thought. The man didn't wear a suit like Mr. M. but was dressed in a black tee-shirt and black leather jacket.

Kaj's heart jumped within his chest to see that Tom carried a machete.

"Don't worry," Mr. M. said with a loud laugh. "He is also my main protector--that's why he must carry this blade."

"I'll take you to my grandfather," Kaj said. "This way, please."

They walked in silence for several minutes. Kaj kept the pace slow, as he knew that the heat and the uphill path made walking difficult for Mr. M. When they reached a flat area with a bit of shade, they stopped.

"You are your grandfather's assistant, yes? Like Tom here who helps me?" said Mr. M as he wiped his brow. Tom stood waiting, looking off into the distance, the machete ready at his side.

"I am the Babu's apprentice," said Kaj. "One day, my grandfather says, I will be the healer for all the people in this area." He winced at his empty boast knowing that the idea of him taking over his grandfather's business was more than ever a thought he avoided. During these several years of serving as an apprentice to his Babu, Kaj had come to doubt that his grandfather possessed the magic that people paid him for with their chickens and millet.

When they reached the hut, Kaj was surprised to see Babu come out to greet his guest. He wasn't dressed in his usual rags but had put on a red western-style shirt that hung loosely to his thighs and a pair of black pants. He wore an orange band around his gray hair, and he carried his decorated stick, a magical object handed down to him by his father, and his father's father. Feathers and beaded bracelets decorated his thin arms and ankles. He bowed his head slightly to Mr. M.

"Let's get started," Mr. M said, his voice almost a growl. "And I want your *apprentice* with us today." He said the word "apprentice" with an emphasis that made Kaj turn his eyes away from his Babu.

"No. He is not yet ready. He stays outside," the Babu said.

"Not today," said Mr. M with one of his smiles.

Babu turned then and led them all into the hut. Just inside the doorway, a tall white candle was burning. Babu had arranged vials and bottles of dried herbs on a board across two flat rocks. He had spread a large piece of woven cloth for Mr. M to sit on. Tom remained standing, keeping one eye on the plastic flap over the door and one on his boss.

Kaj, who had recently been invited more and more into the hut with Babu's clients, stood awkwardly near his grandfather. He knew better than to ask what to do.

"Now you will tell me the kind of problem you are having," said Babu to Mr. M, who did not look at all comfortable sitting on the brightly colored fabric.

"Yes, Babu. We are facing the most important election in the city. We must win. I have come to you for your magic in making sure we are successful."

"I have many potions and herbs for luck," said Babu. "If you want more--a ritual--I will need a longer time and more payment."

"I'm not arguing about payment, old man. In fact, I have heard that you have the power of your ancestors to perform a ritual using the products of a *zeru zeru*."

Kaj's ears pricked up. *Zeru zeru* was a Swahili word for ghost. He knew one such person, a very white-skinned man around his age. They used to be in primary school together. Michael Othman was not a ghost but a flesh and blood boy much like himself. The sisters had let him sit up front to see the board better as his eyesight was poor.

"It is true my grandfather and father provided such rituals," said the Babu. "But I am forbidden by the government to do so now. I would lose my license as a healer."

"Don't worry about that," Mr. M laughed. "We know who to pay."

"I already have amulets with *zeru zeru* hair, and potions and powerful herbs that will provide much good luck," Babu said. "We don't need--"

"I didn't come to hear what you think we need--with all due respect Babu. I'm willing to pay for this ritual, that's all you need to know." He turned then to his assistant. "Isn't that right, Tom?"

Kaj saw the desperation in his grandfather's eyes. He wanted to speak up for him and tell Mr. M and his thug to leave, but he could not summon such courage. He did not have that power.

"We will need one other thing," Mr. M said. "We will need your apprentice to take us to the farm of the *zeru zeru* you told us about. You said he knew the family."

Babu looked up at Kaj, who stood with an open mouth and eyes wide. "I don't know them anymore," Kaj said. "I went to school a long time ago with the brothers--"

"We are sure you can be helpful," said Mr. M. He wrangled a wallet out of his back pocket as he sat there on the ground. He lifted a wad of bills from it and held it out to Kaj. "This is a down payment--do you understand that word? --just for you, your first real pay as an apprentice healer. You will get more when you show us the way to the Othman farm."

Kaj eyed the money, thinking of his mother and her need to see a city doctor, to buy medicine in the city. "No. I cannot do this," he said looking straight into Mr. M's eyes. "I will not do this."

"Tom," Mr. M. said calmly with a brief nod.

Tom brought the machete blade up against Babu's neck. A little blood flowed out in a trickle down to his shirt. Kaj's grandfather gasped and held his head back remaining as still as he could.

Kaj stared at the blood, his heart racing. "Babu--"

"You must do as they say, Kaj. Please." The old man's voice was faint. Kaj had never in his life seen him so frightened.

"You don't have to worry about your old friends, Kaj," Mr. M. said. His words seemed to be covered in honey, but there was something rotten underneath them. "We won't hurt anyone. And anyway, you know that the *zeru zeru* are not truly people. Even your grandfather has told us so. These ghosts cannot be killed! They may even be devils who live among us. They just disappear."

Kaj remained silent. He was not going to argue with a machete.

"Here, take the money. We trust you to do what needs to be done." Mr. M. smiled at him, his bald head shining in the candlelight. He held the wad of bills out to Kaj.

Kaj took the money, wanting to throw it at the man's feet, but he sighed with relief when Tom took the machete from his Babu's throat.

"Two days from now. We'll meet you at the road, and you will show us where to go," said Mr. M. "And then the Babu can perform the ritual to help us win the election. Now, we will find our way back to the car. I'm so glad you have decided to help us, Kaj. Someday, I think, you will be strong and rich like me."

** *

Two days later, Kaj waited in the back seat of Mr. M's shiny black car, which he had once so much admired. Now he wished he could kick it and smash its darkened windows with a rock. It felt like a prison, and every fiber of his body was straining to get out of it. Mr. M. had pulled to the roadside and was talking in low tones to his thug, Tom. "Bring us a flashlight from the glove box," he told him, "and the machete."

"What are we waiting for?" Kaj asked in a tense voice.

"We're waiting until it is a little darker," said Mr. M. "All you have to do is show us the way to the farm."

Kaj clenched his teeth and bunched his hands into tight fists as he sat helplessly behind these two big men. He hated his grandfather at this moment for putting him in this position, and for getting him mixed up with these bad characters. He tried to remember what Sister Angelica had told him about praying to make the right decision. Somehow, her advice didn't seem to apply. And why would the white man's God listen to him anyway?

Finally, Mr. M. and Tom opened the car doors, and the three of them started through the dense tropical greenery that surrounded the Othman farm. They were still able to see in the last light of the day, though it would soon be dark. Kaj had often taken this path on his way to the farm when he and Michael were boys and had gone to school together at the Sister's school. The Othman's place was just outside Kaj's village. Kaj joined Michael and his brothers walking to and from school together every day.

Kaj led the men up the uneven ground through the dense tropical foliage. After walking for almost fifteen minutes, they arrived at a clearing. Kaj stopped and pointed to some trees beyond it. "There are several cultivated fields over there past the trees, and the house is that way." He pointed in the opposite direction.

"When does this *zeru zeru* work in the fields?" asked Mr. M., wiping his brow with his handkerchief.

"I haven't seen Michael in years," said Kaj. "I only know that he works here with his father and brothers. And he is not a ghost," he added, raising his voice, a weak attempt at courage, he thought.

"Don't worry, Kaj," Mr. M. said showing all his teeth in a smile. We just want to watch, to see what he is doing. Perhaps you would like to help us more--could mean a lot of money for you. Eh? What do you say?"

"I've done what you asked. I will not do anymore." He turned then and headed back the way they had come, aware that he could meet his fate at the hands of the man with the machete at any moment. Darkness was upon them now.

"Hey--wait," called Mr. M. "I've got the rest of your money here."

Kaj quickened his steps, and soon he was running down the path at top speed despite the darkness. He continued running when he got to the road, pausing only once to wipe tears and snot from his face. His life had touched evil.

* * *

His grandfather's hut, separated at some distance from the village, was only a little way further. A crescent moon had appeared in the sky.

"Babu! Babu!" he called in a ragged voice outside the ramshackle hut. He could see the light of candles inside.

His Babu came to the doorway, dressed only in shorts. "What is it? Why have you come here at night?" His voice was harsh as it usually was.

"I came to tell you, Babu, that I did the evil thing you needed me to do to save your life." Kaj spit the words like venom. He had never talked to his grandfather in this way, but some fury like an angry crow divebombing a bird of prey had been unleashed inside him. His voice was breaking as he spoke. "I showed those men where Michael lives. If they hurt him, it will be because of you. What magic have you promised them?"

"You are not yourself. Some demon has a hold on you. Come, sit. I will explain it to you," said his grandfather.

Fire burnt in his stomach. "No, Babu, I will not go into your home ever again. Even from out here I can smell the evil. Are you now taking body parts from the graves of the albino people to make your potions?"

"You don't know what you are talking about, Kaj. These men come to me wanting the most powerful magic. They have needs that we don't understand. They are willing to pay a lot for such magic."

Kaj held his head in his hands and then spoke more calmly. "These men, they are not good men, Babu. Don't you see? This is witchcraft. It is evil, and I will have no part of it."

"I am old, Kaj, and this work will soon be yours. People from our village and many others come to us for help. They respect our rituals and our healing. It is what has always been done among our people since the beginning of time. They are not welcome at the white man's shiny hospitals where the healers wear white coats and pretend to have more powerful magic. Your father was foolish enough to go to them for help."

Kaj swallowed hard. "Healing herbs and powders are one thing, Babu. But you have let yourself be dragged into evil ways. You know Michael Othman is not a ghost. You must remember that I went to school with him at the Sisters' school for a few years when I was a kid. We played and ran and laughed together like any children. He is smart, too--the Sisters said so. And his family loves him."

The Babu drew himself up to stand as tall as he could. "You have been spending too much time talking to the Sisters. They have clouded your mind. You are forbidden to go there or to talk with them, to listen to their lies. They do not understand our people, our beliefs, our ways."

Kaj shook his head, his eyes closed before speaking again. "No, Babu. I am almost eighteen now. I have read and heard a little about the world outside of ours. There are albino people in every part of the world--across the oceans even. And nowhere else are they treated as devils or ghosts. These old beliefs are ignorant and wrong."

"And you think the Sisters with their stories about a man who was nailed up on a cross over 2000 years ago is a better story to believe in? A man who got up out of his grave--a *zeru zeru*--three days later? You think he has the magic that can make you live forever?"

"You know the story of their God?" Kaj stared open-mouthed at his grandfather.

"Those people are always talking to everyone they can to change our minds--to make us believe what the white man believes. I do not believe a word of it."

"You may be right, Babu. But in my own heart and mind, I feel what you are doing is wrong. I am not your apprentice. You have chosen to be a witch doctor. I choose not to do this work any longer." The fire in his stomach had nearly gone out now. His voice no longer shook. He had said what needed to be said, and he was free.

"Go then," his grandfather said. "And do not come back begging me for a way to make your living. You are no longer my grandson." With that, he spat on the ground in front of Kaj, turned, and went back into his hut.

18

Tel Aviv, 2008

It was mid-May in Tel Aviv, a beautiful modern city that was only about a hundred years old depending on what point you started counting from. The cold winter rains were over, but the hot, humid days of summer hadn't yet arrived. The evenings were pleasantly warm, and the skies over the Mediterranean revealed the myriad of stars that had always been there behind the winter clouds.

Seth and Jill were seated outside at a popular restaurant along the beach. It was the same place where they had gone for coffee eight months ago after meeting at an evening lecture at the university. Both had stood uncomfortably close in "standing room only" space at the back of the lecture hall, eager to hear Professor Kline's controversial opinions about how Israel and Palestine could peacefully co-exist. When Seth had applauded the speaker for his support of the Palestinians, he could sense a petite and very attractive woman at his elbow staring intently at him.

When the lecture was over, she touched his arm and said, "Do you mind? I can't quite figure you out. You're not a Palestinian, right? But are you Israeli? Are you Jewish?" He had been amused by her bold questions and responded by asking, "And you must be an American?" They had both laughed at that, and he impulsively asked if she'd like to have coffee with him.

Now it was hard to recall a time when he and Jill hadn't been good friends. On this evening in May, they were sharing a platter of fish and chips and a pitcher of beer on the patio of the seaside restaurant. Pop music blared from overhead speakers. He smiled at her, tapping on the table a bit to the beat of the music. He could be himself with Jill whether serious or silly. He admired her generosity of spirit--never seeming to judge anyone, always willing to encourage. And she wasn't afraid to ask uncomfortable questions, a trait Seth attributed, in part, to her being an American, from Colorado she had told him.

"You seem pretty happy," Jill said. "Excited about graduation?"

"I have a bit of surprising news, to share," he said over the steady pounding of the music.

"Tell me," Jill said, her green eyes sparkling with curiosity and interest.

"I've been offered a promotion--an upgrade--to Security Assistant." He had served as an armed guard at the American Embassy for almost two years while attending university in the evenings. Added to the credits he had earned while in the IDF, he was now close to obtaining his degree. The promotion would mean a desk job, greater responsibility for others on the security team, and a higher salary.

"But I thought your work at the embassy was just temporary--until you get your bachelor's," she said with a look that Seth interpreted as either disappointment or disapproval.

He frowned slightly. "Well, yes. I mean, working there was always a way to support myself while finishing my credits. I never expected to be offered another position."

Jill had turned to focus on coaxing a pool of catsup next to her fries. "Are you sure this is what you want to do next?" she asked without looking up at him.

He tipped his head to one side as he watched her wielding the catsup container. "You know, I thought you'd at least be pleased that I'd no longer be carrying a gun to work every day."

She was silent for a few moments, now busy squeezing a slice of lemon on her fish. Finally, she looked up and spoke softly. "Yes, I am certainly glad you won't be carrying a gun around, Seth. But you would still be involved in the business of--violence, right?"

He could feel the heat of his defensiveness rising to his face. "Yes," he began in a controlled tone, "taking responsibility for security necessarily includes the possibility of violence. And injury, and even death for that matter. Sadly, that's a reality in this country."

"I get that Seth. But--and I say this as a friend who loves you dearly, I think you're meant for something else. Something--I don't know--more significant." She closed her eyes briefly as if searching for an answer. "Yeah, that's it, I expect that Seth Melaku will do something significant in this world." She smiled at him.

A friend who loves you dearly?

"You don't think keeping people safe at the American Embassy--in Israel--is important?" he asked trying to keep his expression neutral.

"Oh, of course, I do. I just know that there's more important work waiting for you out there." She waved her hand dismissively.

"Like what, for instance?" He sipped at his beer and looked out over the sea.

"That's totally up to you, Seth. From what you've told me about your father, your culture, your family, your experiences in the IDF, I just don't see you on this path." She touched his arm lightly. "You know what I'm remembering about you right now? I'm imagining you as that ten-year-old boy ready to step off that rescue plane into a new world of possibilities." She paused. "And besides, I just think the position of Security Assistant has no joy in it."

"Joy? What exactly does that mean?" he answered, his brow furrowed in puzzlement. It wasn't a concept he would ever have thought about. "I like working there--I like the people I work with. And they trust me to do a good job."

"And I'm sure you do." She shrugged. "Look, forgive me for my lack of enthusiasm. I don't mean to be telling you what to do. It's just a feeling I have. I truly care about you, Seth."

He grinned as he studied her face. "And what is the joy that you are seeking, Cassandra?"

"Oh, you're making fun of me!" She smiled, dimples appearing on both smooth cheeks. Then, biting her lower lip, she said, "I still have some things to work out before I settle into my joy. That's why I've decided to go to Nepal for a month before returning to the States. To a Buddhist retreat center there where I can reflect on equanimity and peace."

It was Seth's turn to be surprised. "Nepal? I knew you were heading back to the States in June, but you've never mentioned this . . ."

"Listen, let's finish dinner and then go out on the beach. It's a beautiful evening. I'll explain it all to you as we walk."

A short while later, they were strolling barefoot along the beach. Seth fought an urge to pull her close to his heart and kiss her, but she had made it clear early on that their relationship was to be friendship. "I'm going to miss you," he said in what he hoped was a casual tone.

Jill stopped abruptly to look into his eyes. "Seth, don't get all sentimental on me. You knew from the day we met last September that I'd be leaving Israel next month." She paused a moment and looked out at the sea. "And, whether you remember it or not, I told you then that I am a wanderer in search of my peace. I have to keep moving, to learn what the world has to teach me. And anyway, my fellowship at the university was only for a year."

"I remember. But that doesn't make it any easier, and I'm not sure I understand why you're leaving."

Jill stared into his eyes. She put one warm palm against his cheek. "Leaving you, you mean? Please don't tell me you're falling in love, Seth."

"What if I am?" he said lightly as if he were dismissing the idea. He did indeed feel like a child at that moment. He didn't like the feeling.

She sighed. "Oh, Seth. You know how much I love you--but not in the way you want. I have had some-- experiences--that keep me from . . . that make me afraid . . . Come, let's dip our toes in the water." She turned toward the sea.

"I'm listening, Jill. I want to understand you--talk to me." He followed her down the beach.

Close to the water's edge, they stopped and looked up at the sky. Even with the glow of the city lights, they could see a dome full of stars. Jill spoke first. "Looking at the stars always makes me feel like I'm connected to some invisible force in the universe--like compassion or love. When I'm back in the States, I want to remember us standing here on this night just looking as far as we can into the universe." She looked down from the heavens to look into his eyes. "I feel so fortunate to have known you this year. No matter where either of us is in the world, I will always feel connected to you."

"That's a beautiful idea," Seth said, unable to say anything more.

"Seth, there is one thing I haven't told you about myself during all these months that we've become so close. I think I need to tell you now."

He felt a wave of dizziness pass over him as if he could suddenly feel the Earth's rotation. "What is it, Jilly? You look strange--are you okay?"

"Please, just listen. I want to say this quickly." She exhaled a long, shuddering breath. "You know how I feel about guns and violence, but I haven't told you-- exactly why. My older brother--David--was a senior at Columbine High School in 1999. I was a sophomore. I looked up to him. I admired him. I loved him." She paused for another breath. "He was shot for no reason at all by those boys . . . and he died on the way to the hospital. I didn't even get a chance to say goodbye." She looked out into the darkness, keeping her voice low and almost robotic. Then she turned to look at him. "You do know about Columbine, right?"

Seth realized he had been holding his breath. He exhaled and breathed in now as he recalled the name "Columbine" and connected it to the actual incident-- the terrible mass shooting at a high school somewhere in the western part of the United States. He remembered discussing it with his fellow recruits during basic training in the IDF. The States, one guy had said, was as dangerous as Israel, and someone else explained that guns were somehow sacred to the American constitution.

"Yes ... I remember it," he answered her. "I'm ... so sorry, Jilly. Your brother ... That must have been terrible for you and ... I'm just so sorry. I can't even ... Can I hold you?"

Jill nodded her head and buried her face against his chest. She sobbed quietly for several minutes. Seth held her tightly, wishing he could take all that sorrow from her. He listened to the softly lapping waves on the sand. He wanted to keep her safe forever, knowing that was impossible for many reasons.

Jill pulled her head back to speak again. "I didn't want to tell you because I don't want that terrible and terrifying experience to define my life. I wanted you to know me without seeing that empty place, that gaping hole inside me. After it happened, I watched as my dad drank himself to death--a heart attack finally. And my mother just never recovered from the loss of her only son. She became clinically depressed and uninterested in anything outside of her very small world. I came to Israel to continue my graduate study because I could no longer see her like that. Part of me feels guilty for leaving her, but I am fighting for my survival. My mother is being taken care of by her sister, my aunt Hazel, who encouraged me to go."

"My dear lovely Jill." He gently lifted her chin and kissed her on one wet cheek. "You've been more courageous than I can even imagine being. I'm grateful to the universe that you came here, and that our paths crossed. And that we are friends."

She put her head back against his chest, breathing calmly now. He recalled a poem he had studied in an English literature course at the university. A poem by a nineteenth-century poet that had struck him as relevant to the twenty-first century. He had even memorized the final lines of "Dover Beach" and repeated them in his mind as they stood there on the sand.

> Ah, love, let us be true
> To one another! For the world, which seems
> To lie before us like a land of dreams,
> So various, so beautiful, so new,
> Hath really neither joy, nor love, nor light,
> Nor certitude, nor peace, nor help for pain:
> And we are here as on a darkling plain
> Swept with confused alarms of struggle and flight,
> Where ignorant armies clash by night.

The teenage boys who had so thoughtlessly killed Jill's brother had altered the lives of all those who survived as well as the friends and families of those who had loved the victims. And now, they had touched his life too, connecting him to something outside his known world in ways he would only understand later. He felt the warmth of Jill's head against his chest. It wasn't at all the same as what he had dreamed. But he would stand there holding her as long as she needed him to--it was all he could do now.

The stars shone steadily above them, but his world had been overturned as surely as if he had been tossed by an earthquake.

19

Tel Aviv, 2008

It was supposed to be an evening of joy and celebration. Natalie and Benjamin had invited Seth's family to share in the festivities. Seth's sisters, Deborah and Lala, were home taking care of his grandmother Bibi, but his mother and his brother Kofi, now seventeen, made the trip by train from Jerusalem to Tel Aviv. They brought homemade casseroles of Seth's favorite Ethiopian dishes to help celebrate his achievement. Natalie and Benjamin's twins had spent hours making decorations. Colorful crayon posters that read "Congratulations, Seth!" and "Bon Voyage, Jill" were taped to the front door of the house. A bunch of blue and white balloons tied with ribbons hung over the dining room table.

When they all sat down to eat, Natalie offered a blessing. Seth caught a glimpse of the twins with their eyes closed and their heads bowed. A vivid memory of his childhood home flashed through his mind. If only his father could be here today. Was this what his Abba had imagined all those years ago when he was so determined to move his family to the Promised Land? If only he had been able to watch today as Seth walked proudly across the stage to receive his bachelor's degree. If he could only know that his son was now fluent in both English and Hebrew, and knowledgeable about the latest developments in computer science and cyber intelligence.

Benjamin tapped his water glass to gain their attention and rose from his seat. "First, Natalie and I want to welcome you all to our home. It is our great privilege to have you share this meal of celebration with us. I am forever grateful that Operation Solomon brought our lives together all those years ago. Today we are celebrating you, Seth," he said turning his head to face him. Your family has become my family as well, we are all so proud of you and are excited to see where life takes you next. To Seth! L'chaim!"

Glasses clinked. Words of congratulations and hugs were exchanged.

Natalie stood up then. "And it's my privilege to offer a special toast to Jill, who has also become like family in our household over the past year. It's more than the fact that she is Seth's dear friend, and more than our American roots that have brought us close. We--the children and Ben and I--have all fallen in love with her. Though we are sad to see her leave, we are so proud that she will soon return to the States to work with the anti-gun coalition. Her passion and her knowledge will be a great asset to that effort. It's important and urgent work, and we wish her much success. To Jill! L'chaim!" More hugs and best wishes were exchanged among them.

Only minutes later, however, Jill abruptly excused herself from the table. Seth looked after her with concern. He knew she hadn't been feeling well earlier, but she had insisted that she was well enough and didn't want to miss the celebration.

Everything happened quickly after that. Seth heard a muffled scream and then a moan from somewhere down the hall. He found Jill doubled over, her arms wrapped around her stomach. Ben diagnosed appendicitis or possibly a ruptured appendix and made an emergency call in to the hospital. He and Seth wrapped Jill in a blanket and carried her to the back seat of his car where she lay with her head in Seth's lap.

Ben drove with demonic speed to the hospital, while Seth stroked her hair and assured her that she was going to be fine. A gurney was wheeled out as they pulled up at the entrance to the ER. Seth watched, his heart racing, as two orderlies gently moved her from the car to the gurney. Minutes later, she was prepped for surgery and given an injection to relax her. Seth was able to spend a few minutes in a curtained cubicle with her before she was wheeled into the operating room.

Later, when he tried to remember what they had said to each other during those few minutes, he could only visualize her smiling and saying something like, "I guess this means I'll be staying in Israel a while longer, after all." He had mumbled something banal like, "Well, Nepal can wait. We'll get you back to good health in no time." But then, she had asked him to kiss her--for good luck, she said. As he leaned down to touch his lips to hers, she whispered, "I love you forever." He let go of her hand, unable to speak, as they wheeled her through the swinging double doors on the way to the operating room. That was the last time he saw her alive.

PART TWO

20

New York City took some getting used to, Alex discovered. There was something decidedly different about New Yorkers, different than Southern Californians for sure, but different even from the often gregarious and assertive Chicagoans. One morning, as she stood up on the subway, preparing to exit at the next station, a well-dressed middle-aged black woman who had been studying her during the ride looked directly into her eyes.

"Stunning, you are absolutely stunning," the woman said with a smile. "Enjoy your youth, my dear!" Alex smiled back, wondering if she would ever get used to the unfiltered directness of New Yorkers. Nevertheless, she felt a rush of gratitude for the kind intention of the woman's comment.

Ngosi, Alex's assistant at CAPE headquarters, had helped Alex find a one-bedroom apartment in a quiet area of Brooklyn. Ngosi and her husband, Max, had lived in the same building, the Garden Arms, since getting married three years ago. Ngosi was a communications specialist, responsible for scheduling appointments, arranging for translators, and transcribing interviews. Alex appreciated her efficiency, sense of humor, and even her New York straight talk.

Each morning the two women took a commuter subway into Manhattan, often talking about current projects at CAPE. On the way to headquarters, they usually stopped at a favorite coffee shop where Alex ordered a chai tea and Ngosi a soy latte.

One morning as they rode the subway together, Ngosi invited Alex to have dinner with her and Max the next evening. "I've wanted to have you over forever, but I'm not much of a cook," Ngosi said. "And, since you've been curious about Nigerian food, I am going to prepare one of my mother's recipes. I hope you'll like it!"

The next evening, it was Max who welcomed Alex at the door of the apartment and accepted a bottle of wine. "Ngosi is putting the finishing touches on the meal. Please come in and make yourself at home." He extended his hand offering a vigorous handshake. "Welcome to our home."

Max was slim and just an inch or two shorter than Alex. He wore a light gray cotton sweater and gray pants. His skin was almost as pale as hers, his hair was a reddish-blond, and his eyes were blue. Alex tried to guess his family origins, but he looked like so many Americans who were hybrids that she found it impossible.

The first thing Alex noticed once she was seated in their comfortable living room was a large, framed photo that hung over the fireplace mantle. A poignant portrait of two elephants with a baby elephant between them against a background of trees and a clear blue sky.

"What a touching photo. Who is the photographer?"

"Thanks--just a lucky shot. I took it when we traveled to Nigeria to visit some of Ngosi's extended family two years ago. Unfortunately, elephants are disappearing from that country."

Ngosi came in from the kitchen wearing an apron. "Welcome, Alex!" She was at least a foot shorter than Alex and had to reach up to hug her.

"Whatever you are cooking smells divine, Ngosi."

"It's my mom's recipe for pounded yams and *egusi* soup--Nigerian favorites."

"And I can attest that it is even better than her mom's," said Max putting an arm around his wife's waist.

He poured wine for all of them while Alex helped carry the aromatic serving dishes to the dining table, which was decorated with African print placemats and napkin rings in the shape of zebras.

"I've never traveled to Africa," said Alex after admiring the table setting. "I'd love to go. Have you been to any other countries on the continent?"

"No. My mom wanted us to visit my grandmother and some cousins after we were married," said Ngosi. "Both Max and I grew up and went to school here in Brooklyn, so that trip was quite an adventure. Nigeria was truly a foreign place to us."

"But we loved it," said Max. "English is the official language, but Ngosi's grandmother spoke only Hausa. She couldn't have been more welcoming--even to me."

"And my younger cousins all spoke at least some English--made us feel right at home."

"Where is your family from, Max?"

"Oh, I'm a combination ethnicity--you know, the one people check off as simply "Caucasian" on a form checklist. I recently paid one of those genetic ancestry companies that analyze your saliva to tell you where your ancestors are from. Mine included Scotland, Ireland, England, and central Europe--maybe Poland. A mutt, if you will, with a tiny percentage of Neanderthal from way back to boot."

"A very good mutt," Ngosi smiled at him. "His Irish grandmother is ninety and still going strong, so we're hoping for her good genes."

As they talked, Ngosi served the *egusi* soup and yams. All agreed that the dinner was superb. Max poured another round of red wine.

"And what about you, Alex?" Ngosi asked. "What do you know of your family background?"

"Well, that's a bit complicated. I've never done DNA analysis--but perhaps I should. My story is a bit mysterious. I was adopted by a couple in Southern California. My adoptive mother is an immigrant from India who went to graduate school in the States and stayed on when both her parents died. My adoptive father is a mix of German and Norwegian ancestors. They met in graduate school in California. They adopted me through a colleague--a doctor who lived in England apparently, but just how all that happened has never been clear to me. I don't know where I was born--or to whom."

"They don't want to tell you?" Ngosi asked, looking at Alex with a furrowed brow.

"It's not that. They were always so good to me. I'm their only child, and they made me the center of their lives--though both had professional positions at a university. I never wanted to upset them by asking."

"I understand, Alex. But--please, tell me if I'm being too curious or too blunt, which is probably a fault of mine--but do you know anything about how you, a baby with albinism, came to be placed for adoption?"

Alex looked at her new friend in awe. No one had ever asked her point blank about her albinism. "No, though that is something I've thought a great deal about--since learning when I was eight years old that I have albinism. A boy in my third-grade class called me a 'white nigger.' I assume that my ancestors are African--but that's all I know."

"But you always knew you had been adopted?"

"Oh yes, of course, but I became more aware of the significance of adoption when my parents took me to see the musical, *Les Miserables* when I was in high school."

"I loved that show," said Ngosi. "So, let me think--Cosette's single mom died of some awful disease, and then she was adopted by Jean Valjean, the hunted prisoner, who had become a success and a good man."

"It made me wonder about whether my own mother had died like that--though I never mentioned it to my parents. What really hit me was how fortunate Cosette was to be adopted at all. She could have died living with those awful people. Instead, she grew up feeling much loved and lived a comfortable and secure life."

"Like you," Max said, looking intently at Alex.

Alex smiled at him. "Yes, quite like me though my kingdom was among beaches, palm trees, and the Pacific Ocean in Southern California, a place I love dearly."

"Brooklyn and New York City must seem quite as foreign to you as Nigeria was to us," said Ngosi. They all laughed.

"Did you know, Alex," Ngosi continued, "that CAPE has done some preliminary research into the mistreatment of albinos, er--people with albinism--in several African countries? We've been so busy researching Syria during these past months, but I've always hoped we would get back to that issue. I did begin research some time ago."

"I have to confess that I know nothing next to nothing about albinism in Africa."

"I'll dig out some of the articles for you. But briefly-- people with albinism are an endangered species in many African countries, particularly in Malawi and Tanzania--but in other places too. Some people believe their bones contain gold dust and magic. Those body parts can be made into potions that are sold to people who believe such things will bring them wealth or sexual prowess or good luck. People with albinism--including small children--are sometimes maimed and often killed for their body parts."

"Why haven't I ever read anything in the news?"

"If it has been mentioned, it doesn't make front page news here in the States. We all live in our bubbles of self-protection, I think. The fact that black people are killing other black people in some distant, almost unheard-of country--even if those black people happen to look especially white--is not a concern of most people in the United States. It would be considered a local problem. Think of how different it would be if it were black people maiming and killing the actual white people, the Caucasians, living there. *That* might make headlines."

"You're right. And you've totally captured my interest, Ngosi! Listen, I'd love to team up with you on a project like this if you're interested. We both have a connection to the African continent. Who would be better suited to writing and sponsoring a proposal?"

"Of course, I'm interested."

"It's a deal. Next week, will you show me what you've researched so far?"

While Max was busy in the kitchen preparing coffee, the two women moved to the living room and talked excitedly about how they might propose an investigation of the treatment of people with albinism in Africa to the Executive Director and her board.

Over a dessert of lemon sorbet and coffee, Alex steered the conversation back to more personal topics.

"Tell me more about you two--how did you meet?"

"That's easy. I saw this super beautiful, highly intelligent woman across the room at Brooklyn College on the first day of a course on International Relations. I fell in love," Max said looking at Ngosi.

"Life has been good to two kids from Brooklyn," Ngosi said. "And now we're hoping to become parents. We've been trying to get pregnant and have just entered the scary and expensive world of IVF." She sighed. "That's probably why I'm so curious about your adoption. I'm sorry if I overstepped --"

"Not at all," said Alex. "I heard your comment about good genes and assumed that a family is in your future. I've been observing you two--and I know you will make wonderful, loving parents, no matter if you adopt or have success with IVF. Some child--or children--will become the center of your lives, and they will be very fortunate, indeed."

Later, as Alex brushed her teeth and got ready for bed, she thought briefly about the world and the plans she had left behind--law school, Quincy, and a lucrative job at a law firm in DC. And here she was, by who knew what stars, living in a wholly different universe, engaged in ideas and actions that felt significant and meaningful. Ngosi had shown her a new pathway toward understanding the suffering of other people who looked like her. How had she not known? A new sense of energy filled her as she imagined herself on the wheel of time heading toward something significant. And she was ready for whatever time would bring.

The old folk song that her father loved so much played softly in her mind as she lay down to sleep. *To everything, turn, turn, turn, there is a season, turn, turn, turn, and a time to every purpose, under heaven.*

21

New York City, 2013

Alex spent the morning in her office at CAPE poring over both surface and aerial maps of Syria as she read various articles and eyewitness reports from the ongoing war there. She made a note of any city or village, building or street, hospital or detention camp that was mentioned. When photographs were included, she printed them and pinned them up on a corkboard on one wall of her office. Then she attempted to locate them on the maps. She had discovered in doing this research that if she could orient herself to specific buildings or streets and imagine herself there walking or driving, she could better understand what was happening on the ground. She could imagine the sounds of traffic noise, locate shortcuts and alleyways, and identify possible sources of shelter or help. Taking note of places and memorizing the foreign names, she was able to map out a world in her mind that she could enter and move about in as clearly as if she were in a virtual reality game. After an attempt to explain the process once to a colleague, she kept it to herself. As with other aspects of her memory, most people found her ability hard to believe or thought it was a kind of parlor trick.

On this May morning, she was reading a report from a pile of folders on her desk about a sixteen-year-old girl, Haba, a citizen of Australia who, after traveling to visit an older brother two years ago, had been seized and held in the al-Hol detention camp in Northern Syria. Thousands of others, mainly women and children and many of them from other countries like herself, endured horrific conditions at the camp. Haba was sick, alone, and frightened. Through UNICEF representatives on-site, she begged for help by posting a desperate plea on social media. CAPE had made inquiries and contacted Australian officials to push for repatriation and to demand basic medical care for detainees, Haba's best hope of getting out of the detention camp.

Alex tapped the location of the camp on her imaginary mind map before continuing to read. A bleak desert encampment, al-Hol was a place she already knew well from her research. She was not ready, however, for what she read in the rest of the report. Haba had died in the camp only a week earlier, from malnutrition and heart failure. She weighed only ninety-six pounds. The report included a blurry selfie that the girl had managed to send along with her pleas on WhatsApp over a year ago. Alex stopped reading, got up from her desk, and walked to the employee lounge at the end of the hall.

Looking down on the city of New York from this height was usually a good distraction, one that allowed her to regain some semblance of composure. She noted that the line of plane trees along the western entrance to Washington Square Village was a hopeful blur of spring green. But today she couldn't erase from her mind the hollow-eyed girl in the tiny picture. Just a child, so much suffering.

For perhaps the hundredth time, she asked herself if she was doing enough in this position. CAPE's mission did not include halting or even identifying the aggressor in any situation. It did not delve into the politics, the accusations, the acts of revenge by any one side. Its sole purpose was to bear to witness the suffering of people--no matter who, no matter where, always remaining neutral in hopes of bringing their suffering to the attention of those who could help. Alex understood and agreed with the organization's policy, but now she asked herself how that principle had helped sixteen-year-old Haba. Surely they could do more?

She paced the empty lounge, glancing out at the city below, wishing she could go for a run in the nearby park, where she often spent her lunch break jogging a few miles. But she had a lunch appointment with the organization's Executive Director at 12:30. During the eighteen months since being hired at CAPE, she had met Elizabeth Hampton only twice: when she was introduced to her colleagues during the first week at a company-wide meeting, and again just six weeks ago when she happened to be riding up the elevator before eight in the morning, intent on completing a Duolingo lesson on her phone before work. The Director, who had stepped into the elevator just as it was about to close, smiled at Alex when she heard a chime from the language program signaling a correct response. Alex smiled back and quickly shut down the program.

"Good morning, Dr. Hampton."

"Elizabeth--please. And you are Alex Carter. That's that language-learning app, isn't it? I recognize the sound--my daughter uses it for learning French at college."

"I'm fascinated by the Arabic program--a bit more challenging than some others, I find."

"Good for you! I'm not much good at languages myself," Elizabeth said. "My daughter tells me it's all a matter of mindset--you know, forget about age and such. But I'm not so sure."

Alex had laughed politely.

* * *

The meeting began with the requisite small talk exchanged between two women of different generations, statuses, and backgrounds. While they ate their veggie sandwiches, ordered up by Elizabeth's assistant from the deli on the first floor of the building, the Director asked a few questions. Did Alex's family still live in Southern California? Yes, her mom and dad still lived and worked in Los Angeles. How did she like New York City? She doubted that she would ever be mistaken for a real New Yorker, but she found it interesting and stimulating. Did she enjoy her job here at CAPE? She did. Alex answered that this position allowed her to use her skills and also live her values.

But where is this conversation going?

"I'm so glad to get to know you a bit better," said Elizabeth. As you know, I'm often off traveling to our other offices and away from New York for weeks at a time. But I want you to know that I've read all your analyses and reports, all your thoughtful applications for policy and next steps. And I am very impressed."

Alex had not expected praise for her work, nor had she feared complaints. But as she looked at the Director's expression, she sensed that something more was coming.

"Alex, I have a proposal to make, and I want you to know ahead of time that your job does not depend on accepting it. We, all of us at CAPE, are proud of your work here, and we want to keep you, but something urgent has come up. A situation where we could very much use your particular set of skills."

She paused. Alex didn't know how to respond.

"Okay," Alex said, tipping her head to one side. A shiver of excitement ran through her, but she kept a calm expression on her face.

"Not to be mysterious, let me lay out a proposal for you to consider. We would like you to go secretly into Syria with a trained field agent to gather and then communicate first-hand information directly from the people who are suffering under intense wartime conditions. We need a woman who can talk to the women there, to understand and be their voices so their situation will be known to the world. I understand that you are now fluent in Arabic-- quite a feat, I have to say. First, you would receive a few weeks of field training at our facility in London. And meet your partner, of course."

She paused, and Alex knew the woman was trying to read her reaction. Alex lifted her chin to indicate that she was listening and intrigued. Her head was spinning as she imagined herself going into a war zone.

"It is, no doubt, a dangerous assignment, Alex, but it's a very important one. CAPE and other human rights organizations have been able to interview victims and survivors at the borders, but we need to tell the world about what it is like on the ground for the people-- especially women and children--who are not able to escape. If you accept, you will go to London within the next two weeks to begin training." After a slight pause, she added, "And then slip over the border from Turkey into Syria by night."

Alex leaned forward a little in her chair. "I can't tell you what a coincidence your proposal seems to me. I was just reading about a young Australian woman who died in one of the Syrian detention camps. I was wondering what more we can do. How we can make a difference for people like her."

"Your empathy and your determination to bring about change are the very reasons you are here, Alex. As you are aware, our policy is not to get involved in politics, not to engage in accusing or prosecuting, not to force change in any country's policies. But we can, through our reporting, influence policy. It's our job to uncover the inhumane treatment of people wherever that is occurring in the world."

"Yes, Dr. Hampton--Elizabeth. I do understand that. I just get so--frustrated."

"Some of us here have been at this work for a long time. And believe me, we get frustrated at times too. But sometimes, and there are no guarantees, we do manage to get through to world leaders when they understand the human suffering that is happening under their watch."

"I'm aware that I'm just a beginner here--and I'm grateful for all you and your colleagues have done to build CAPE to a well-respected organization. I'm honored to be a small part of that. I very much want to say yes to your proposal, but do you mind if I take a few days? I want to talk to my family--to my parents."

"Of course, Alex. We want you to consider it carefully, and of course feel free to discuss it with your mom and dad. You might also want to do a little research into the young man you would be working with--a most lovely human being originally from Ethiopia. His name is Seth Melaku. Besides his native language, he is fluent in Hebrew and pretty good in English. I think the two of you will get along well."

A few minutes later, Alex took the elevator down to her floor, aware that the wheel of time had just ticked forward a notch with a new opportunity presenting itself to her. A way to make a significant difference. She would have to tell Ngosi that their proposal for an investigation into albinism in Africa would have to be placed on hold for a little longer.

22

Southern California, 2013

Alex took a 4:00 pm flight on Friday afternoon from JFK to Los Angeles. She always looked forward to flying westward because it amused her to contemplate going backward in time as the plane sped through several time zones. The thought that time wasn't the same everywhere had fascinated her since learning about it in elementary school. The plane landed a bit ahead of time--good tailwind according to the pilot. Alex called up an Uber and arrived in time to enjoy the red gleam of the sun sinking into the Pacific as she sipped a glass of sauvignon blanc with her parents on their rooftop patio.

The next morning, Alex was up at dawn and ready for a run along the beach. Her dad had declined to join her because of an arthritic knee that was acting up. Alex found a tube of sunscreen in the medicine cabinet and her old running hat on a hook in the laundry room. Stepping outside, she stood still for a few moments breathing in the familiar scents of the sea. She headed for the paved pathway for pedestrians and bikes, referred to by locals as the strand, which stretched for miles along the white, sandy beaches of several cities and towns in Southern California.

Alex joined bikers, runners, and all manner of dogs and their human companions, delighting in the comfort of being so close to the ocean again. She had experienced one of her visions while on the plane the day before, and she wanted time to think it out. Sipping a ginger ale and nibbling a packet of peanuts, she had been surprised to feel the faint nausea and to see the familiar halo of light in front of her eyes that signaled the onset of one of her visions. She leaned her head against the window and closed her eyes, knowing that whatever it was that took over her consciousness, it would be gone in a few minutes.

In the vision, she felt herself an infant, startled from sleep, awakened by the loud hum of an airplane. She felt herself looking up at one of the light people nearby--a man with a gray mustache and a beard. She had seen him in visions before, but his features remained a blur. He wasn't looking at her. But then, she was being held in the arms of a woman who was talking softly to her and smiling. The woman looked somehow familiar, but she wasn't one of the light people she had seen before. The woman rocked her gently, and again she fell into sleep.

When the vision disappeared, Alex looked at her watch. Only a couple minutes had passed. She sat up straight as she realized that the woman holding her in the vision was Zara, her adoptive mother. Was that a memory or just her imagination? She had kept her world of visions secret since early childhood, but perhaps, she thought, now it was time to do some investigation. She had always wanted to keep from hurting her mom and dad who had been so good to her, who had, indeed, loved her. But now she needed to find a way to ask her mother about the time they visited Dr. Espinoza. He had asked her questions about the visions, which he and her mother had mistakenly referred to as dreams.

She looked out at the sea as she ran. She had not wanted to think about that visit to the doctor, but now it loomed larger than ever. It was time to know more. She made a U-turn on the strand and ran back toward her parents' home.

* * *

The jacaranda tree in the small backyard was in bloom, its purple blossoms showing off amongst the graceful fernlike leaves. Alex knelt at the base of the tree lifting flowering plants out of a plastic carrier and placing them in holes she had prepared around the tree. Her dad sat at a small table in the shade of the tree, a book open on his lap.

"I figured you might want to add your own touch to Nacho's resting place," he said as he watched her work.

"That was thoughtful, Dad. Thank you. These white impatiens are perfect--and they'll grow well in the shade."

Her mother smiled as she placed a tray on the table. "California avocado toasts," she announced, "and some lemonade." Time to take a break."

"Let me just finish watering these new plants," Alex said. She finished watering and rinsed her hands under the hose. *Good-bye, Nacho. You were the best of friends.*

"Okay, Lexy," said her dad when they were all seated at the table. "I've had the feeling that this quick visit home was not just to visit Nacho's grave or to check up on us. Is there something you want to tell us?"

"Ah, you know me well, Dad. And yes, there are a couple of things I wanted to talk with you about. So much has changed in my life these past couple of years, and even though we talk on the phone and text a lot, I wanted to see you in person--to ask you some things about the past, and to ask your advice about something that has come up for the future."

"Well, we've always enjoyed your questions," her mom said. "Want to start there?"

"Thanks, Mom. I think when I was a kid living at home with you, I was afraid to ask you about the circumstances of my adoption. I'm not sure why. Lately, I've been thinking more about it, and I was hoping you would tell me more details--about my past."

She saw her parents exchange a quizzical look. Dad raised one eyebrow slightly, and Mom nodded almost imperceptibly.

"I guess I hold the most information--but not much more than we told you long ago," Dad said. First, we don't know who your birth parents are, Lexy, and we don't know why you were given up for adoption." He folded his hands under his chin and looked into her eyes. "But there are some things we didn't tell you. If you wish, I will tell you now." He turned to look at his wife. "Please chime in wherever you want, Zara, I don't always remember details these days."

"Okay. I'm listening, Dad. What *didn't* you tell me?"

"When you were tiny--I'm talking maybe two or three years old, we told you that we got a call from a doctor overseas who told us that you needed parents and a good home. We told you then that we traveled to England to pick you up and make you our very own child."

"I remember," Alex said.

"We found out later that we couldn't modify that story," said Mom. "Because you remembered every word of it, and you wouldn't accept us making any changes to it."

"Why did you want to change the story? I don't understand."

"We wanted to tell you everything when you were a bit older, just so you would know your history," said Dad. "Part of the story we told you was true. We did get a call from a doctor I had met at a medical conference in London. His name was Oliver Canfield. He lived just outside London, and after adopting you, we stayed in touch for a while. But we lost contact with him many years ago. Anyway, he told us that he and his wife had been in Africa for a couple of months, where he volunteered his services as a pediatrician in several clinics."

"Do you know where he traveled in Africa? What countries?"

"No. I don't think we ever talked about it. But something was wrong with his wife's vision at the time, and when they got back to England, she was diagnosed with retinitis pigmentosa, a degenerative disease that could eventually lead to severe vision loss--even blindness."

"What does this have to do with my adoption?"

"Oliver Canfield claimed that you had been in great danger in Africa. He said he was helping a family who wanted to keep you safe."

"By giving me away to strangers? Sending me out of the country where I was born--separating me from my parents? But how could anyone--?" Alex stopped so she could control the tears behind her eyes.

"He was able to forge a birth certificate in Africa and take you on the plane with them. Babies didn't need passports back then."

Her dad stopped talking. Her mom reached over to put her hand on his arm.

"This is hard for you to talk about," Alex said. "I'm sorry--"

"It's all right, darling," said Mom. "It was an emotional time for all of us. We learned that Dr. Canfield's wife was severely depressed after her diagnosis, and he knew she wouldn't be able to care for you." She poured more lemonade in their glasses.

"So he called Dad?"

"I had told him how much we wanted a child--how we had been trying for so long and had just about given up," Dad said. "We were afraid that as a couple who identified as Christian and Hindu that we would not be good candidates in the eyes of American adoption agencies."

"We jumped at the chance to adopt you," Mom said. "But we didn't fly to England as we told you back then."

"Then, how--?"

"Dr. Canfield, who had the forged birth certificate, brought you himself on an eight-hour flight to New York from London," said her mom. "He said you slept most of the way."

"We were waiting at the gate--you could do that in the old days--and Dr. Canfield put you into your mom's arms."

Her mom smiled. "We fell immediately in love with you. And then we flew another six hours back to Los Angeles--thrilled with this beautiful little girl who has become a most lovely young woman--more amazing than we could have dreamed." Her eyes shone with tears.

Alex looked from her mom to her dad. She wiped tears from her face and put an arm around each of them. "I must have been quite the dictator not to allow you to change the story."

"Well, I wouldn't use the word 'dictator' but you were quite convincing," Mom laughed. "You have always had such an incredible memory." She paused a moment, looking at her daughter with affection.

"Thank you--both of you--for always looking out for me. I love you."

"Have we answered all your questions, Lexy?" said her dad.

Alex smiled. "Just one more topic if you don't mind too much."

"Go ahead," her mom said softly. "But please eat--I made plenty and we've hardly touched them."

"Remember that doctor we went to see when I was four going on five--in that tall building at the university, I think. We took an elevator--my first elevator ride. Just you and me, Mom."

"Yes, of course. Dr. Espinoza. I'm only slightly surprised that you remember." She grinned. "He is no longer in private practice but is now a professor at the university in Irvine--doing research. I saw an article by him a year or so ago in the *Journal of Neurobiology*."

"We only saw him that one time--yes? Why did you take me to see him?"

"Oh dear--we're going back a long way here, my darling. He was a colleague of mine, and I was worried about some dreams you had--you would tell me about something called the light people. I couldn't understand. One was about an elephant, and some others seemed violent--someone screaming or holding on to you."

"And what happened after that? Why didn't we go back to see him again?"

"As I remember, you didn't want to talk to him about your dreams. When I spoke privately to him, he seemed to want to do some tests--some research regarding memory. I said no. You were too little to be a guinea pig."

"And what do you remember about the dreams, Mom? Did I continue to have them?"

"You know, I think you never mentioned such dreams again. I thought that somehow going to see that doctor made them go away. Did they?"

"Not exactly," Alex said with a slight smile. "Once in a while I may have a similar dream, so I was just thinking about that time. It's nothing, really, just my curiosity."

"Good to be curious!" said her mom. "That is how we learn what is real."

* * *

Toward evening, the three sat together on the deck of Kincaid's, a restaurant on the Redondo Beach Pier, drinking wine and sharing an artichoke and crab dip that had long been Alex's favorite appetizer. Seagulls and lines of pelicans flew over the ruffled water, busy with their own lives.

"How I love sitting here with you," said Alex. "It really is a bit like traveling back in time--except we all look a bit older. I'm sorry that this visit is so short."

Her mom placed her hand on Alex's arm. "My Alex, we are delighted to have you visit, but I cannot take one more moment of suspense. You said you wanted to talk to us about something that has come up for the future--a new project?"

"I did say that didn't I? And yes, I have something to tell you that I hope you'll see as something positive. I guess I want your blessing."

Her parents were both looking at her, waiting.

Alex took a sip of wine and smiled at them. "The Executive Director at CAPE, Elizabeth Hampton, has asked me to consider a special mission. They want me to go with a trained field expert to Syria, where I would talk with the women who are suffering there. We need to tell their stories to the world."

"Syria!" her parents said at the same time.

"I've been researching and writing about the war there for months. I have a detailed map of several Syrian cities and towns in my mind--you know how I can memorize such things. I've read many reports from people who have escaped, many of them in refugee camps outside the borders. Conditions are terrible for those who cannot get out. CAPE can make a difference in their suffering by verifying those stories and publishing them."

"But there is a war going on--bombing and killing. We hear about it every day on the news," said her dad. "Why you, Lexy?"

"Why not me, Dad? I've become fluent in Arabic--you know how I am with languages. And I already know a great deal about Syria from my position as a researcher. I'll be with a partner--a man who is experienced in fieldwork. He was a special forces soldier in the Israeli Defense Forces, so he has skills that I lack. And I will be in almost constant touch by satellite with my colleague and friend, Ngosi, at the New York office."

"Oh, my sweet Alex," said Mom. "I do understand why you want to do this. That you want to make a difference. But as your mother, who loves you more than life, I can't advise you to accept this job."

"I understand, Mom, but you probably know that my mind is quite made up?"

"We do know that," said Dad. "I have no doubt you would do a good job of gathering information and reporting it. But you are asking us to accept a terrible uncertainty about your safety when it has always been our job to keep you safe."

"You have both taught me, in your own ways, that life itself is uncertain. What is certain, I wonder, in this world? Is there a god or a prophet or a witch somewhere who could tell me one certain thing--besides the fact that we are all facing death? Look out at the ocean here right below us and beyond. It changes not only the direction of the tides every twelve hours or so. It is changing every moment. And within it are millions of creatures who are being born, living out their lives, and dying. Nothing about it is certain."

She paused and looked at the two dear faces of her adoptive parents. "Yes, I am asking you to accept uncertainty. I love my life and I will do everything I can to stay safe, but it is no longer your job. Gaining an understanding of what is happening to those women and children in a war zone is the best way I can help relieve suffering in this world of uncertainty and constant change. I have to go."

Her dad and then her mom, got up to hug their daughter. "We are very proud of you, dear Alex," Mom whispered. "Go in peace, Lexy," said Dad.

23

In transit from California to New York, 2013

FROM: AlexCarter@cape.org
TO: NgosiObiakaHarrison@cape.org

Ngosi:

Sorry I missed you before I left for California. I'm writing this as I fly home. I wanted to let you know that I have accepted Dr. Hampton's proposal (I've emailed her) and will be leaving almost immediately for training in London--possibly Friday of next week. Will you please look into plane reservations to Heathrow? I'm excited, a little frightened, but mostly just itching to go and learn what is really happening on the ground in Syria. An unexpected opportunity.

As I understand it, you will be my main contact throughout the mission. I will be sending you reports, which you will review and edit, and provide to Dr. Hampton or whoever else needs access. I will also be depending on you for news stories and research when needed. We will make a great team, I think. I will be depending on you.

Speaking of teams--I've done just a bit of research on the experienced field researcher, Seth

Melaku, who will be my team leader. Do you know anything about him?

Hope IVF process is progressing?

Best,
Alex

FROM: NgosiObiakaHarrison@cape.org
TO: AlexCarter@cape.org

Alex:

Wow--just wow. I can't believe you are going into a war zone--but I know with your memory, your ability to speak Arabic, and your cool demeanor, you will be perfect. I have to say that I can't help but worry about you. But I know that CAPE pays careful attention to security issues for agents, and I'll have to go with that.

I've done a bit of research about your future partner, Seth Melaku. Interesting history--a Black Jew from Ethiopia, who made it out of Ethiopia on a secret airlift in 1991 when he was only eight years old. Has a family (grandmother, mother, two sisters, a brother) living in Jerusalem. He was an outstanding soldier with the Israeli Defense Forces (IDF)--made it to an elite special forces unit and is an expert in Krav Maga, but apparently he left the service after a few years and later joined CAPE. I don't know the details.

We'll talk this coming week before you leave. Anything I can help with--packing I mean? Max and I can take you to the airport. Just let us know when.

Peace,
Ngosi
P.S. Nothing new on the baby front. I'll keep you updated.

FROM: AlexCarter@cape.org
TO: NgosiObiakaHarrison@cape.org

Ngosi

It has occurred to me that this new venture will mean that we will have to delay our proposal regarding albinism in Africa. I know you've worked really hard on that, but don't think I've forgotten it (ahem, at least only for a little while in the excitement of the moment). I think we have a good case for renewing efforts to investigate--possibly sending a field team to Malawi and Tanzania and--elsewhere? I'm indebted to you for bringing this urgent issue to my attention, and I want to make this project a priority when I return from Syria. Of course, I take a personal interest in this issue. I hope you will keep working on it while I am in London and then Syria.

Best, Alex

24

London, 2013

On Alex's third day in London, she endured several hours of physical and psychological assessments at CAPE headquarters--just routine, she was assured. Relieved to have the afternoon free, she borrowed an umbrella and walked through a steady rain to the Palace Athletic Track just two blocks from where CAPE was located in central London. Emily, a senior researcher in human rights for children, had told her about the indoor facility that featured a six-lane running track.

Alex paid a small fee to rent a locker where she left everything but her phone and earbuds. Although she had arrived at Heathrow Airport two days ago, she was still experiencing the weird time disorientation of jet lag. Perhaps a good run would help to clear her brain.

The track was in a high-ceilinged space that looked as big as two high school gyms. In contrast to the leaden clouds outside, the room was brightly lit, a pleasant simulation of sunlight--but happily without the necessity for her usual sunblock, Alex noted. Having changed into tights and a tank top, she sat on a bench to lace up her Nikes and watch a few solo runners making their way around the track. An overweight woman of middle age who seemed to be concentrating on her breathing, an elderly man who ran slowly but with grace, and a teenage girl with short brown hair who had a wiry build and multiple piercings on her face.

As she stood to enter the track, Alex noticed a man standing with hands on his hips on the opposite side of the room. About twenty-eight, she guessed, his skin was very dark, and he was tall, slim, and muscular--like a basketball player. He wore navy blue shorts and a white tee shirt. When he turned his head and looked over at Alex, their eyes met for a few seconds. Then she knew. This was Seth Melaku, the "experienced field agent" with whom she was preparing to enter a war zone, the person on whom her life might soon depend. That jarred her out of her fog.

When he waved and dipped his head slightly, she knew he had recognized her as well, although they had never met. She waited for him to walk to where she was standing.

"You're Alex Carter, the American lady lawyer." His broad smile seemed genuine, but she took offense at 'lady lawyer.' Either he was joking, culturally ignorant, or intentionally insulting her. She decided to put off judgment and ignored the comment.

"And you are Seth Melaku--a former soldier, outstanding field agent, and apparently a barefoot runner."

"Whoa! That's your summary of me? You are a quick study." His eyes were bright with amusement.

"Of course, I studied your picture, and I've read your profile--as I assume you've read mine."

"I've come here to run," he said. "You must have the same idea. We can talk as we run."

Was this a challenge? *Take it easy. Perhaps I'm being a bit paranoid.* They started jogging at a leisurely pace on the two middle lanes of the track. Within moments, they were matching strides.

"Did you know I'd be here--I mean, did Emily tell you I asked about a place to exercise?" Alex asked.

"Actually, I come here several days a week. A good way to de-stress, no? But you're right. I read your profile, and I recognized you from your picture--though it doesn't do you justice. You are more beautiful than your picture indicates."

Alex ignored the compliment. "We're scheduled to meet tomorrow--eight in the morning, I believe."

"Yes, and I already told the assistant to order chai tea for you," he said with a sideways glance.

Alex was quiet for a moment. "Then you did read my profile. I remember that I spoke in an interview about my parents and my childhood--and my mother's chai." She smiled as the memory of the spiced tea comforted her. "I'm afraid I don't know your morning drink preferences."

Seth smiled. "Coffee, black, no sugar." They ran easily for another minute. Seth broke the silence with a question. "Can I speak frankly, Alex?" He was no longer smiling.

"Of course," Alex said, but she was already putting invisible shields in place.

"I'm thinking that this proposed partnership is in some ways like an arranged marriage. We must hope those doing the arranging know what they're doing. You know, choosing a partner or having one chosen for you is a very serious step. It could make all the difference-- whether in a marriage or a partnership such as ours."

"The difference between life and death, you mean." Alex didn't break stride and looked straight ahead. She was mulling over the words "proposed partnership."

"Ah, you have already considered the facts of this situation and been honest with yourself. Of course, you are a barrister--excuse me, a lawyer. I imagine you are trained to weigh facts before making any decision."

Alex couldn't help looking at his bare feet as they continued. Did he always run without shoes, or had he forgotten them today?

"Well, while we're speaking honestly, I have to say that I don't think it's a coincidence that you're here at the track today, Seth Melaku. But I wonder if you forgot your shoes?"

His eyebrows lifted, and then he threw his head back and laughed heartily as he slowed to a stop and bent over laughing.

Alex stopped too and grinned at him. "If this is some kind of a test, let's make it real," she said. "Are you ready for a sprint--how about to the halfway point? Come on--let's race!"

With that, Alex took off, stepping out with a lengthened stride. Seth followed close behind and then ran alongside her. There was no question of speaking now. Both ran to win, and both were breathing hard. Near the finish, Alex found the energy to kick and think beyond the finish as her dad had taught her. She stepped over the line two long strides ahead of Seth.

"I think," Seth said, bending over and catching his breath, "I think you are telling me something here. I like you, Alex Carter. I think we might make an excellent team."

25

Beaconsfield, England, 2013

Alex stood looking at number 112 Warwick Road, in Beaconsfield, her destination after a forty-five-minute train ride from London's Marylebone Station and then a short Uber ride. The home was one of several two-story, attached housing units, all identical in red brick with white wood trim. Sycamore trees, just leafing out from buds, lined the streets in a quiet neighborhood.

Alex had fussed over what to wear and what to bring for this visit. She had finally decided on a trim gray suit and black pumps with a blue silk scarf. She carried a shopping bag from Fortnum and Mason's containing a Biscuit Selection Tin and a pomegranate and rose scented candle, which she had found pleasing as she sampled several possibilities in the store. Fortnum and Mason's had been Seth's helpful suggestion when she had mentioned her plan to visit an acquaintance in Beaconsfield, though she didn't tell him the purpose of her visit.

Nothing about this place, she realized from where she stood at the curb, looked even vaguely familiar. No reason to be nervous, she told herself again. She had thought a great deal about this meeting after talking on the phone to Charlotte Canfield a week ago. Mrs. Canfield had been polite and seemed to welcome a visit when Alex explained who she was. Her husband, Oliver

Canfield, had died after a stroke eight years ago. She had kindly invited Alex to lunch.

Alex walked toward the house and started up the steps when she heard the sound of live piano music. Within seconds, she was tumbling backward through time toward the realm of the light people. She felt herself lying on a small bed against a wall barricaded with soft pillows on the opposite side. A slight breeze blew over her, and she could hear music, which she knew came from the big piano in another room. The vision shifted and she could see the blond woman sitting at the piano, her hands moving over the keys, but tears were falling from her eyes. The man with hair on his face was standing behind her yelling angrily. Something was wrong. Alex could feel it in her body, even when the woman picked her up with cold hands and held her. The woman's face was often wet with tears.

Alex stood outside Charlotte Canfield's home, paralyzed by the visions. She knew that they would fade, so she waited for the music to finish. She didn't know the name of the piece, but she knew every note as if she had listened to it many times.

When she rang the doorbell a few minutes later, she heard unhurried footsteps coming toward the front door.

"You must be Alex," a thin, gray-haired woman said. "I'm glad you've come. Please come in."

"Thank you for inviting me here. It means a lot to me, Mrs. Canfield," said Alex trying to study the woman's face, which was vaguely familiar, although thinner and more lined, but something else was different, something she couldn't quite put her finger on.

Once inside the foyer, Alex was again transported to one of her visions, this time by the medicinal smell of eucalyptus. A lovely blue and white porcelain bowl on a side table held the round blue-gray leaves. The smell made Alex cautious as if something in this place was dark or unhappy. She couldn't put a name to the feeling.

She followed Charlotte Canfield down a hallway, past a neat white kitchen, to a room at the back of the house where French doors let in a flood of daylight. The room was sparsely furnished with two comfortable white armchairs, a small round tea table, and a baby grand piano.

"Let's sit for a few minutes here. Then ... I thought we'd have lunch outdoors in the garden," Charlotte was saying. Alex was doing her best to shake off the visions. She noticed that Charlotte did not look directly at her but somewhere just past her head.

"That sounds lovely. Oh--and I've brought these for you," she said holding out the shopping bag.

Charlotte held out her hand to accept the bag. "I have so much to explain to you, Alex. I need to tell you first that I am almost totally blind. I see some light, and I can make out shapes, but I've suffered from a degenerative eye disease for many years. You are kind to bring me gifts, but you'll have to help me understand what you've brought."

"Yes, of course. I'm so sorry. I should have remembered--"

"I didn't tell you much during our phone call. Oliver made sure that I would be comfortable here in a small home so that I could continue to take care of myself when he was gone. But in the eight years since he died, my condition has deteriorated further. So, I now have help with shopping, cleaning, and a bit of cooking. Mrs. Chu comes three days a week. And I have some friendly young neighbors next door who check on me quite regularly. And a sister in London who visits from time to time." She smiled.

Alex listened to the stream of words, not knowing what to say next. "And you play the piano," she said after an awkward silence. "The piece you were playing before I came in. What is the name of it?"

"That piece is an old favorite of mine--a nocturne by Chopin--Nocturne in E flat major."

"You play it beautifully. I feel that I—that I can remember it--remember you playing it."

Charlotte looked toward Alex. "Remember it? But you were not even a year old when you were with us," she said softly. "It's a famous piece. You've probably heard it somewhere--in a movie, perhaps."

"You're probably right. But, Mrs. Canfield--"

"Please call me Charlotte."

"Charlotte, as I mentioned on the phone, I'm trying to understand more about my adoption and my biological parents. Whatever you can remember--"

"Yes, child, I will tell you what I know. Mrs. Chu is preparing our lunch. Let me take you upstairs for a few minutes, where I have a couple things you will want to keep."

Charlotte stood and reached for a cane that was propped against the piano. "I use one of the rooms as a bedroom, of course," she explained to Alex as they slowly ascended the stairs, "and the other room still holds some mementos of my life with Oliver as well as some of his books and his professional medical certificates. I like to sit there sometimes and just remember him and all his kindness to me."

"You must miss him very much," Alex said. "My father gave me his name. I guess they knew each other professionally."

Charlotte led Alex into a room that included a small blue couch, some crowded bookshelves, and an old television. Several photographs and certificates hung on the walls.

"If my memory serves, they met at a medical conference in London," Charlotte said. "Over drinks at the hotel bar, I believe. Oliver shared that I had retinitis pigmentosa. He had suspected it when we were still traveling in Africa, but I got a definite and devastating diagnosis soon after we were home. We were both still in shock over it. I was convinced it would ruin my life. I believe I was suicidal."

"How terrible for you. I'm so sorry."

"Then, perhaps because Oliver had been open about sharing his own problems, after that, your father told Oliver about how much he and your mother wanted children but had been unsuccessful even after going to a fertility specialist. That, my dear child, was the beginning of your adoption."

"I see." While Alex kept her voice calm, a deep pit seemed to be opening inside her like a sinkhole. "How long was I with you and Dr. Canfield?"

"About five or six weeks, I think it was." She bowed her head as if she were praying. "I'm sorry, Alex. I was intent then on becoming a famous pianist--a pipe dream as it turned out. I was looking forward to practicing as soon as we returned home from Africa. It had been Oliver's idea to rescue you--and I told him that I didn't want a child. He was very disappointed, I think. Angry even." Charlotte raised her head in Alex's direction. "When I look back, I feel great regret. Yet from what you've told me on the phone, your adoption by Paul and Zara seems to have been most fortunate for you. I couldn't have taken care of you in the state I was in." Charlotte put both hands up to her trembling mouth. "I thought about you these many years--about my selfishness, hoping everything worked out for you. I always hoped I would have an opportunity to apologize to you. I am so, so sorry, Alex."

"I'm not judging you, Charlotte." Alex put her hand on Charlotte's arm. "I can hardly blame you for your decision, and I do indeed feel so fortunate to have my parents--they are good people. They love me dearly and I them. But there is so much more I want to know--"

"I understand, but wait, let me give you something." Charlotte moved toward the shelves that held a few books and some mementos of travel--some wood carvings of African animals, a woven basket perhaps from the Amazon, and a bronze begging bowl possibly from Tibet. From the top of a shelf near the window, Charlotte lifted a square white box. She brought it to Alex.

Alex sat on the couch and lifted the lid. A small, stuffed white elephant stood atop a framed photo. Sam! Her dear friend all these years. For a moment, she was afraid she would black out and faint right there on Charlotte's couch. Her heart was beating fast, and a shadow was rising before her eyes.

"Are you okay, dear?" Charlotte asked.

"Yes. Yes, I'm fine, it's just--I think this toy, this little elephant, was mine."

"Of course, it was, dear. I meant to send it along with you, but somehow it got left behind."

Alex held it to her nose. She couldn't pick up any familiar scent, it just smelled dusty. Then she reached into the box for the framed photo. She looked at it in silence, aware that she was looking far into her past. It was a photo of two young black people, a man and a woman, the woman holding a small bundle in her arms. They were standing in front of what looked like a hospital. Alex held her breath, unable to speak.

Charlotte waited. "It's you and your mother and father. The picture was in your nappy bag. I met them only once--the day we brought you from Africa to England by airplane."

Alex tried to keep her voice calm even as part of her was detached and watching herself sitting there. She took a breath. "Their names--do you know their names?" she asked.

"Your mother's name was a flower of some kind-- Rose? Violet? I'm sorry, I don't remember. Your father worked at the hotel where we stayed. I'm sorry. I don't remember his name either."

"Thank you, Charlotte, for keeping these things safe all these years," Alex said. She wanted very much just then to be alone, to stare at this photo of her mother and father. To hold the tiny elephant that she had always thought of as Sam close to her heart. And to figure out how this information was related to her visions. Could she really remember so much from infancy?

"Anyway, these are yours now, as they should have been all along," Charlotte said with a sigh. "Let's go down to lunch. Mrs. Chu will be ready for us with some chicken salad sandwiches and a bit of fruit."

Charlotte didn't have much more information to offer. As the two women sat under a huge beech tree in the narrow but well-cared-for garden, Charlotte could only recall that Oliver had been intent on getting some papers that he said would help them rescue a baby from great danger in Tanzania--or was it Malawi? Or Kenya? She couldn't quite remember anymore. Charlotte remembered very little of what happened after that. Or perhaps she wasn't willing to talk about it.

A short time later, Alex said goodbye at the front door and headed down the stairs to await her ride to the train. As she stood at the curb, she heard the beginning notes of a piano piece--the Chopin nocturne again. The music perfectly expressed the longing and sadness that filled her now. She remembered what she had whispered to Sam long ago: *I'm only eight, Sam, but one day, we will find them, and then we will understand.* But she had surely received what she came for, she thought, as she looked down at the box she was holding close against her chest. It held treasures that she had only dreamed of and, for a short while, allowed her to travel backwards on the wheel of time.

26

London, 2013

After several weeks of training with Alex for their assignment, Seth sat down across from his boss, Graham Fortier, head of security operations, on the tenth floor of CAPE's London headquarters. Fortier was in his late fifties, with neatly trimmed gray hair. He was clean-shaven and perhaps a few pounds over his ideal weight, but his animated features and his manner of speaking in fast, clipped sentences made him seem younger than his years. His assistant had brought in a tray with a pot of tea and one of coffee along with a plate of Irish shortbread biscuits, Fortier's favorite.

"Please, pour yourself a coffee," Fortier said with a welcoming smile. "I know you're still training for this assignment, but I wanted to touch bases to go over our checklist. You'll be leaving on . . ." He rifled through some papers on his desk.

"One week from today, sir."

"Right. Your British passport is ready. It won't show any connection or travel to Israel. You will use the biography created for you on your previous assignment-- your emigration to the UK as a child. By the way, you've developed a convincing British accent since you've been with us, Seth."

Seth smiled. "I try, sir."

"Do you have all the equipment you need?"

"I've worked with Monroe to set up satellite phones and an in-country communications network. We'll be able to send reports as they are written. I still need the name of our initial contact and drivers on both sides of the border."

"We'll give you that and the address of the safe house just before you leave.

Fortier changed the subject then. "So--how is the training going with your rookie partner, Alex Carter? I hear good things about her."

Seth took a sip of coffee, then ran his hand over his closely cropped head before answering. "You know, to be honest, I had my doubts about doing this--taking an untrained agent into a war zone, sir. But now that I've had a chance to observe her and get to know her a little, I have to say that I'm impressed."

Fortier stirred a spoon of sugar into his tea. "Tell me what you mean."

"She's super bright, a really fast learner, quick on her feet, and apparently fine with taking orders."

"But," Fortier prompted when Seth hesitated.

"But there is something else that worries me a little. Something I can't quite put into words. Perhaps it is summed up in the word "heart." She is a particularly determined human being who wants to make a difference. She . . ."

"Go on. I'm listening," Fortier said as he picked up a biscuit.

Seth ran his hand over his head again as he looked out the window into the distance. "That heart, or whatever one calls it, could make her take chances, put herself in danger. I mean--I'm not saying she has a savior complex or anything like that, but she might let her emotions get in the way of her thinking. I don't know." He shrugged. "I could be wrong. She is a barrister after all--reasonable and logical.

Fortier smiled. "You sound protective, Seth, and perhaps a bit defensive."

"Do I? I'm just trying to figure her out. It will be my job to keep her safe." His eyebrows came together and his forehead furrowed in a frown. "And there is her appearance--she's--very white--"

"Albinism. Isn't that mentioned in her file?"

"Yes, yes. But I was going to say that her whiteness-- even her hair--and her height make her stand out. She is easy to notice."

"And you think this is a problem?"

"I'm not sure. She doesn't seem to purposely call attention to herself but . . ." He shrugged again. "We've talked about how she must dress, of course."

"Tell me about how the physical aspect of training is going," Fortier suggested.

"Oh, she's strong, a runner you know. And no complaints, ever. She gives her all and wants to learn whatever we can teach her."

"And her understanding of what you'll be facing? Does she know Syria's situation and its history?"

Seth thought for a few moments. "Amazing, actu- ally. She has this memory-- She knows the names of streets in some towns and villages. Arabic names! Like maybe she has a photographic memory or something. She has also been teaching me some basics of Arabic."

Fortier sat back in his chair and folded his arms. "Despite what seems to be some earlier reservations on your part, you make her sound rather extraordinary. So I have to ask. Are you committed to taking on this assignment with her as your partner? And can you accomplish it safely?"

Seth grinned. "You are right, sir. I do feel protective--it is my job after all. But I believe we'll be a good team. I understand the importance and the urgency of this mission. Alex has skills that I lack--more than I knew. That will be most valuable."

"Excellent. And just as a heads up--we are following daily intelligence reports about possible offensive action in the northern part of Syria, but you will have the latest information as we receive it. We'll talk again before you leave."

When Seth walked out of the office a few minutes later, he wondered if he had said too much. He no longer had doubts about Alex's abilities. But he couldn't know how this young, untested American woman would react to a radically different environment. He had grown to trust her, but how well did he know her? What he didn't say to Graham Fortier and barely acknowledged to himself, was that he found Alex Carter a bit mysterious and quite fascinating.

They would be walking into a version of hell that Alex could not yet imagine. He was determined to keep his focus on keeping them both safe.

27

Turkey–Syria Border, 2013

The country roadway was dark and full of potholes. No lights were visible in any direction. It was 4:30 am. Alex peered out the smudgy windows from the back seat of the car, which smelled of years of sweat and cigarette smoke. She thought she could make out fields stretching into the distance to the east. Seth sat next to Adem, whose job it was to safely deliver Alex and Seth to the place where they could steal over the border from Turkey into Syria.

"What if we meet gendarmes or border guards?" Seth asked.

"You must go with them," Adem said calmly.

After another minute of silence, the driver said, "When we get to the border, very soon now, you must move quickly."

"Yes, we understand," said Seth. Alex handed him his pack from the back seat and adjusted the black scarf on her head.

"Get ready, I'm turning off the headlights. When you get past the fence, you must run. The road is not far."

Adem pulled the car over to the side, the engine running. "Now!"

Alex was out the door, slamming it behind her, pulling on her backpack as she ran. Seth was right behind her.

They heard the car pulling away, but they didn't glance back.

Alex was pleased to see a pink and yellow glow appearing on the eastern horizon. Grateful for the faint light, the two ran through tufts of grass toward coils of concertina wire, which seemed to stretch for miles in either direction. Here they had to move more slowly and deliberately to deal with this obstacle.

Alex went first, her backpack hoisted high on her back. Dark tights and socks protected her legs as she took one step at a time, pausing after each step to check for movement in the shiny coils, which could spring up like a den of angry silver snakes at any sudden movement. They had practiced this maneuver but not in such dim light. Seth followed in her footsteps, keeping an eye on Alex's progress.

The sleeve of a sweatshirt that Seth had tied around his waist suddenly hung down toward the waiting coils and got caught in the steel barbs. "Keep going, Alex. I can get this."

"Where's your knife?"

"Backpack."

From the corner of her eye, Alex saw a faint light far down the fence line, a flashlight perhaps. She pulled her penknife from her jacket pocket. "Here, let me." Within seconds, she had cut the sleeve free.

They adjusted their packs on the other side of the malicious fence.

"Thanks, Alex. Good work."

"I guess this is our welcome to Syria." She looked at Seth and smiled. "Ready?"

And then they ran hard until they reached a narrow dirt road. Within thirty seconds, a small Hyundai pulled up, and they climbed into the back seat.

"You made it," said their driver. "I'm Yousef. Thank you for coming to my country."

* * *

That evening, after reviewing maps and plans and establishing communications with security contacts, Seth stirred a pot of soup that Yousef had left for them at the safe house as Alex sliced up fresh cucumbers and tomatoes for their dinner. They had already contacted London using a satellite connection to confirm their arrival in Syria.

"You know," Seth said as they sat down to eat with only a candle for light, "I must confess to you that a few weeks ago I was reluctant to have you come on this assignment. Now I recognize your value. You have what we called in the Army 'good instincts.'"

Alex raised her eyebrows, slightly amused but grateful for his words. "My value, eh? I hope I can live up to your expectations. Hey, Seth, can I ask you a question?"

"Of course."

"I know a little about your background and your experience in CAPE, but I find myself wondering why you--why anyone-- is drawn to doing this dangerous work."

Seth sat back in his chair and took a deep breath. "To answer, I must tell you a story. When I was in the Israeli Army, I was taught Krav Maga. Do you know it?"

"Some kind of martial art--like karate or jujitsu?"

"Yes, it combines the best techniques of many martial arts, but it has some unique aspects. It's said to be the most efficient way to counter any attack."

"And that's good, right?"

"But that good comes with a dark side. Krav Maga requires an ability to act with physical aggressiveness--including killing one's opponent in rather terrible ways when necessary. But my point I is that I was very good, an expert, at this so-called art. I don't know why exactly, but my instructor told me it had to do with my instincts in stressful situations. That is what I've discovered about you--good instincts under stress."

"But why did you leave the IDF if you were such an expert?"

"Ah, yes. That is what I am getting to. One day, when I was observing a crowd of angry people at a village on the West Bank, watching for possible violence, a sixteen-year-old Palestinian girl surprised me and stabbed me with a screwdriver. My training would've allowed me to disarm her within seconds, capture her, or even kill her if that became necessary. Instead, I backed off--and ran."

Alex put her fork down and looked into Seth's eyes shining in the candlelight, his mouth in a tight line, and his forehead furrowed. "But why--?"

"It was a moment that made me realize that everything I loved about being in the IDF was based on a lie. I had told myself that being a soldier made me a man--a hero, and that I was finally accepted in my adopted country, that I belonged. I felt good about my physical and mental fitness, and I took pride in telling myself that I was protecting my country and its people."

He paused, placed his elbows on the table, and rested his chin on his hands. "When that girl was desperate enough to stab me, I realized that what I thought I valued was based on the capacity for violence against other people who felt cornered and desperate. Who were outsiders."

"And you have compassion for those outsiders," Alex said. She squinted her eyes at him.

"When I learned about CAPE and their fight for basic human rights, I knew I had found my place in the world." He stopped talking and stared down at his plate.

Alex reached over the table to put her hand on his arm. "Thanks for telling me that, Seth. Being an outsider is something I've dealt with all my life although I lived in such a privileged bubble that it didn't affect me directly. Made me think, though."

Seth stared at her for a few moments as if he would say more. He was surprised to find himself wanting to tell her about Jill and how she was so opposed to violence and to guns. How her personal suffering--the loss of her brother--had influenced his decision to do this work. And how his heart still ached at losing her.

What was it about Alex that made him want to confide in her, even to feel vulnerable in her presence? Then he moved to pick up their plates. "We will talk more another time. Now, let's clean up and get some sleep. We have a busy day tomorrow."

28

Aleppo and Serrin, Syria, 2013

The next morning, Yousef showed up in the blue Hyundai to take Alex and Seth to Serrin, a rural town about an hour's drive from the safe house in Aleppo. He said that just a week earlier he had heard reports of violence against civilians there after increasing protests against the Assad regime.

Alex wore a burqa with black socks and shoes. She thought of it as a cloak of invisibility. Her white-blonde hair was hidden under the black cloth, and she wore sunglasses over her almost colorless eyes. Seth, who could not hide his dark skin in a country where few people of African ancestry lived, would have to rely on his British passport if they were picked up by gendarmes or soldiers. While his papers identified him as a British citizen and an immigrant from Africa, they didn't reveal his Israeli citizenship.

As they drove into Serrin, Alex was thinking ahead to the report she would write and send to Ngosi in New York later that evening. She would describe the town center, which consisted mostly of small, run-down shops, block apartment buildings, a dusty market square, and a mosque. Rubble and other evidence of violence were everywhere in the poverty-stricken town. Alex watched a few men as they went about their business riding through the streets on motorbikes. Suffering and death had visited their town, and life went on. Several small children were running and laughing with each other on the sidewalk in front of an apartment building that had gaping holes, perhaps from explosions. Jagged pieces of cement hung precariously from half-demolished apartments on an upper floor.

Alex listened as Yousef explained to a committee of town officials why they had come, to bear witness to the illegal attacks on civilians. Several men dressed in fresh-looking dress shirts accompanied them on a tour, hopeful that Serrin's story would get the attention of world leaders. Two of them spoke some English and were surprised to learn that "the foreign woman" spoke Arabic. They stared at Seth's dark skin, but they asked no questions. After walking through streets of bombed-out buildings and walls full of holes, the group stopped at a damaged two-story home on the edge of town. It had been partially destroyed, and the exterior walls were riddled with bullets.

"In this place, government tanks surrounded civilians," said one of the officials, who was wearing a red-checked kufiyah. They were killed inside--I will show you."

They all went inside into what must have been a living room, and the man knelt on the floor in front of a wall that was lined with holes at a height of about a meter from the floor. "This is where they shot them," he said. "And then they burned all nine bodies."

Alex's blood felt like ice water in her veins during this demonstration. *Someone must have had to clean a lot of blood from this wall, and these floors.* For just a moment she was paralyzed, envisioning the man in the kufiyah kneeling there in a pool of blood. She shivered uncontrollably. It occurred to her then that her cloak of invisibility was not one of invulnerability. With great effort, she willed herself to action. Scrambling for a pen and pad of paper from her bag, she went to work as she had been trained. Were all these people civilians? Were women and children involved? Why was this home targeted? How do you know these were government tanks? Can you provide the names of the victims? How many soldiers were there?

She and Seth would ask the same questions of various people several times over in order to verify the information. She took suggestions from Seth, translating when he needed her to do so. He was able to speak to those who knew some English. They knew that people sometimes lied or exaggerated for any number of reasons, but CAPE was determined to provide only an objective, factual account backed up by the stories of multiple witnesses, about what happened. It was not within their purview to prescribe remedies or interventions.

Later, when Alex and Seth were nearly exhausted from listening to tragic stories, Yousef told Seth that he had located a woman who was willing to talk to Alex about the death of her sons in the recent attack. He would make introductions and then leave the women to themselves.

"Only if you want to, Alex," said Seth when he told her about it. "I know you are tired and that such stories are difficult to listen to."

"Don't worry about me, Seth. Whatever difficulty I might have in listening to a story is nothing compared to what these people have suffered. I can hear one more story."

A small boy, perhaps six-years-old, wearing a ragged tee-shirt, cutoff jeans, and a blue baseball cap followed them up the dim stairway of an apartment building. The child, who had enormous hazel eyes and long, dark eyelashes stood alone a little way behind his mother, who was covered in a black burqa. Her round, puffy face struck Alex as a face of grief, her mouth drawn downward, her eyes heavy-lidded and swollen as if she had been crying.

Her name was Leena, a name Alex did not write in her notes but that she would keep safe in her memory. Leena invited her to sit on an ottoman.

Alex removed her sunglasses, and she could see that the woman was looking at her eyes with their white lashes. "I'm a friend, Leena, please don't be frightened."

Leena nodded and looked down at her lap. She was holding a gilt frame, but the picture was turned face down.

"My Arabic is not perfect, but I hope you will understand me," Alex said.

"So far, yes. I understand you," Leena said.

Alex spoke slowly to be sure of choosing the right words. "I'm not a journalist. I'm with an international human rights organization. We believe it is extremely important for the world to know what has happened here--that's why we've come. I understand that it must be very difficult for you to talk about your family and what happened to them."

"God willing, it will be a blessing if others hear what has happened here." Leena looked up at her guest.

"Yes, I hope so. I want to hear your story. We will tell the world about it."

"Alex," Leena began, seeming anxious to talk. "I am a mother of three sons." She put her hand on her heart, then gestured to a narrow couch against the wall. "My oldest was sleeping right there. It was just past 6:00 am when Assad's men came to our home."

Alex glanced at the little boy standing still and silent behind his mother.

"Did they wear military uniforms?"

"Yes. And my son said to them, 'There is nothing here, sir.' But the officer told him 'Shut up,' and the others hit him with their rifles and knocked him down."

Tears rolled down her cheeks, but she kept talking. "They took him outside. And after a little time, I went outside. All my sons were lying on the ground. Two were executed. Bassam had been shot right here," she said pointing to her forehead through the burqa, "and his body was burned. Yasin was also executed, and his body was burned."

The little boy watching Alex and Leena was silent. He brought his arms up to his chest. He moved closer to his mother, his eyes wide.

"Was anybody in the family a fighter or an activist? Was there any specific reason they came after your sons?"

"I don't know." Leena's face was shiny with tears that she didn't bother to wipe away. She turned over the framed picture from her lap and held it up, as if to illustrate her agony, to make it real to Alex. It was a composite photo of three mustached men, presumably her husband and the two sons, who Alex guessed to be fifteen and seventeen.

Alex stared at their portraits, feeling a weight in the pit of her stomach. "Were your sons armed?"

"No! They were not armed," she said almost screaming.

"I am so sorry for what has happened to you and your family," Alex said. She could not torture this woman further with her questions. "Your words--your story--will be heard by many people, and we hope that it will help to bring about change. I am so grateful to you for your courage in telling us about your sons."

Leena wailed. "If we could save them by weeping, we would do it. Our tears could fill gallons and make a river--for all our people who are dying, for our women, our children. For the things they are doing to us, our tears could make a very big river."

"Yes," said Alex. "A river of tears." She put her hand on Leena's arm. "Your little boy--what is his name?"

When Yosef called up to her from the stairwell, she hugged Leena goodbye. "May this be a blessing on you."

The little boy stood in the doorway, looking at her with his large hazel eyes. "Be a good boy, Daniel," she said in Arabic. "Help your mom now, yes?" He nodded solemnly, and she could feel his eyes on her as she descended the stairs.

29

Aleppo, Syria and New York, 2013

FROM: NgosiObiakaHarrison@cape.org
TO: AlexCarter@cape.org

Alex:

Your excellent report electrified all of us here in NY.
I'm still thinking about that poor woman who lost
her sons. Heart wrenching. No other human rights
organization has been able to obtain this kind of
on-the-ground information. You tell it so vividly
and at the same time objectively--that's hard to do,
I think. You are very brave, Alex.

Director Hampton was especially pleased, and
I know there has been talk about sending your
reports to the White House. Surely somebody will
be moved by your descriptions of innocent civilians
suffering in a war zone. I wish I could put a copy
of it right on President Obama's desk--he'd read it
for sure.

There is also a lot of discussion here about how
safe--or unsafe--this mission is for you and Seth.

We are, in a word, worried. Please, please be careful. We need you. Please be safe.

Peace
Ngosi

FROM: AlexCarter@cape.org
TO: NgosiOblakaHarrison@cape.org

Hi, Ngosi,

By some cyberspace miracle, I've received your email on my phone, but connections are very unreliable here as you can imagine. I want to dictate about this surreal experience on my voice recorder while it is happening and hope to send the recording to you when we have a better connection back at our safe house.

At the moment, Seth and I are at in a chaotic scene in what is left of the lobby in a hospital in Aleppo. We rushed here after one of our contacts managed to contact us and let us know that the hospital had been bombed. We are talking with witnesses, most of them stunned as we are. All of this is so devastating.

Oh, Ngosi, what terrible acts are we humans capable of? Much of the hospital has been destroyed, people--whether patients, doctors, or other staff-- are wandering amidst the smoke and rubble, confused, crying, and bleeding. We are doing what we can to help, but the situation is chaotic and overwhelming. I just talked to a nurse who is heading to the obstetrics floor and has agreed to take me there. She was able to talk to another nurse--lots of damage but patients needing care. Not sure when they might be able to move them somewhere else.

Signing off for now. Hope you get this.

30

Aleppo, Syria, 2013

Alex picked up the hem of her burqa so she could follow Dima, a young Syrian nurse, up three flights of the hospital stairwell. She pressed the cloth of the burqa against her face as they made their way through clouds of smoke and dust. Shouts and cries seemed to come from everywhere, human pleas for help full of fear and despair. An unreal world. She listened for the sound of planes overhead. Would they come back around to bomb the hospital again? Damaging the hospital was not an accident, and whoever it was might want to finish what they started. Her muscles were tensed, ready to dive or run at any moment.

She glanced at her watch. She had promised Seth that she would meet him on the ground floor near the reception desk in fifteen minutes.

As soon as Dima pulled open the heavy door to the obstetrics floor, they could hear screaming and crying. The unit had received a direct hit. Parts of the ceiling were lying in the hallway, wires hung from holes in the roof, and a layer of gray dust covered everything. The electricity appeared to be out.

"I must help where I can," said the nurse. "Are you okay on your own?"

"Yes, thank you, Dima. Don't worry about me." She looked into the young woman's liquid brown eyes, sensing both pain and panic. "I am so sorry, Dima." Though they had met only ten minutes earlier, the two women hugged each other tightly.

Alex made her way down the littered hallway and stepped into a room where she thought she heard a baby's cries. It took her a moment to take it in what she was seeing. A single hospital bed was piled with debris that had fallen from the ceiling. A woman's pale and bruised face was looking at Alex from that bed, her face contorted in pain.

"Please," the woman called weakly in Arabic. "Please help my baby."

"You're alive," Alex mumbled in English.

"Please help my baby," the woman pleaded again.

"Listen, I am not a nurse, but I will help you and your baby if I can," Alex managed to say in Arabic. Her entire body was trembling as she listened to the baby's muffled cries. *Where are you, little one? Help me find you.*

A portable infant crib was overturned next to the woman's bed, covered with pieces of drywall and dust. Hazy light streamed in through holes in the ceiling. Weak cries were coming from somewhere on the floor. Alex could hear short, gasping sounds as she pushed rubble aside, her own heartbeat pounding in her ears. When she spotted a pink and yellow bundle under the hospital bed, she knelt and reached out with shaking hands to pick it up.

She brushed dust off the baby's face and mouth. No blood. The tiny infant, still swaddled in its cotton blanket, cried louder now, taking full breaths, and producing what Alex thought must be instinctive cries for survival. She kissed the baby's cheek and held it against her heart. "You're all right now, sweet child. You're going to be all right," she soothed in English. Standing up, she turned her attention to the woman in the bed.

She cleared off as much rubble from the bed as she could while holding the baby against her shoulder. She had hoped to be able to place the baby in its mother's arms, but now that she was close, she could see that the poor woman was in no shape to hold her child.

"What can I do to help you?" Alex asked. "Do you want water?

"I'm afraid," the woman said breaking into sobs. "My little Aziza was born two days ago, and they say that I have an infection. And now this! They are trying . . . to kill us! . . . Even in . . . our hospitals."

"I will try to find a nurse for you."

"Wait," the woman said. "Please--please stay a moment."

Alex reached out to hold the woman's hand. "Yes, I am here."

Over the next few minutes, the woman, Yura, spoke in a barely audible voice while Alex listened and jostled the baby to sleep.

"You must take care of my baby girl. I think I am going to die here soon. And no one is coming to help. And I am afraid the bombs are coming through the roof. Please, lady, you must take care of Aziza now."

"Yura, please listen to me. I'm not a nurse. I'm with a human rights organization. But I will try to find a nurse for you now."

She went out into the hallway, still carrying the baby against her shoulder. She saw a nurse down the hall and called to her. "Please, this woman needs help."

"I will come when I can," the nurse said. "Many people have been hurt. Many need help."

A low hum reached Alex's ears. *Are the planes coming back for another shot at the hospital?* She ran back into the room.

"Please, please take care of my baby," the mother was moaning, trying to lift her head from the dusty pillow.

"I have an idea, Yura. Is there someone at your home who can take care of Aziza?" Energy raced through Alex's limbs now. She was ready for action.

Yura's eyes opened wide. "My mother is there with my other children. I will tell you the address. You will take Aziza there?"

Alex memorized the address and then listened, terrified, to the whine of a rocket somewhere nearby. "The nurse--down the hall--she said she is coming soon. She will help you."

"Yes, thank you. Please lady, you are beautiful, like an angel, I think. You will take Aziza to be safe? You will save my baby?"

"Yes, yes, I will take her to your mother, I promise."

"Go, go now--"

The hum of a plane somewhere seemed to be growing louder. Alex ran for the stairwell, holding the sleeping Aziza in her arms. She couldn't do anything about the hospital or all the people suffering there, but she would take this baby, this one tiny being, to safety.

Her burqa tripped her up once on the stair, but she was able to grasp a railing to keep herself from falling. Aziza still slept.

Seth would be looking for her at the hospital entrance by now. What would he say about the baby?

When she got to the ground floor, she couldn't open the heavy door out of the stairwell while holding the baby. She rapped on the door and shouted for help. No one came. Then she noticed another door to the outside behind her. She put Aziza inside her burqa and pushed. The door opened easily.

She found her way through the dust and rubble to the front of the hospital, crying out when she came upon parts of a body--an arm, a leg--she didn't want to see any more. She lifted her head trying to find her way through the smoke and dust. Her heart was racing as she held the baby tightly against her chest.

Seth was waiting outside what had been the main glass entrance doors. "Alex! I was worried. Are you all right?"

"I'm fine, but I have something to--"

Seth's right hand was wrapped in a piece of blood-soaked clothing. "Seth, are you okay? You're bleeding. Let me see your hand."

"It's okay, Alex. I cut myself on a piece of glass. The bleeding has stopped. Let's just get away from this hospital. It's very likely that they will send more rockets or drop more bombs here."

"I know where to go. Follow me." Alex took off with long strides toward the back of the hospital. Seth followed her as they crossed several streets and made their way down a narrow alley.

"You seem to know where you are going, Alex. Where are we?"

"There is a mosque down this next street--just a little farther. We can rest there. Just a little farther."

When they reached the mosque, they sat partly hidden behind a column near the entry steps.

A muffled cry came from within her burqa. Aziza was awake. Alex brought the baby out and held her against her chest. She had grabbed a bottle of infant formula from the overturned crib and offered it to the baby now.

"Oh no, Alex. What have you done? A baby!" He paused as he peered at the tiny being. "We are here only to be witnesses to these horrors. We can't get involved. We can't save all these people."

Quickly, Alex told him about Yura and how she had to leave her behind. "I had no choice, Seth. The mother might have been dying. I promised her that I would take the child to its grandmother. We're close to her home now."

"What if we can't find her home? What will we do?"

"We will find it, Seth." She placed her hand on his shoulder. "I know the way. You're right. We can do nothing here, nothing to stop these terrible acts of hate and greed. But we can save one little child."

Aziza was fussing. Alex held her up to her shoulder and began singing softly.

"A lullaby, yes?" Seth smiled as he reached over to caress the child's head. "And I believe you are singing in Swahili--I recognize a couple words. I didn't know Swahili was one of the languages you know."

"It's not. I'm--I'm not sure how I know this song--this lullaby. It is perhaps--an old memory. I'll tell you more about it later."

They both jumped when they heard an explosion in the direction of the hospital. Seth pulled Alex to her feet.

"Let's go, we'll find the baby's grandmother, and then we'll find our way back to the safe house," Alex said. "And I'll take a look at your bleeding hand."

"You are nothing short of amazing, Alex," Seth said staring at her. "Let's go."

31

New York City to Syria, 2013

FROM: NgosiObiakaHarrison@cape.org
TO: AlexCarter@cape.org

URGENT - Security ordering you and Seth out of Syria. Your presence has been noted and your position may be compromised. Plans are underway to extract you--use secure code for instructions.

32

Aleppo, 2013

The only sounds from outside the safe house were the occasional car passing and the screeching of cats in the alley behind the house. Alex and Seth were in the kitchen eating scrambled eggs with tomatoes and cheese by the light of a single candle when they heard four staccato knocks at the entry door. Seth moved silently to the front room, briefly touching the knife strapped to his leg under his jeans. He listened. Another four knocks.

"It's me, Yousef."

Seth opened the door to let him in, shut it carefully, and turned the bolt in the lock. Alex joined them in the living room.

Yousef's voice was calm as he spoke in heavily accented but rapid English. "You must leave here now. I will take you to another safe place. There you will await help in crossing the border to Turkey perhaps close to midnight. Do not clean up here, take only your essentials, you must come right away. You understand?"

Seth and Alex both nodded their heads.

"One at a time, please. Walk at a normal pace. To my car parked around the corner and a short distance north of here. You will see it." He pointed to the west. "One of you must go out the back door. One out the front. Understand?"

Again they nodded in agreement. Yousef disappeared through the kitchen and out the back door of the house.

"I'll go first," Seth said as he stuffed a laptop into his backpack. "Out the front door. Count to fifty and then slip out the back way. Are you okay?"

Alex was struggling to put the black burqa over her head. "I'm fine. Go. I'll be right behind you."

Yousef had the car's motor running, and he sped off the second that Alex hopped into the back seat and shut the car door. No one spoke until they had zigzagged through the narrow streets to reach a main road. Seth watched carefully to determine whether they were being followed.

"I think I may have interrupted your dinner--I'm sorry," said Yousef with a quick smile when they were out of the city. "It is time for you to go home now with our thanks for coming here to listen to my people."

"We are grateful to you, Yousef, for all you have done for us," said Alex. "And we will do our best to let the world know about conditions here." She paused and then continued, "I have one more favor to ask you please, Yousef."

Yousef glanced at the rearview mirror to see Alex's face. "Of course, dear lady. If I can help--"

"When we were at the hospital two days ago, we carried a newborn baby from her injured mother to her grandmother's home nearby. The mother's name is Yura, and I can give you the address of the grandmother. Can you find out for us if Yura made it out of the hospital alive and was reunited with her family?"

"I will try. Yes, I will find out for you. Do not worry."

Alex found a pen in the pocket of her backpack and wrote the address on a scrap of paper.

"Where are you taking us now, Yousef?" asked Seth. "Are we--and you--in danger?"

"We believe the house where you were staying has been discovered. Intelligence indicated that someone was suspicious of you. Your security boss in London decided that we should not wait, that you must leave as soon as possible."

"I see. Thank you, Yousef."

They drove west for forty-five minutes, a route that took them into the countryside. Alex saw some empty fields and smelled farm animals through the open car windows.

"You will wait in a shed at the rear of this family farm, not close to the house. The farmer and his wife are friendly to us, but you will not meet them. Someone will come for you within a few hours to lead you over the border." He looked at Alex. "I think you will not need the burqa now, Miss Alex. You will have a little hike over the fields, but you will soon be safe on the other side."

With that, Yousef stopped the car and indicated a small outbuilding alongside the dirt road. "There is water there, and perhaps a bit of food from the farmer. May Allah protect you."

"And you," Seth said as they scrambled out of the car.

* * *

The shed held various farming implements, neatly hung or stored along the walls. A jug of water stood on a small workbench next to a plate of dates and nuts that was covered with a dish towel. There were no windows. Seth turned on a flashlight, and they made themselves as comfortable as they could on the floor of the shed.

"What if no one comes for us?" Alex couldn't help asking aloud. "I mean, I trust Yousef, but what if something goes wrong?"

"We're near the border. If we have to, we will set out on foot alone when it is still dark. Yousef said around midnight. We'll wait and see."

"Well--then let's finish dinner," Alex said with a grin. These dates look luscious."

"I'll show you how the Israelis like to eat them." Seth pulled out his knife and cut one of the dates part way through and stuffed some nuts into it. "Try it--my mother and sister make these with a bit of sugar for weddings."

Seth opened the door a crack to get some fresh air. They could hear only the sound of crickets and then the howl of a dog at some distance.

"Tell me something I don't know about you, Seth Melaku," Alex said as they lay back with their heads on their backpacks. "I think we have been through an amazing--and rather traumatic--experience together, and you know, I can't think of anyone I would rather have shared this time with."

Seth met her eyes in the dim light. He smiled. "Yes, I will tell you something about me, but then you must also tell me something I don't know about you."

"Agreed."

He lay back and looked up into the darkness as he began his story. "Several years ago, when I had just graduated from the university in Tel Aviv, and before I joined CAPE, I had a friend, a very dear friend. Her name was Jill--and I was perhaps in love with her. She was American, like you. And she was optimistic, you know-- she laughed a lot and never complained. And she truly cared about other people, so they liked her immediately. Then, one day, she told me that she had lost her brother. He was one of many killed in a mass shooting at his high school. And his death had destroyed her parents. She was trying very hard to find a path forward for herself. And I think she was doing so. But then--" His voice broke.

"You don't have to continue, Seth. I can feel your grief . . . Perhaps I shouldn't have asked you--"

"It's okay, Alex. It's a relief to speak of it--if you can bear to hear it."

Alex heard him take a deep breath. She wanted to reach out and hug him, but she sensed he had more to say.

"Soon after she told me that, Jill died as a result of a ruptured appendix--or perhaps the doctors did something wrong when operating. I'll never know for sure. But in her own way, she did say good-bye to me."

"I'm so sorry, Seth. You must miss her very much."

He looked over at Alex, her white-blond hair shining in the dim light. She had turned toward him, her face mirroring his expression of grief.

"But since I have met you--and come to know you--I feel that grief softening somehow. I think I'm accepting . . . what happened. You have shown me a more hopeful world. Dearest Alex, I guess I'm trying to say that I've fallen in love with you."

Alex sat up, a smile spreading across her face. "Seth Melaku--couldn't you have chosen a more romantic setting to tell me this?" They laughed like children whispering secrets. She leaned over to kiss him lightly on the lips. Then she lay down next to him again and took his hand in hers.

"I will be careful of the cut on your hand. Is it feeling okay?"

"It's fine. You won't hurt me."

"Now I will tell you a bit of my story as I promised. I had a boyfriend before I joined CAPE--his name was Quin. We were both offered positions at law firms in Washington DC after graduation, and I think he wanted to get married. But it became obvious to me at some point that we were not meant for each other, and I left the relationship. It was the right thing to do though I know he was hurt by that." She was silent for a few seconds.

"Thank you for telling me--"

"Wait, please, I want to say a little more." He squeezed her hand.

"I have been thinking now and then in this environment of chaos and violence that I am so fortunate to be here with you--I would never have met you if I had followed the path I was on, and I couldn't possibly have imagined this one. Here we are in an old farm shed many miles from home--just two human beings from radically different pasts who have somehow been brought together. I find that fascinating, I don't even know how to describe it . . . But I guess I'm saying that I've fallen in love with you, Seth Melaku."

He leaned in close to kiss her. Then he grinned and said, "Maybe this is a romantic place after all, eh?"

33

London and Stonehenge, England, 2013

Seth knocked at Alex's hotel room door just before 9:00 am. After being extracted from Syria, he and Alex spent two long days of debriefing at the London CAPE headquarters. They were praised and applauded for their courage and the valuable information they had gathered under fire. Messages of congratulation and gratitude came in from several people at the New York office as well.

Alex opened the door dressed in faded jeans, a pale-yellow sweater, a blue Chicago Cubs baseball cap, and sneakers.

"I'm almost ready. But I wish you would tell me where we're going. Should I bring a jacket?" She paused a moment to look at how he was dressed. She smiled. "Hey, Seth Melaku, it's good to see you looking relaxed and wearing clean clothes!"

Seth laughed. "And you, Lexy, look--gorgeous. Sure, bring a jacket. You're a visitor here in London, and I want to show you one of my favorite places for R&R. Do you know this expression in America--R&R?"

"Of course. Mostly in a military context, but it's in common usage for anyone who needs time to chill."

Seth smiled. "Exactly, so I thought we deserve a little R&R. We will chill! But first--I have some very good news from headquarters."

"Tell me! Is it news of the baby--and Yura?"

"Yousef learned that Yura is still in hospital care, but she will survive. And the baby, Aziza, is safe with her grandmother and siblings. Her brothers have given the baby a nickname --Alex!"

"We saved her, Seth. Just think of that. Only one small person, but who knows what her future may be?" Alex sighed deeply. "I think I'm just now beginning to take in what we experienced. I texted my parents to tell them we're home safe. But soon, I'll have to call them. I've been trying to think of how to talk about--all that. Life in Syria almost seems like a dream to me now. Maybe that's how our minds protect us from walking around terrified, I understand better now why soldiers are often reluctant to talk about their war experiences."

"Ah, we can talk about that later. For now, it is a beautiful June day in merry old England, and we are going to enjoy our rest and relaxation. Come!" He held the door open for her.

They took the tube to Waterloo Station where they bought takeout coffee and chai tea before boarding a train. Alex couldn't help but see that they were headed to Salisbury, which could only mean a visit to the famous and eternally mysterious Stonehenge.

On the train, and then on the short bus ride from Salisbury, Alex told Seth about the proposal she and Ngosi were working on to convince the CAPE executives that it was worth sending a field team to Africa to investigate the allegations of violence against people with albinism. Seth listened carefully.

Alex said, "While we were in Syria, Ngosi has continued researching about albinism. One of my emails from her is a report from NPR--that's the well-respected public radio station in the States--from a few months ago. The article is a pretty good summary of what's happening. For example, there have been albino killings in a dozen African countries, including South Africa and Kenya, but things are worse in Tanzania. During the past six years, more than a hundred people with albinism were violently attacked in that country. Seventy-one died and thirty-one escaped, though most of those were maimed--their limbs or other parts cut off. Many of these victims were children who were attacked in broad daylight. The brazen violence has forced the government to open boarding schools for those children, but Ngosi says those schools are more like warehouses than schools. Their parents are afraid to have them at home or to send them to public school."

"Why are conditions in Tanzania worse than the other countries?" asked Seth.

"It's not really clear. But Tanzania has one of the highest rates of albinism in the world--nearly one in every 1,400. Compare that to one in 20,000 worldwide. Some scientists believe that East Africa may be where the genetic mutation that causes albinism may have started."

Seth's eyebrows came together in a frown. "I find all this horrifying and just kind of unbelievable--not that I doubt you and your colleague." He shook his head, seemingly stunned. "I'll read the draft of your proposal when it's ready. Perhaps I can help get it the attention it deserves at CAPE headquarters in London."

"That would be helpful, Seth. Perhaps you could help us understand more about security concerns if we were to send a field team into say Malawi and Tanzania."

Seth hesitated a moment. "Lexy, please tell me that you are not envisioning being part of such a team. I doubt that CAPE has a strong network of contacts to help with protection in those third-world countries. Security for a team would be quite difficult, I imagine."

"Other human rights groups have done some investigation, and the United Nations is also on the alert to this problem. I'm passionate about this, Seth, and so is Ngosi. And yes--I want to go there and find out for myself what is happening and why. It's just so hard to fathom these horrific incidents here in the twenty-first century."

Seth shifted in his seat and stared out the window, his brow furrowed in thought. "Okay, let me read the research you and Ngosi are putting together. Then I can make a better recommendation for security. I will do whatever I can to make this happen." Determination shone in his dark eyes.

When the train arrived in Salisbury, they boarded a tour bus. They first glimpsed the circle of giant monoliths as they drove through the wide-open country to the Stonehenge visitor center.

Alex looked up at the cloudless sky--like a huge, blue bowl above the Salisbury Plain, protecting them in this space that many had held sacred over thousands of years. Whether Stonehenge was an astrological observatory or a mystical burial ground, or even the landing site for aliens, she was fascinated by the meaning it held for human history.

"Seth, you couldn't have known this, but when I was maybe twelve, in junior high, I think, we studied Stonehenge, and I was sure--for about six months--that

I wanted to be an archaeologist when I grew up. Mostly, I wanted to solve the mystery not so much of who designed and built all this--but why."

"I can imagine you as a little girl wondering about that." Seth smiled at her. "I knew almost nothing about this place until I was about to leave Israel. People at the embassy liked to tell me what I should see while in England. So, one day, not long after I arrived, I came out here by myself--even walked around on those rolling hills beyond the site. As it turned out, this is where I made a big decision."

"To join CAPE?"

"Yes, and the other side of that--to leave my family and my adopted country--the Promised Land. Somehow being out here made me feel--I don't know exactly-- clearer about my life and what I want it to be. It's hard to explain. Maybe it just reminded me a little of my home country, my childhood."

At the site, they had to stay on a pathway lined with ropes some distance from the actual stones. They did their best to separate themselves from a crowd of tourists as they gazed at the stones and tried to imagine human beings perhaps as early as 3100 BC standing in this very place. Seth had picked up brochures at the visitor center and read aloud, "Around 180 generations have passed since the stones were erected at Stonehenge.'"

"I like the sound of that better than just how old the place is--it puts people into the story," said Alex. "Do you think that the people who lived here--and all the generations that followed--continued to believe whatever it was the first builders believed?"

Seth frowned slightly before he answered. "You know, I lived my first ten years in an isolated, rural region of Ethiopia. We were shepherds, and my father was a faithful religious man who followed the Jewish teachings handed down over perhaps two millennia. By the time I was born, our people were no longer completely ignorant of the outside world, but for almost all those years, they thought they were the only remaining Jews on the entire Earth. They knew nothing of the changes and additions to Judaism over the centuries."

"You are so fortunate to have such a rich history behind you--the history of both your family and a community of believers," Alex said.

Seth searched her face. "Yes, yes, I am fortunate for that. We lived very simply, but we had each other, our language, our customs and rituals, and especially our hope that one day we would go to the Promised Land-- which we could only read about in our ancient scriptures. Our beliefs and our hope were part of us, like DNA, and they kept us going through many hardships."

"And was the Promised Land all you hoped for?" Alex asked.

They had wandered away from the paved path to go through a gate that took them outside the fence toward one of the small grassy hills.

"I was only ten, so I'm not sure what I expected. My father had just died, and my brother was born on the airplane that brought us to Israel. It was a time of upheaval for me--for my whole family. My hero then was an IDF soldier who had been assigned to our airplane during Operation Solomon. His name is Benjamin Bendler--a doctor, and he became a friend to me and my family, helping us to get settled in a new country. My old hope of reaching the Promised Land was replaced by a more private wish. I wanted to become a soldier like Benjamin--to be respected, perhaps to be a hero." He paused here to give a lopsided smile. "But mostly to belong."

"I understand," Alex said. "I understand wanting to belong."

Seth offered her his hand as they walked up the dirt path to stand atop the hill. She was surprised to feel her heart speed up as she casually took his hand. The air was clear, so they could see for miles in all directions past the rolling hills of the Salisbury Plain to woods and villages beyond.

"Later, when I left the military, I went to see Benjamin and his family in Tel Aviv. He is no longer a soldier. He is still a medical doctor but he also works with Peace Now--trying to negotiate peace between Israelis and Palestinians. Perhaps you know of this organization?" Seth's eyes were wide as he looked at Alex. "Ben is still my hero. I want so much for you to meet him and for him to know you."

Alex tipped her head to one side and studied Seth's face as she felt a smile widening on her own. "I would like that, Seth." She was conscious that he was still holding her hand as they surveyed the scene before them in silence. She gently squeezed his fingers. He tightened his grip, the two hands seeming to communicate independently of their owners.

"Look over there, see that rough-looking, jagged rock standing all alone over there--the one that looks like it is leaning? That is the Heel Stone, an important part of

Stonehenge's history and mythology. If we were to come here in a few weeks, we would be among a giant crowd of people celebrating the summer solstice, chanting, and dancing, and celebrating life around it."

"I remember reading about it long ago. Something about casting a shadow into the stone circle during both the summer and winter solstice--yes? A key part of the astrological observatory?"

"Ah, for a moment there I forgot about your superpower memory." Seth grinned. "What I want to tell you is that I was looking at that very stone when I knew that I wanted to spend my life helping to give a voice to people who weren't able to speak up for themselves."

"I think your father would be prouder of that choice than anything else you might have chosen, Seth."

He put his arm around her waist. She leaned her head on his shoulder. She felt a warmth in her belly and her skin tingled.

"During all that time in a war zone, I wanted so much to touch you, Lexy. I told myself that if we got out of there in one piece, I would bring you to share the magic and the peace of this place--to have you feel it too."

She reached out both hands and placed them on either side of his face as she stared into his deep brown eyes. "Since I am with you, Seth Melaku, how could I not?"

34

Near Arusha, Tanzania, 2012

Kaj was worried about his mother. She had taken to sleeping long hours into the day, and she no longer had dinner for him when he arrived at her hut. She didn't have the energy to create the beaded bracelets and baskets that he sold for her on the roadside or occasionally took into the Arusha marketplace. A few neighbors brought food and laid it outside her door, but she ate little.

Layla had been a widow for almost ten years. No one mentioned her husband, Biko, anymore. He had died of the wasting disease, and most villagers remembered only that about him. They would not enter Layla's hut because of it.

Kaj couldn't remember much about his father, but he knew well the stigma of the wasting disease that had killed many people in his village and other villages as well. His father refused to go to the Babu for help. When Kaj told Sister Angelica about his mother and how she had become so thin, the Sister offered to come to Layla's hut.

"Boniface," she said after examining his mother, "I have been trained as a nurse--in the ways of modern medicine. I want you to listen carefully now, as I have something difficult to say to you. Let's go outside. Your mother is sleeping."

"Yes, Sister. I'm listening."

"Your mother most likely has what is called AIDS, and I believe she is dying. She believes this as well. I would like to arrange for her to go to the hospital in Arusha where she can be more comfortable."

"I can't pay for that, Sister. I'm no longer working for my grandfather, and as you saw, my mother can no longer make the things I used to sell for her."

"It's all right, Boniface. I know a way that she can stay at the hospital. She will be treated kindly as she faces death. You will be able to visit her. She will not be alone."

Kaj looked down at his feet. "I thank you, Sister Angelica. I think my mother would like that very much."

"And I would appreciate it if you would come live with us at St. Cecelia's--as a member of our staff. You know the school and the Sisters well, and we trust you. We need someone to do a variety of odd jobs around the place and to help with the garden and the chickens. You would also have some responsibilities for our security."

Kaj looked up at Sister Angelica with his eyes wide. "I would live there--with the Sisters and the orphans?"

"Yes, you would have a bed, food, and a small salary. And you could continue to learn at our school and from our books."

"That is most generous. I cannot say no to that." Kaj smiled briefly. Perhaps this God who died but didn't die was looking out for him after all.

35

Near Arusha, Tanzania, 2013

Boniface helped with whatever needed doing at St. Cecelia's--cleaning, repairing, weeding, and sometimes riding a rusty old bicycle the two miles to Arusha for fresh vegetables or other supplies. He had taken on the job of checking and repairing the wooden fence around the compound of white-washed brick buildings that housed the children and staff, a schoolroom building that included a tiny chapel area, and another small storage structure for garden supplies and tools. He was easy with the children and often spent time with them twisting balloons into animal shapes for the little ones or kicking an old soccer ball around with the older kids just inside the gate after classes. He listened in at school lessons, and Sister Bernice helped him choose books that he could read from their small library.

He mourned the loss of his mother, but he was grateful to Sister Angelica for arranging to have her moved to the hospital, where she had been cared for and kept comfortable by kind nurses. Kaj sat at her bedside and held her hand in the last hours of her life. She was able to smile at him and tell him he was a good son. She told him how much she loved him and urged him to always follow his heart. Sister Angelica helped him arrange for her burial in their small village. On the day they buried her, he kept vigil at her grave throughout the night, unable to cry but filled with the pain of loss.

One evening in early October, Kaj lay on his narrow cot after making a final check of the fences and locks on the gate at St. Cecelia's. It gave him great satisfaction to walk the perimeter of the compound each evening when everyone was in bed. He liked listening to the insects chattering and clicking from somewhere in the undergrowth, and he took comfort in the shushing sound of the breeze blowing through the palm fronds above.

Every day at St. Cecelia's, he was learning more about the great world outside of Arusha and his village by listening to the Sisters and reading whatever he could get his hands on. He studied the globe that stood on Sister Angelica's schoolroom desk, fascinated by its possibilities. Placing his fingers on oceans and continents, he located his own small country on the eastern edge of the African continent. The world was so much larger than he had known. He begged Sister Bernice to explain the international date line and time zones. She did her best, but the idea of time being different in various locations was a bit beyond his grasp. Time, he decided, must be magic, and he wanted to know if he could go backward in time. Sister Bernice gently told him no, that was impossible as far as she knew.

Tonight, he was trying to read an English-language newspaper that he borrowed from Sister Angelica. He kept a pencil and paper next to his bed to write down words that he would look up in the thick dictionary the next day. His vocabulary was quickly increasing.

On the front page of the local paper, a headline caught his eye.

Danger! Election Year!

According to a recent United Nations report, there is an increased demand for body parts of people with albinism in the lead-up to elections. People who are wealthy and educated may turn to witch doctors for good luck potions. The people who harvest the parts are usually impoverished and willing to do something dreadful simply to make a bit of money. These criminals can gain up to $100,000 U.S. for the sale of a whole body according to the U.N. Few attackers and witch doctors have been brought to trial, let alone convicted.

During the past twelve years, a string of murders has left at least 72 Tanzanian albinos dead.

Last month, a United Nations report on albino persecution put Tanzania at the top of a list of African nations—mostly in East Africa—where albinos are targeted for murder.

There are fears of more murders ahead of an election later this fall because of the risk that some politicians could turn to witchcraft to improve their chances.

Kaj sat up, swung his feet to the floor, and threw the paper down. He needed to move, to take the jitters out of his body, but he couldn't leave the confines of his small room so late in the night and risk disturbing the

Sisters or the children. Pacing the few steps from his bed to the door and back, he couldn't block out an image of Mr. M. and his evil smile appearing in his mind's eye. He hadn't seen him and his thug since that night at the Othman farm. Just the thought of how he had agreed to their demands and shown them the farm made him lower his head and put his hands over his ears.

It was his job now to keep everyone at St. Cecelia's safe. That included the two albino children who were especially at risk. He thought of how little Nico loved kicking the soccer ball around with him, and how Lilia loved to dance, spinning in circles with the other little girls. These sweet children were both seemingly unaware of how their lack of skin color put them in grave danger.

At that moment, he decided that he would make up for his lack of courage by doing everything he could to protect them.

He picked up the newspaper from the floor and scanned the front page. Another headline, this one in a corner near the bottom of the page made him draw in a quick breath: "Local Man Found Murdered." Closing his eyes, he took several deep breaths and sat again on the bed.

Last week, Tanzanian authorities announced the recent murder of 17-year-old Michael Othman who had gone to watch a soccer match with his brothers in Arusha and disappeared sometime just after the match. The human rights organization Amnesty International quoted the Tanzanian police's description of the gruesome murder of Mr. Othman: "About four men trafficked him to

Mozambique and killed him. The men chopped off both his arms and legs and removed his bones. Then they buried the rest of his body in a shallow grave."

If there was more, Boniface couldn't bring himself to read it. He knelt next to the cot and put his hands together the way he had seen the Sisters do in the chapel. He didn't know any of the prayers he sometimes heard them reciting softly as they ran strings of beads through their fingers. But kneeling seemed the right thing to do somehow.

36

New York City, 2013

Alex and Ngosi were seated for lunch at a small square table at Ahimsa, a popular Indian restaurant a few city blocks from CAPE headquarters. Alex had returned to New York near the end of June, and now July had arrived bringing high temperatures and humidity to the city.

"This looks like a great place for lunch," said Alex. I love the pictures and the statues of Buddha and Ganesha."

"Who is Ganesha?"

"See that huge wooden statue over there--the one with the elephant head and a round belly and four arms? Ganesha is extremely popular and perhaps the most worshipped of deities among Hindus, but some Buddhists also like him."

"Kind of a funny looking guy. An elephant head?"

"Oh, there are all kinds of stories about Ganesha and how he got that head. You have to read them for yourself. My mother, who was brought up in India, keeps a small shrine to Ganesha in a corner of our kitchen. He is known as a Remover of Obstacles. Though he can also create obstacles when he thinks it necessary."

"And does your mother pray to Ganesha?"

"I can't really answer that," Alex said, her eyebrows coming together in a thoughtful frown. Mom's shrine, which includes pictures of her deceased parents, some flowers, a little bell, sometimes some fruit--was always there in the kitchen. When I was growing up in southern

California, I thought everyone had such a shrine. She made us all chai tea in the morning, and I like to think that was her time to think about things beyond everyday reality. You know, a more spiritual plane of existence. It wasn't something we talked about."

A young woman with multiple piercings and a warm smile arrived to take their order. Ngosi urged Alex to order for both. "You're the expert on Indian food. We can share a few things to enjoy more tastes."

While Alex ordered, Ngosi stared at the Ganesha statue, a slight frown appearing on her forehead. "I'm still thinking about that odd looking elephant Ganesha--do you think he could help remove the obstacles to getting pregnant?"

Alex laughed. "Sure! Try rubbing his belly. That should do it. How is that project going by the way? Last I heard you had harvested eggs."

"Yeah--that was successful, and then we had to, you know, get the eggs and the little swimmers together. We're waiting to hear about embryos."

"I have a good feeling about this, Ngosi. A little more patience--it will work."

"My parents both attended Catholic schools in Nigeria--which was a good thing, of course. It was the beginning of their education. But the Catholic beliefs-- dare I say dogma--sit quite deep with them. I'm sure my mother is lighting candles at St. Theresa's in Brooklyn and praying for me to get pregnant in the natural way. And really--I can't fault her for that."

"I get it," said Alex as the waitress arrived to set several platters of food before them. "We all fall back on those early beliefs. When I fly in an airplane, I feel compelled to pray that I will arrive safely even though in my rational mind, I don't necessarily believe in the intervention of God or any deity in my everyday life."

"You've just reminded me of a piece of research I've done on albinism in Africa. It was actual footage on YouTube of a witch doctor doing an exorcism on a young woman who was having difficulty getting pregnant. She was in his hut--a nasty looking mess, and she sat on the ground with a blanket on top of her. He lifted the blanket a bit and made her smell the smoke of some burning herbs and then drink some potion. Sometimes he even slapped her in the head! Eventually, she lay down and moaned and writhed around on the floor. When the exorcism was finished, she claimed that the demon possessing her had come out. It was scary. I actually felt like vomiting."

"I suppose it is what the people there--especially outside the cities where education is sparse--must put their trust in," said Alex They don't have the knowledge or the money to seek help from modern medicine."

"They can't inject hormones and harvest eggs to get pregnant as I can," said Ngosi.

"I've been reading all the articles you've sent me on violence against people with albinism, and I think we can write a strong proposal to convince the higher ups. And Seth--my partner in Syria--is willing to review our proposal to make sure that security concerns are met. Actually, I'm hoping that he will want to be a part of the team that would go to Africa to collect information."

"Alex, I've wanted to ask you about Seth, but I didn't want to pry. You got along well with him?"

Alex tore off a piece of garlic naan and looked toward the huge Buddha portrait on the wall nearby before answering. Her slight smile matched his. "Yes, we got along well--better than well. I think about him. A lot. Right now, he is in Israel visiting with his family. But we are in close touch."

"I see." Ngosi smiled. "Do you know you are glowing pink through that super white skin of yours?"

"It all feels a bit surreal, Ngosi. I've never felt like this before, and I'm still kind of walking a few feet above the ground. I will talk more about it another time, okay?"

"Of course. "I'm just so happy to have you back safely, Alex. I lost sleep during your time in Syria--worrying about you."

"I appreciate your concern, my sweet friend, but It was so worth being on-the-ground. The suffering of everyday people there is just incredibly terrifying. I hope our reports will have some influence in Washington D.C."

"I heard a rumor that Elizabeth was contacted by President Obama--but I can't swear to the truth of that. Are you--I don't know if 'glad' is the right word--glad that you went?"

"Oh, yes. For several reasons. First, I want to thank you, Ngosi, for engineering all our communications and keeping us apprised of new developments in Syria--and for helping to get us out safely. I know you were instrumental in editing our reports and getting them into the right hands. I really can't thank you enough. You were my right hand all the way."

"You made me feel like I was there with you--though I have to say that I was happy not to be. I admire your ability to be so calm in a situation like that. How do you do it? I think you must have a special gene or some other secret for holding it together in dangerous circumstances. I wish I had that."

"I don't know about any of that, but I know that I loved being there and doing that work. I've always enjoyed running and have recognized the 'high' that running can make me feel--adrenaline, endorphins, whatever. This work--in the field--is something like that only much stronger and more meaningful."

Ngosi looked at Alex, put her fork down with a clatter, and put her hands up in a tent to her chin, like a child praying. "Oh no, Alex! I'm just realizing--please tell me that our African proposal would not include sending you to that continent. People with albinism are in great danger especially in countries such as Malawi and Tanzania. The United Nations has recently put out an alarm--perhaps I sent you that article? You would be walking into a lion's den."

"Don't worry, Ngosi. It is *because* I am albino--and of African descent--that I want to be on this team. We will pay close attention to security. CAPE makes sure of that. And we will read all the research to understand what is happening as much as possible beforehand. With your help, we will not walk in as ignorant outsiders. I am really interested in getting at the root causes--the deeply held beliefs of the African people. In addition to being aware of the greed of some people who take advantage of those beliefs."

Ngosi looked at her watch. "Oh, we better get back to headquarters. We've hardly paid attention to this delicious food. I'll ask the waitress to bring us a few boxes--and we can enjoy the leftovers for dinner. Come over to our apartment and have dinner with me and Max. We can talk more about what to do next.

On the way out, Alex paused at the large Buddha statue. "Do you know the meaning of this restaurant's name--Ahimsa?"

Ngosi shook her head.

"In Sanskrit, it means something like 'non-violence,' embraced by Mahatma Gandhi and others. It is about not causing injury through deeds, words, and thoughts." She sighed deeply. "That would be my vision of a better world, but oh, we have such a long road ahead."

37

New York City 2013

It was late on a rainy Friday afternoon in September, and Alex was still at CAPE headquarters. She paced back and forth in her office, her thoughts jumping among the past, present, and future. She couldn't help smiling to herself. She had just come from a meeting with Director Elizabeth Hampton and CAPE's executive committee. They had approved--not without controversy--the proposal regarding an investigation into the widespread violence against people with albinism in several African countries.

The main concern of the committee had been security for the investigating team: Alex Carter and Seth Melaku. But the team's excellent work in war-torn Syria and Seth's military background had finally been enough to convince committee members that the risks were worth what they might learn from victims and their families in Africa. She could hardly wait to tell Ngosi, who had already left the office for a doctor's appointment, and Seth, who was just returning to England from visiting his family in Israel.

She glanced at her watch, reminding herself that she was expecting a call at 5:00--in ten minutes--from Dr. Espinoza. She had googled him after talking briefly to her mother about the visit they had made to see him when Alex was not yet five years old. She had skimmed through the website of the Center for the Neurobiology of Learning and Memory at the Irvine campus. Their research looked interesting. The more she read, the more intrigued she became, so she emailed Dr. Espinoza, requesting that he call her when convenient. He responded immediately by email. He clearly remembered her coming to his office with her mother, and he would be happy to talk with her.

As she looked out on the New York skyline, an image of the nearly blind Charlotte Canfield appeared unaccountably in her mind. She had avoided thinking about her visit to Beaconsfield though she could recall it in detail. She didn't want to think about the things that had triggered the visions there--the piano music, the eucalyptus smell, even something about Charlotte's face had the power to take over her conscious mind.

During all these years, she had feared what such visions might mean about her sanity. What would anyone say if they knew about them? That they were simply products of her imagination? Or hallucinations? Or perhaps that she was crazy? Even as a four-year-old, she had understood that there was something wrong, perhaps even shameful, about them. Back then, she didn't have the words to describe what she experienced. Even her mother had thought her little daughter was describing dreams she had in the night. As a child, Alex had vowed to tell no one. Seth was the only person she had talked about her visit to Charlotte. But she hadn't yet told him about the visions.

Suddenly, the office lit up in a flash of lightning. Alex flinched as a thunderclap seemed to shake the building. The rain was coming down harder, and the wind had picked up and was blowing sheets of water against the windows. The storm must be right overhead.

Her cell phone vibrated on the desk. She glanced at it. Marcus Espinoza.

"Hello. This is Alex Carter." She could picture the man as he looked when she was still in preschool. She had been fascinated by how his mouth moved within the hair of the beard and mustache. And he had reminded her of one of the light people. She could remember telling him why she called them the light people, but he hadn't really understood.

"Hello, Alex. Marcus Espinoza here. "I was both surprised and delighted to hear from you."

"Thank you so much, Dr. Espinoza. You must be wondering what prompted me to get in touch after more than twenty years--"

Dr. Espinoza laughed. "It was indeed a bit of a surprise, but quite coincidentally, I recently came across the notes I took back then of your visit to see me. Before our visit, your mother had described to me your detailed dreams of strange people and places. We had hoped you would tell us more. Your mother worried that the dreams were memories, though that seemed impossible at the time. I have always regretted that we were not able to follow up on that initial visit."

"I can't say I've regretted it. I'm sorry, but as a child, I didn't feel comfortable talking to you. Or to anyone about those dreams--and by the way, they were never 'dreams.' I have come to call them visions over the years, and they can occur at any waking moment."

"I see. And now you are hoping to understand more about these visions?"

"I'm working in New York City now--I'm an attorney--but when I visited my parents in California recently, I reminded my mom of our visit so long ago, and she mentioned your current research regarding memory. So I googled you--and your Center."

"Can I ask why you're interested, Alex? Is this a professional or a personal interest?"

Alex hesitated, remembering how she had refused to confide in this doctor as a four-year-old. It's . . . personal. I mean, I've always wondered--worried--about the visions. And I'm wondering if they could actually be memories of some kind."

"I understand. Perhaps it would be helpful if I tell you a little about the research we are doing on memory."

"Yes, I'd like to hear that."

"None of this research existed when you were a child. During the last six or seven years, we've been investigating a rare phenomenon that we have called Highly Superior Autobiographical Memory or HSAM. As of now, we only know of ten cases of HSAM in the world. But we expect to learn more as time goes on. Each case has its own peculiar characteristics, but basically, it's a condition that leads people to have the ability to remember an unusually large number of their life experiences in vivid detail." He paused.

"Go on," said Alex, her curiosity piqued.

She watched the rain dripping down the window, the droplets joining other droplets and making tiny rivers that ran down to the bottom of the window. The thunder and lightning had moved on, she could still see the lightning at a distance.

"The people we have studied describe their memories as uncontrollable associations. They 'see' a vivid description of something that happened to them on a given day--without any hesitation or conscious effort. You can learn more simply by googling HSAM or even looking it up on Wikipedia."

"Wait. Wait." Alex had been holding her breath as she listened. "My visions, as far as I can tell, seem to be associated with my infancy. Could they possibly be memories?"

"Interesting. Let me ask you a question or two, Alex. In my notes, I wrote that you had memories of an elephant--but you didn't want to tell me more about it. Can you perhaps tell me about that now?"

Alex bit her lower lip. She had kept this secret for so long, and she had no particular reason to trust this doctor. But what if he could help her understand? "Yes, I will tell you what I can. The elephant is small, not large as I told you then. Actually, it is something quite small--a plush toy. Long ago I named it Sam--I don't know why. Sam became a sort of imaginary companion to me--a source of comfort. But when I was in England a couple of months ago, I visited a woman, a widow now, from whom my parents adopted me when I was barely a year old. It's a long story, but she had kept the small, plush elephant along with a photo of my biological parents." Alex took a long breath in. Her heart was racing.

Dr. Espinoza hesitated. "As far as I know, we have not yet found someone with memories that go back so far. Before a child has language. But what you are describing is definitely in line with what I might expect if you are one of these rare patients with HSAM. I'll be happy to send you some articles and other references. But let me say that if you find that any of what I've described fits your situation, you might want to be tested."

"There is a test?"

"There are several tests--verbal tests, including tests of memory as well as physical tests such as an MRI to take a look at certain structures in the brain."

"Can we perhaps talk again when I've had a chance to read more of your research? I'm about to go on a work trip to Africa, so I wouldn't be interested in any testing until later."

"Of course, Alex. HSAM is rare, and your ability to recall images from before the age of a year would be even more rare. Still, I hope you will seriously consider the idea that your visions are likely actual memories, not figments of your imagination, not hallucinations."

"I will, Dr. Espinoza. Thank you for responding to my request. I look forward to reading more about your research."

When she hung up, Alex sat at her desk for a long time watching the streams of raindrops find their inevitable way down the pane of glass. *Actual memories, not figments of your imagination, not hallucinations.* She whispered his words. Perhaps there was no reason to fear the visions after all. They were still somewhat mysterious, but she would now have a different perspective as she tried to figure out what they meant.

PART THREE

38

Kilimanjaro International Airport, Tanzania, 2013

Alex stood waiting in the baggage area of the Kilimanjaro International Airport. This place looked nothing like the airports in the States. It felt like a huge warehouse space with a concrete floor and a few small windows near the ceiling. She noted that although most of the men were dressed in western-style clothing, many of the women wore long skirts and head coverings. Hoping to blend in, she had changed into an ankle-length skirt and a long-sleeved blouse at the Amsterdam Schiphol Airport hours earlier.

It was mid-morning, but her body had yet to register the journey across time zones. She was vaguely aware that she had lost eight hours somewhere, and that she had traveled forward in time to find herself in these unfamiliar surroundings. After too many sleepless hours on two flights, the first from New York to Amsterdam and then another to Tanzania, she didn't want to even contemplate what time zone her body inhabited.

She tried her phone again, hoping for a connection while keeping an eye on the line of luggage in front of her. Just as she spotted her bag, her phone dinged, and several messages started coming through. Her mom had written to tell her again to be careful traveling. And there was a message from Seth:

Flight delayed. ETA 8:00 pm (Tanzania time). Let's meet at the hotel. Can't wait to see you.

She smiled as she texted back:

Looking forward to a new adventure together. I hope we can make a difference here.

When she picked up her bag, which she had tied with a yellow ribbon, she noticed that people were openly staring at her. She was used to such curiosity, but her appearance here seemed to demand more than usual attention. Her height and her white skin drew more outright stares than she was accustomed to. *They know I don't belong here.* Two men who were also waiting for baggage were laughing as they looked toward her. She caught bits of what they were saying in Swahili--"what a deal" and "here comes money." She thought of Ngosi then, of the warnings she had repeatedly made. Okay, the first order of business, she told herself, was to hire a taxi to go to her hotel where she could stretch out on a bed and go to sleep.

Just outside the exit gate, she pulled a gray silk scarf from her bag and wrapped it over her white-blonde hair. When she exited through the glass doors of the airport, she saw a few men standing with signs to identify passengers who had pre-arranged transportation. As soon as she took a few steps out the door, many other men accosted her to offer their taxi services.

"Madam, vous voulez un taxi?"

"Taxi, Lady? Cheapest to Arusha!"

Then she heard, "Money! Money! Here comes money!" spoken in Swahili.

She had read about this expression. It meant that she--or rather her albino body--was worth a lot of money to someone. Nevertheless, she was shocked to hear it spoken so brazenly in a public place. She felt vulnerable in these surroundings, which contained no English signs, and no obvious way to hire a taxi. Surrounded by several men at once, she nodded at a young man who was dressed neatly in a white polo shirt. She asked him how much to the Four Points Sheraton Hotel in Arusha. The other men began to call out to her again, offering cheaper rates, but she allowed this driver to take her suitcase and clear a way for her through the pressing crowd of men.

Desperate for sleep, Alex was hoping to rest on the hour drive to the city. Her driver handed her a bottle of water and held the door for her to climb into the back seat after placing her suitcase in the trunk. The car smelled of cigarette smoke and the pine tree deodorizer that hung from the rearview mirror. It was not the cleanest taxi she had ever ridden in, but she felt grateful to be out of the airplane and the crowd at the airport entrance. She put her head back against the seat with a deep sigh.

"You are English?" the driver asked as they pulled out of the airport.

"American," Alex said, reluctantly lifting her head from the seat back. "From New York," she added to be polite.

"You come on vacation or work here?"

Although the driver was speaking in English, she decided to switch to Swahili. "A little of both. My husband is coming in on a later plane." They had decided on this deception in conversation with the CAPE security team.

"Perhaps you will want a guide to our country?" he said turning his eyes from the road to look at her and smile. "I am Rabee, a very fine guide."

"Perhaps."

He was silent for a few minutes. The breeze from the car windows helped lessen the oppressive heat. Alex could feel her eyes closing.

"Your husband. He is like you?"

Alex saw him look at her in the rear-view mirror. She felt her heart speed up. She had faced such questions before from those who wanted to define her by her appearance.

When she didn't answer right away, Rabee said, "Maybe you want protection here, to stay safe in Tanzania."

"What do you mean?" She closed her hands in tight fists. *I'm being paranoid. He's offering to help. Why does it sound like a threat?*

"A lady like you alone here. It might be safer for you to have a security person. How do you say in English--a bodyguard."

"I told you, my husband will be coming in a little while." Alex felt the blood rising to her cheeks, as if a small fire of fear had been lighted somewhere inside her.

"Uh-huh," he answered.

Alex put her head back against the seat again. "It's been a long plane ride. I need to rest a little." She was on high alert now and too agitated to doze.

Almost an hour later, Rabee pulled up in front of the hotel. As he retrieved her suitcase from the trunk, Alex got out of the car and reached into her bag for the envelope of Tanzanian shillings that she had thought to get at a currency exchange kiosk in the airport.

She wheeled her suitcase to a comfortable-looking couch in the airconditioned lobby of the Sheraton where she sat down and pulled out her phone. The directions for connecting to the internet were printed on a small card on a nearby table. She spent a few minutes on the phone and then walked to the reception desk.

A short time later, she stood outside with her suitcase waiting for a taxi. She texted Seth:

Change of plans. Moving to a different hotel. Follow this link: https://kibopalacehotel.com/ Will explain later.

39

Arusha, Tanzania, 2013

Alex and Seth were among the first guests for breakfast in the Kibo Palace Hotel dining room. Early morning sunlight streamed through windows that looked out into a small courtyard garden. When a waiter arrived to take their order, Alex smiled and greeted him in Swahili.

"Good morning, Mister--Mister Juma," she said reading his name badge. "I'm new to Africa and I want to learn everything I can while I'm here. Can you tell me about this beautiful tree in the garden? What kind is it?"

"Good morning, madam and sir," the waiter said in English with a wide smile and a nod to each of them. He was a slim man of fifty-something, his hair mostly gray, his shoulders slightly stooped. But his voice was confident, a man who was experienced in serving his customers.

"You speak English," said Alex.

"I have learned a little from hotel guests over many years," he said. "That is an acacia tree. This kind with the greenish bark is also called a fever tree. If you are going on a safari in the Serengeti, you will see many more such trees. Can I bring you coffee or tea before I take your order?"

When he left, Alex whispered to contain her excitement. "I'm still pinching myself that we are actually here, Seth. Have you thought about the fact that we are on the continent where, more than likely, both of us were born? Is it a coincidence? Destiny? Karma? Or just the randomness of the universe?"

"You ask difficult questions, Lexy," he said with a grin. Some people would claim that our every choice is predetermined by genetics. Some would name a deity as the supreme controller of every action. Me, I'm still floating on air just to be with you again." He smiled and reached his hand out to take hers. "I love watching you and listening to you. Your curiosity and your determination are infectious."

"I know I've said this a lot already, but--I missed you! I am so--well, so filled with joy to be here with you, Seth." They stared into each other's eyes for a few moments.

"Okay. Let us begin to talk about business," said Seth. "In looking at our schedule, I see that tomorrow we will attend a community awareness presentation by Under the Same Sun. I was able to locate the village on a map, it's several miles north of here. We'll ask our waiter about the possibility of hiring a driver or renting a car."

The waiter arrived at that moment with a pot of coffee, creamers, and sugar. He took their order, and after a brief exchange, he said yes, that he would be able to recommend a driver who was an excellent safari guide.

"We are grateful for your recommendation," said Seth, "but actually, we're not planning to see your country's wildlife on this trip." He frowned slightly as he explained. "We are hoping to talk to people who can tell us more about the people with albinism here in Tanzania. We are working for an organization that investigates the violation of human rights anywhere in the world. And we will need a driver who can take us to many places."

The waiter's eyes grew large. "I understand." He looked directly at Alex. "I couldn't help but notice, madam, that you are an albino person," he said lowering his voice. "Excuse me if I am being too bold, but I must warn you that it's very dangerous for you to be here in this country. Terrible things sometimes happen here to-- people like you." He glanced around the restaurant, where only a few other guests were having breakfast. "Tanzania is a friendly country. But there are some greedy and dangerous people who you must avoid."

"Thank you for your concern and for telling us that, Mr. Juma," said Seth. "We'll be careful."

"He seems genuinely concerned," said Lexy when the waiter left. "Perhaps a bit dramatic though?"

"I think we can't underestimate the effect of your appearance here, Lexy. We are foreigners in this land, and we will have to carefully choose who we trust. Right now, I trust this man--a gut-level feeling. But in any case, I don't want you to worry. I will keep you close."

The waiter returned with a tray of eggs, toast, and pancakes and placed the food carefully in front of them.

"I will leave a note under your door with the name and number of a driver, not for going on safari but for driving anywhere you want to go. I know this man well, and he is a friend. He will also watch out for your safety." In a louder voice, he asked, "Is there anything else I can get for you?"

"Thank you, Mr. Juma," said Seth. "We are grateful to you and hope to talk with you again."

The waiter looked from Alex to Seth. "Please. Please be very careful."

40

Seth stood looking at a large, colorful world map encircled by dozens of small portraits of people with albinism from a variety of countries and ethnicities-- from China to South America, from the United States to Europe. On the table in front of the display were brochures in English and Swahili. Seth picked one up as he glanced around at the crowd of perhaps two hundred or more villagers who were chatting and laughing as they waited for the presentation to begin.

> Should both parents have the gene, there is a one in four chance of their child being born with albinism.

> But it doesn't just affect the colour of their skin, hair, and eyes: it can also affect their eyesight. Many people with albinism are considered legally blind in Europe and America.

He looked up from time to time scanning the crowd of villagers who were sitting on low walls and leaning against the white-washed buildings. Experience had taught him that violence could erupt without warning in any crowd. In his research into conditions in Tanzania, he had realized that they were not going to have the kind of security backup they could rely on in other countries. CAPE hadn't yet developed a reliable network in Tanzania or Malawi, though there were certainly organizations and people in sympathy with their concerns. Cell phone service could be spotty as well. He understood then that they would have to rely mainly on themselves for security.

He observed that many of the villagers were curious about Alex, this tall, strikingly beautiful woman who had features like them but who had white skin and hair. He watched her animated expression as she stood talking with Victoria Akaro, the host of the Under the Same Sun presentation. What, he wondered, was Alex feeling with all these people staring and pointing at her? Surely, she wasn't as oblivious and relaxed as she appeared.

A few minutes later, their host gave Alex a hug and walked to a microphone that had been set up in a dusty courtyard among the buildings and huts. Alex joined Seth who had found a bit of shade under an acacia tree. The villagers quickly hushed as Victoria welcomed them and told them about the work of Under the Same Sun. She said that she hoped everyone had had a chance to look at the posters and brochures that would help them understand that people with albinism were people just like them.

"That is what the scientists and medical doctors tell us about albinism," she said. "They also tell us that there are individuals with this condition among many animal species and even in some plants. But I want to talk to you about us humans. Under the Same Sun believes that every human being has a basic right to live freely and without fear. I am here today to urge you to see people with albinism the same way you see any other people."

The crowd was quiet. Seth shifted his eyes around at the crowd of men and women and children who were listening to Victoria Akaro.

"First, because I know you've all been wondering, I want to introduce two guests who have traveled all the way from America and England to visit Tanzania, Alex Carter and Seth Melaku. She extended her arm toward the two foreigners encouraging them to wave so everyone could see them. "Alex and Seth are here to study the attitudes toward people with albinism and the ways they are treated here in our country. They work for an organization called Compassion for All the People on Earth, or CAPE. Thank you for coming here today, Alex and Seth." Polite clapping and much murmuring in the crowd.

"And now, I want all of you to listen carefully to a very special speaker, who will tell you her story of what it has been like living with albinism. Magdalena's story is difficult to hear, but it is important to learn of this woman's suffering and of her bravery. Please give Magdalena your attention now."

Victoria began clapping, and the audience followed as a young woman of about twenty, walked to the microphone. Her left arm was a stump, which she didn't try to hide. She wore a flower-print dress, and her plump cheeks were marked with brown, crusted sores. Her eyes were an almost transparently blue, fringed with white eyelashes. Her hair was closely cropped in what looked like a pale-yellow cap covering her white scalp.

Her voice was soft, shy, hesitant. "My name is Magdalena. I used to live in a village just a little way north of here. I want to tell you my story because too many people don't understand what it is to be albino. Our skin is white and most of us can't see too well, unless we have glasses." She paused and looked around at the crowd. Seth thought she looked terrified, but she continued.

"We are not ghosts, we are not evil beings, we are not stupid. We want the same things that you want--to enjoy our families and friends, to love, to work, to be useful. I was never allowed to go to school as my father thought it would be too dangerous. Instead, I made breakfast for my sisters and brothers, and it was my job to care for their uniforms."

She raised the stump of her arm and held it in the air. The crowd was silent. "This is what happened to me one night when I was fifteen years old." She let them stare and then added, "And I was one of the lucky ones."

Her voice grew hoarse as she spoke into the microphone. "Five men entered the bedroom where I was sleeping. They began to hack off my arm with a machete, and I woke up screaming. The pain was . . . indescribable. When I saw my arm lying there all bloody on my blanket, I wanted to keep it, and I said to them--let me keep this arm! And I screamed again. I think they became afraid because they wrapped my arm in one of their jackets and ran out of the shed that was my bedroom."

Magdalena wiped tears from her face and looked toward Victoria, who quickly moved beside her and put an arm around her shoulders.

"Magdalena has been through a great deal of pain since then, but as you can see, she has healed well. Our organization, Under the Same Sun, gave her a safe place to live with other people with albinism who also need help. She will soon be fitted with a prosthetic arm, but meanwhile, she has learned tailoring at one of our education centers, and she can knit with one hand! She also goes to school, which she was never able to do before."

Seth watched Alex's face as they listened to Magdalena and Victoria. It was one thing to read about the maiming and killing, but quite another thing, he thought, to hear about it first-hand. Her forehead was furrowed as she listened. He knew she was feeling the young woman's pain.

As Victoria stood in front of the microphone to thank Magdalena for telling her story, Seth looked out at the villagers, who had been listening attentively. Were they convinced that a person with albinism was just like them and should be respected like any person?

As he scanned the crowd, he saw two men who stood behind the others and had the look of outsiders. One was a heavy man who wore dark pants and a white dress shirt with the sleeves rolled up. The other, bald and muscular, wore a tee-shirt and a black leather jacket. Were they government officials who were interested in the presentation? Or officials from a nearby town or village? It would make sense that they would want to know what was being taught, as the government had recently sworn to discourage discrimination and violence against albinos. Or could the presence of these two men be more ominous? He would be vigilant, and he would keep Alex close to him.

When the presentation was over, Seth waited, keeping an eye on Alex, who stood with her arm around Magdalena as they talked to Victoria and others who came to greet them. He was surprised when his cell phone buzzed in his pocket. Cell reception had so far proven unreliable at best. He looked at the text message:

Mr Melaku, what is it you think you are doing? Watch your back. You don't know Africa.

He looked to where the two men had been standing. They were gone.

He made a mental note to make a visit to the local police station to find out more about Tanzania's emergency systems. He would also try to spend some time with the police chief to learn about how the police protect people with albinism.

41

Goodluck Kombe, the driver who had been recommended by the hotel waiter, quickly became a trusted guide. He arrived in a tan Toyota Land Cruiser with "Overseas Adventure Travel" painted on the door. He not only drove Alex and Seth to their various appointments, but he suggested other contacts and also made sure they were well fed. Goodluck was a solid, good-looking man in his late thirties, married, with three small children. He had trained and worked as a safari guide in the national park for two or three private tour companies, but he was also sometimes available as a personal tour guide. He owned the Land Cruiser and kept it in good condition.

During their first few days, Alex and Seth were able to interview several maimed victims of violence along with their families. Like Magdalena, the victims had faced horrendous terror as well as physical suffering. Although they had always faced discrimination, even within their own communities and families, once they were victimized, they often became, even more than before, outcasts in their villages. Some were very young children whose parents were too frightened to ever let them go to school or even play outside with other children.

Goodluck helped Seth arrange an interview with a police officer in an Arusha precinct. The officer, he explained, spoke pretty good English, and he had been involved in a case where thieves had dug up the graves of two people with albinism and stolen their limbs. Unfortunately, the case did not result in prosecution, a not uncommon outcome.

Ngosi had been able to contact a United Nations representative, Maria Omari, who was working to bring awareness of the problem of violence against people with albinism to a larger audience. Ms Omari was happy to meet with them to talk about the situation not only in Tanzania but other African countries as well. She talked about what was being done in the United Nations in an attempt to resolve the situation. And she was able to help them arrange a discussion with several local politicians. Though people were polite and answered any questions Alex and Seth asked, Alex often sensed a reluctance, and perhaps some defensiveness, when it came to talking about the role of witch doctors and the beliefs of the population. They had pointed out that the government now had a licensing procedure which required that the witch doctors--there were more than 75,000 in Tanzania--be registered with the government.

"Perhaps," Seth said to Alex after one session with members of a town council, "we should be going more to the source--talk to a witch doctor. These people seem afraid to talk about who goes to the witch doctors--for their magic--for wealth and luck. Perhaps Goodluck will help us arrange a meeting with a local witch doctor."

But when they approached Goodluck and asked if he could help them find such a person, he discouraged the idea. Smiling politely, he told them that it would be far too dangerous to introduce Alex to a witch doctor, even one who claimed not to ever use body parts of albino people. They were not to be trusted, he told them, and any witch doctor would be hostile to questions from outsiders. He didn't know any witch doctors anyway, he told them solemnly. He and his family were Christians. They had nothing to do with the black magic of the witch doctors.

* * *

One very early morning, as Seth and Alex were seated for breakfast at the hotel, their waiter greeted them warmly. "You have been very busy during your stay here, I think," he said as he poured coffee for Seth. "I will bring you a pot of tea, madam. And what will you both have to eat this morning?"

"Mr. Juma, good morning to you. Yes, we've been busy--but I've wanted to tell you thank you for recommending Goodluck Kombe to us," said Seth. "He has been most valuable."

"I'm happy to hear that, sir. You are learning a lot about the threat to people with albinism in my country?" he asked in a soft voice.

"Yes, Mr. Juma. We have learned a lot," said Seth. "You have been a great help to us. By the way, I'm Seth and this is Alex. Please call us by our names."

The waiter nodded his head and smiled in acknowledgement. "And please call me Samuel." He took their order, but then he seemed to hesitate at the table. "I didn't have a chance to tell you earlier." Again, he hesitated. Finally, with a quick glance around at the still mostly empty dining room, he said, "I have two grandchildren who are also albino people. They are in danger every day."

Alex glanced at Seth, her eyebrows raised. "Oh, Mr. Juma--Samuel. Thank you for telling us that. We'd like to know more about your grandchildren if you're willing to share with us."

"Thank you. Of course, I am pleased to tell you about my grandchildren," he said. "I will put in your order and return to show you a picture of them."

The photograph showed two smiling children, a girl about eight and a boy about ten. Both had the same white-blond hair as Alex. Neither seemed to have the kinds of brown blemishes on their pale faces that Alex had seen in many internet photos. Albino skin, lacking melanin, was especially vulnerable to sunlight, and many people with albinism in Africa developed serious and life-threatening skin cancers. Because of that and various other causes, the average lifespan of someone born with albinism was less than forty years.

The waiter spoke softly as he poured more coffee. "They are Nico and Lilia. Their mother, my daughter, boards them at St. Celia's Orphanage and School during the week to keep them safe while she works. She is a nurse's aide at a clinic in Arusha. You may want to talk to Sister Angelica, who is in charge at St. Cecelia's, a very kind woman."

"We would very much like to visit at the school," said Alex. "And meet Lilia and Nico," she added.

"Goodluck is familiar with the orphanage. He can take you there--not far. I will give you Sister Angelica's number."

"Well, that's a surprise," said Alex when the waiter left to put in their order. She sighed. "I hope that is a sign that we are to be trusted. I feel an undercurrent of something--suspicion? fear? distrust?--wherever we go in this country."

"What are you thinking, Seth?" she asked. He had a faraway look on his face.

"Hmmm--just thinking back to my childhood. I was, of course, surrounded by black people like me. I never knew of a person with albinism, but I can't help but wonder now if such a person was born--were they killed as they sometimes are here in Tanzania?"

"A dark thought. What is it about us humans that makes us distrustful of those who don't look like us? It's enough--almost--to wish everyone was blind. That distrust has caused so much death and destruction in our world."

Seth put his hand over hers. "Shh, my sweet Lexy. We are doing what we can. That is all we can do for now. Let us see what this day brings."

42

New York and Arusha, 2013

TO: AlexCarter@cape.org
FROM: NgosiObiakaHarrison@cape.org

Thank you for your initial report. We have all read it with great interest. I can only imagine what it must be like to be albino in a place where many would consider you not-human. I know you don't like me to voice my worries, but I feel compelled to warn you once again. I have just read an article from a BBC undercover reporter from several years ago--2008, I believe. She visited ten witch doctors asking for help for some imaginary problem. Several offered a solution that involved obtaining albino body parts, and they even offered a way to obtain them. But an undercover policeman discovered her scheme, and she received death threats. So, even the police are not to be trusted.

On a more optimistic note, I doubt that the news has reached you that the United Nations has just released a preliminary report on albinism. There is talk that an independent expert may be established to look into the situation further. And there has been a resolution to have a more in-depth report written on discrimination and violence committed against albinos in Africa. The information that you and Seth uncover will be an invaluable contribution to this work.

Please forgive me for my lack of courage, Alex. I do not mean to discourage you in the least. I just want you to be safe.

TO: NgosiObiakaHarrison@cape.org
FROM: AlexCarter@cape.org

Ngosi:

There is no need to ask for forgiveness, my friend. You are quite right that this country is dangerous for people with albinism. As you will read in my report, I've learned from a local social worker whom I talked to that one of the major causes of this discrimination is the deep-rooted beliefs of the people. According to a recent poll, 93% of the population of Tanzania believe in "witchcraft." That is, they will go to traditional healers--many of whom also claim to practice witchcraft (3,000 are currently registered with the government to practice) as their ancestors have over many centuries.

The amazing and dedicated founder and CEO of Under the Same Sun, Peter Ash, who is a businessman and a person with albinism from Canada, has written that he "can't understand the evil that motivates someone to do something like this." Personally, I don't believe in evil as an independent entity. Rather, our human minds are vulnerable and can be swayed in ways that are indeed destructive to ourselves and others. History has surely shown us that we are all capable of "evil."

As I talk to all these people, I am more than ever aware of myself as a person with albinism--a fact that in my past used to make some people curious and that caused me to wear glasses and protect my skin from the sun. It is so much more in this culture.

Seth and I have talked to many people by now--many people with albinism but also to families who have lost their albino loved ones. We traveled to a village in northern Tanzania where a twenty-eight-year-old woman with a four-year-old is trying to live without her arms (and rather ill-fitting prosthetic arms). Her mother, who has other children to care for, is currently helping her daughter, feeding, dressing, and bathing her--and helping her take care of her child. The young woman was attacked during the night when she was pregnant. She lost that baby. She has two teenage albino sisters (the parents are black) who are now hiding out with their grandmother and spend their days in the forest.

Among the most horrific of stories is the one of an albino woman with an albino baby. One evening, she had applied ointment to the baby's head (skin conditions are common) and went outside her hut to wash her hands. Two men with machetes accosted her and tried to take the baby's limbs. Fortunately, the woman's screams brought the neighbors who were able to scare them off. She showed us the long scar resulting from the machete wound on the child's leg.

What is the answer to ending these horrors? We are still studying that problem. Thank you for sending me the UN resolution. While I'm delighted to see this growing recognition, I am too impatient for effective action. All these people are in danger on a daily basis--now--while someone or some group studies the situation . . . How can we educate an entire population, not only in Tanzania but many African countries, about the genetic basis of albinism? One of the most hopeful efforts as far as I've seen is from Under the Same Sun. This NGO has established workshops and albinism awareness sessions during the last two years. They are educating the professional class--social workers, teachers, and medical staff--but they have also been going into villages to educate people more about what it is to have albinism. I support this, of course, but again, I'm so impatient. There are so many people to reach, and education is sorely lacking here.

It's late, but as you can tell, I'm in an excited state about this situation. To me, it calls out for some immediate remedy, but my rational mind tells me I must be patient.
Must get some sleep. Please let me know your news if there is any. I'm thinking about you and Max often with great hopes for your success.

Alex

TO: AlexCarter@cape.org
FROM: NgosiObiakaHarrison@cape.org

You are the first to hear this--we are pregnant! It is a bit too early to tell anyone--not even our families yet, but we agreed that this news would be a bright spot for you among the difficult issues you and Seth are dealing with. I know you will rejoice with us! Please stay safe.

Ngosi

43

St. Cecelia's School and Orphanage, 2013

A line of eucalyptus trees half-way up the hill shielded the complex of small, white-washed buildings that housed twenty or so children, three Catholic Sisters, and a caretaker at St. Cecelia's Orphanage and School. When Alex had spoken to Sister Angelica, the director, on the phone explaining a bit about CAPE and their investigation into the treatment of people with albinism in Tanzania, she had warmly invited them to visit.

Sister Angelica, dressed in a plain, blue, ankle length habit, greeted them at the gate and introduced Boniface, the caretaker and a former student at St. Cecelia's.

"We don't get many visitors here, so the children are very excited to sing a welcoming song for you," the Sister explained as she led them to a one-room building that served as a classroom.

Inside, the room was lighted only by the sunlight coming through the open windows. The children were seated on benches in front of wooden desks. A blackboard at the front of the room read "WELCOME TO OUR SCHOOL." The students had chalked in their name around the welcome message. There was an excited buzz among them when Sister Angelica introduced Seth and Alex. She told them that they had come on an airplane all the way from England.

The teacher, Sister Bernice, a stout woman with cheeks that glowed pink, greeted them with a smile. "The children have been learning English," and they would like to sing you a song they have been learning." With that, she hummed a note, and they began:

It is better to light just one little candle
Than to stumble in the dark!
Better far that you light just one little candle
All you need's a tiny spark!

If we'd all say a prayer that the world would be free
The wonderful dawn of a new day we'll see!
And if everyone lit just one little candle
What a bright world this would be!

"That was very beautiful," said Alex, who had been genuinely touched listening to the children's voices. She glanced at Sister Bernice and then looked back at the children. "Thank you from the bottom of my heart."

Her attention had been immediately drawn to two of the children whose white skin stood out among the group, undoubtedly Mr. Juma's grandchildren. She guessed that Nico was about ten and Lilia a year or two younger.

Lilia and Nico. They look like me as a child! Except my mother allowed my hair to grow to a fluff of curls.

It was decided that Alex would stay and observe the class for the last lesson of the day. Seth would go with Boniface, the young caretaker, to take a tour of the grounds. The two of them would later join Sister Angelica in her office for a glass of iced tea.

Alex sat down in the back of the room to watch Sister Bernice teach a geography lesson. The sister assigned a map of Africa to color for the younger students and reviewed the current names of all the African countries with the older students.

Alex couldn't keep her eyes from Lilia and Nico. She studied their clothes, listened to them speak, and observed their facial expressions and their mannerisms. She felt great empathy and an unmistakable connection with them.

She understood as she watched that she was looking at what could have been her life if she had not been taken to England under mysterious circumstances. These children seemed protected here and happy enough, but she knew now after so many interviews with victims and their families, that there was always a possibility of danger. She had learned from Sister Angelica that their mother was single, that her husband had left her because he was suspicious of her giving birth to two very white babies.

When the lesson ended and Alex was thanking Sister Bernice, she felt a tug at her arm. It was Nico.

"How come you look like us?" he asked. His sister stood a few steps away, her head bent shyly toward the floor.

Alex laughed and put her hands out to both children. "Yes! the three of us do look alike with our white skin and our yellow hair, don't we!" She spoke in Swahili, and both children took a hand and moved closer to her.

"You are very pretty," said Lilia. "I want to have hair like yours."

"Well, you will when you let it grow--perhaps when you are a little older. But you are very pretty now, Lilia."

"You live in England?" asked Nico. Does it rain every day there?

"No! Not every day, though more than here in Africa I guess. My home is in the United States. Do you know where that is on the globe, Nico?"

He walked to the teacher's desk and proudly pointed to the United States. "Across the ocean. My mother says we may go there one day!"

"And perhaps you will. Listen, I am going to talk with Sister Angelica now, but I want to talk to you again another day. And I'd love to meet your mother."

"She comes for us on Friday," said Lilia.

"We go home with her for the weekend," said Nico. "She has a lot of work to do on the other days."

"Then I will come on a Friday if I can. And I will bring a few little gifts from the United States. Okay?"

The children smiled and then ran out to play with their friends. Alex promised herself that she would find time to see them again.

* * *

Seth walked the perimeter of St. Cecelia's School and Orphanage compound with Boniface as his guide. The younger man's English was halting, but Seth listened carefully and understood well enough to know that he was earnest about his work and determined to keep the Sisters and the children safe. Here and there, Seth shook a portion of the stick fence to test its strength, silently nodding his head to approve the repair work that Boniface had done.

"Soon," Boniface was explaining, "Sister Angelica will send for battery-powered lights that will go on when something moves in the yard at night."

"Excellent. Do animals ever enter the yard? Any dangerous animals?" Seth asked.

"Oh yes, it can happen. Two times I've seen an old hyena sniffing at our chickens. Then I discovered the place where he crawled under the fence. I was able to repair it."

"Good work, man. Sister Angelica told me you are good with the chickens and also with the vegetable garden. How did you learn these skills?"

"In my village, I helped my mother after my father died. I was just a boy."

"I'm so sorry. That must have been difficult for you."

They had circled to the front gate, where Boniface showed him several padlocks and his ring of keys.

"How long have you worked here at St. Cecelia's?"

"Almost two years. I am learning English from the Sisters." Boniface ducked his head to hide a smile. "I left school when I was ten. I worked as an apprentice for my grandfather to take care of my mother. I also sold some bracelets and other jewelry she made. Unfortunately, she died."

"I'm so sorry, Boniface. St. Cecelia's is fortunate to have you."

"It's all right. I am very sad, but now I am again learning many things about the world."

Seth inspected the padlocks. "Sister told me that your grandfather is a traditional healer. And a witch doctor."

Boniface glanced sideways at Seth. But he remained silent.

"Come, I will show you our chickens."

Behind the school and housing buildings, Boniface opened the gate to a wire-fenced coop. A healthy-looking flock of seven chickens ignored them as they pecked at the ground. Boniface bent down to scoop up a fluffy rust-colored bird.

"Looks like she knows you," Seth said with a smile.

"She is a friendly chicken." The young man held her against his chest and petted her before putting her down to join the others, "And she knows I will not fail to feed her."

"Do you know why Alex and I are visiting Africa?" Seth asked.

"Sister Bernice told me you have come from far away to learn more about the children of Africa."

"Hmm. That is true, but perhaps you noticed that Alex is an albino person who also looks like an African person?"

Boniface frowned. "Yes, and I have known such people living in this area. Here at St. Cecelia's, we have two albino children, Nico and Lilia."

"Yes, I'm looking forward to meeting them, and I know you are helping to keep them safe. Alex and I work for an organization that believes all human beings have the right to be respected and safe from harm. No humans are better than some other humans."

"You mean the *zeru zerus*."

"Do you call them that?"

Boniface looked down at the ground. "No, I know I should not. It's just common here. I believe as you do--to respect all people."

They left the chicken coop and walked toward the main school building, where Alex was talking with Sister Angelica.

Seth spoke to Boniface again. "It is because people with albinism are in danger here that we are talking to people who can help us understand why that is true. We were hoping that your grandfather could talk to us about the beliefs some people have about the magic of people with albinism."

Boniface stood still and looked at Seth. "No, no," he said, his eyes flashing in alarm. "Talking to my grandfather is not a good idea, sir. He has told me I am no longer his grandson. I think he may do deals with evil men who hurt and even kill . . ." His words faded out as he turned his head away.

"I'm sorry if I've upset you. Don't worry. We have other people to talk to. No need to bother your grandfather."

"Can I perhaps ask you a question?" Boniface said looking down at his own hands.

"Yes, of course. What do you want to know?"

"You are a black man, but you live in a country that is mostly white, no?"

Seth laughed briefly under his breath. "You have no idea how complicated that question is. I was born in Africa--in a country called Ethiopia, far north of here. Until I was ten, I was surrounded only by other black people. But since then, I have lived in several countries that are, like you say, mostly white."

"And in your country now--"

"England."

"Yes, in England, it is acceptable that you are a friend of an albino woman?"

Seth looked at Boniface, but the younger man kept his eyes on the ground. "I'm not sure how to answer you, my friend. You seem to be asking two questions. In England, it's fine to be friends with any woman. And as far as I am aware, there is no discrimination against albinos--male or female. We have a scientific explanation for people being born with this condition. They are the same as everyone else, with the same opportunities for education and careers."

"And that is true for black people in your country as well?"

Seth nodded. "Yes, for all people from any race or nation." He paused. "In theory at least." He sighed.

"That is good. I would like to go to England one day," Boniface said looking up with a smile.

44

Tanzanian Prison, 2013

Seth studied the man sitting in front of him at a rural detention facility located among the fields and farms about forty miles west of Arusha. In his late thirties, he was short but muscular, a grim look on his clean-shaven face. He was a farmer, and he and four other men had killed and mutilated his neighbor. Seth shivered as he involuntarily placed himself in the man's shoes, imagining how they ambushed Lucas, a twenty-eight-year-old albino man as he cultivated his fields, which were some distance from the farm where he lived with other family members.

Seth felt his stomach turning as he looked at the prisoner, but he spoke calmly to introduce himself and Alex and to tell him why they were there. Alex translated for both Seth and the prisoner.

"We're trying to understand," Seth said. "We're not here to judge you, but I may ask you some difficult questions. The prison officer has assured us that you will cooperate."

The prisoner sat silent in a chair a few feet from them. Neither his hands nor feet were bound. He nodded. He never looked at Alex although she was speaking the only words he understood.

"Why did you kill this man--Lucas?" Seth heard himself asking in a voice harsher than he had intended.

The prisoner looked away as if he might find an answer outside in the prison compound. Seth had seen him glance at Alex and quickly avert his eyes when the prison officer first brought him into the office for the interview.

"Some people sent us to that place to do it. He was just a ---" He did not finish his sentence.

Alex translated and then asked him in Swahili, "Did you mean to say that the farmer was just a *zeru zeru?*"

The prisoner looked at the floor as he folded and unfolded his hands. He remained silent.

"They must have promised you something for doing that?" Seth suggested in what he hoped was a neutral tone.

"They promised to pay ninety million shillings."

"For you?"

"For the five of us--to share."

"What did they tell you to do for that much money?"

"To go to the man's garden near the river to-- commit the offense."

"Who has so much money to spend on an act like this? And why?"

"I don't know. I don't know anyone with so much money."

"The brother of the murdered man took us to that garden near the river today," Seth said. "He told us that the body was mutilated and that many parts--limbs, tongue, internal organs, private parts--were taken. Did you help with this?"

Alex translated as best she could, her voice faltering as she remembered the gruesome details that Lucas's brother had related to them.

"I did." The prisoner's voice was steady, though he wouldn't meet Seth's eyes.

"How did you know what to do?"

"There was a man who gave us instructions, what to cut, what to take."

Seth remained silent as he took deep breaths. Then he asked, "Do you think it is acceptable to kill someone for money?"

The man glanced up at Seth's face for just an instant before staring down toward the floor. "No, it is not."

"Then why--?"

"Sometimes a man doesn't know what he is really doing. Satan takes over his body and his mind, and he does these things."

"Do you believe in witchcraft?"

"Yes, I do. Everyone here believes in witchcraft. It is part of who we are. The witch doctors are very powerful. I can only ask God for forgiveness now."

"You are a farmer?"

"Yes."

"If you have a good year after your harvest, how much could you expect to earn?"

"Maybe 400,000 shillings if things go well."

"So even splitting the money with the others, you would be a rich man. Did you get paid?"

The prisoner closed his eyes. His chin trembled slightly. "No."

"How long will you be in prison?" Seth asked.

"I don't know."

"Time's up," announced the prison officer who had been standing outside the open door. He took the man's arm to usher him out of the office. But the prisoner turned and, for the first time, looked directly at Alex. "People will look at you only as a deal. You are in great danger here."

"May God forgive you," Alex said softly in Swahili as she watched him leave.

Seth reached out to hold Alex's hand as Goodluck drove them back to Arusha. From time to time he glanced in the mirror, alert to the black car that followed them. He had noted it on several occasions. He had dismissed it at first, but by now, he was sure. He would not alarm Alex, however. Their security was his responsibility. He felt for the knife he kept strapped against his right shin.

45

Arusha, Tanzania, 2013

"Can I bring you a chai tea, Miss Alex?" the waiter asked she took her seat at their accustomed table near the courtyard window.

Alex smiled. "You are making me feel quite spoiled, Samuel. Yes, I would love a chai tea. How are you this morning?"

"Very well, thank you," he said with a slight bow of his head. "And your husband--he is coming soon? Shall I bring coffee?"

"Yes, he'll be here in a moment. Thank you."

Alex looked out at the smooth, greenish-yellow bark of the acacia tree. She had googled the species after talking to the waiter at the beginning of their stay almost three weeks ago. The "fever tree" variety was unusual in producing chlorophyll in its bark instead of its leaves. How had it evolved so differently? She knew only the basics of genetics, but she had learned in a high school science class that not all mutations proved to be advantageous. In certain isolated human populations where intermarriage was common, mutations that were ultimately harmful had appeared and were passed on to the following generations.

Is that what albinism was here in Africa--a harmful mutation? A death warrant? But for most other human populations, albinism often went unnoticed or was at least hardly worth noticing. In Tanzania and other

African countries, however, being born with white skin seemed almost synonymous with being evil. How had that idea begun and when? Was it built into humans to reject what was "other," to deny the reality of other beings because they were different from oneself?

"I see you are somewhere far away this morning," Seth said as he sat down across from her. "Is it one of your visions?"

"There you are! And you managed to find a newspaper. In English?"

"No, only Swahili, but I hoped you would read me the headlines." Seth grinned.

"I haven't had a vision," Alex said responding to his question. "But just being here makes me feel some vague sense of--I don't know, recognition--or recollection? Déjà vu? As if I can almost touch the thread that will lead me to an answer. Something I can't quite put my finger on."

The waiter appeared with two pots--one of chai tea and one of black coffee.

"Ah, good morning, Samuel," said Seth. "I would love to have some of those delicious *vitumba*."

"Just toast for me," Alex said, "but I'd like to ask you a favor, please."

The waiter nodded.

"We're planning to go back to St. Cecelia's today. I just fell in love with your beautiful grandchildren when we visited there, and now I'd very much like to meet your daughter. Please tell me her name and what time she usually picks the children up on Fridays."

"She will love to meet you--I have told her about you. She is not white like the little ones. Her name is

Miriam. She picks them up after work--around five o'clock after work."

When he left, Seth looked at Alex with raised eyebrows. "Are we thinking of going back to St. Cecelia's? Did you forget that we have an appointment this afternoon with Dr. Jackson--the surgeon at the hospital who has studied traditional healers? He knows a great deal about the witch doctors and how they have been registered by the government. I think it is important to speak with him."

"Yes, I agree. But I want to make the most of these last few days, and I've had an idea that I want to run by you." She took a sip of tea, frowning a bit. "Of course, I hope our work--our interviews and reports--will make a difference for people with albinism in this country, but I'm feeling frustrated. Impatient. Angry too if I'm honest. Change is so very slow."

"I understand, Lexy. But that's the nature of our work. We are the voices for those who are suffering. That's what we're here for."

"You're right, of course. But I have an idea. Please hear me out."

"I will always listen to your ideas," Seth said with an indulgent half-smile. He reached out to gently brush her cheek.

"I want to help those two kids, Nico and Lilia. To stay safe, to protect their skin, to make sure they can get glasses, to continue their education, and--to give them a chance to outlive the average age of people with albinism here in Africa. I know I can't help everyone, but I can do something to help them." Her eyes were bright with determination.

Seth put his coffee cup down in its saucer. "What exactly are you proposing, Lexy?"

"I want to make a long-term financial investment in these children. We know their grandfather is a hard-working man and a gentleman. We know their mother is also hard-working and determined to protect her children and send them to school. There is something about them that makes me feel--I don't know--close to my own roots, I suppose. I'm not wealthy, and I can't snap my fingers and change the deep beliefs about albinism in this society, but I can at least do something to help these two children. Does that sound ridiculous?"

Seth was silent, remembering how Alex had been determined to save a baby in Syria when bombs were dropping nearby. He loved this about her, yet he hesitated. They were there as agents of CAPE, with a job to do. Their interviews and analysis of the situation could help shape policy in the country and contribute to changing the current attitudes toward people with albinism. He understood her impatience. Many people were still in danger from those who would profit from the superstitions about them.

"No, not ridiculous. I love you for your kind heart, Lexy. I really don't know how much you can realistically do to protect Nico and Lilia. And I don't want to see you hurt, disappointed I mean, if you can't do it."

"Look at me, Seth. I was probably born here in this country, maybe right here in this city. For some reason--good or bad--I was taken away or stolen or even given away by my mother and father. I'll probably never know what happened. But if my parents were trying to protect me from danger, I can at least try to help Nico and Lilia.

They have a right to live safely and to have a chance to become the best people they can be."

"I understand this is very personal for you, Lexy." He reached for her hand and squeezed it. "I will do what I can to support you."

"Thank you, Seth. Now--this is what I must ask of you today. I want to be there at St. Cecelia's when their mother comes to pick them up. Goodluck can drop me off there before you go to interview Dr. Jackson at the hospital. It is only a couple of miles away and--"

"Wait! You know that I can't leave you there alone, Lexy. It's what we agreed to back at headquarters as a condition for allowing you to come to Tanzania. I am your only protection here. I can't allow you to be exposed to danger."

"But, Seth, it will only be for an hour--two at the most. And I won't be in any danger. I just want to take the baseball caps and sunglasses for all the children and talk to Nico's and Lilia's mother. It will be my way of paying back for the opportunities I've had in my life. I will be safe there. Please don't worry so much. I'll be fine." She smiled as she looked intently into his eyes. "You inspected the fencing and the locks yourself, and you know that Boniface will be there to keep us all safe."

Seth looked at the pleading expression in her violet-blue eyes. He recognized her lawyerly skills in laying out an argument. This idea must have been forming in her mind since their first visit to the orphanage. It was true that Boniface seemed a reliable and responsible young man--strong too. He thought of the planned interview with Dr. Jackson--a man who had studied and published articles on the ancient medical practices in Tanzania. His information would be valuable for their final report to CAPE.

He shook his head as if to clear it and then sighed. "Okay. I know how much this means to you, Lexy. I'll join you at St. Cecelia's after the interview. But you must promise to stay close to Boniface. I'll talk to him ahead of time." He paused, frowning. "It's a good thing this doctor speaks English," he added with a grin.

Alex reached over the table to touch his hand just as their waiter arrived and served their breakfast.

She took a bite of toast. "And now would you like me to scan the headlines of that paper for you?" She picked it up and glanced at the first page. She decided not to read an article with the headline, "Human Trafficking on the Rise in Region." It would only make Seth worry more. "Would you like to hear about the shortage of safari guides in the Serengeti?" she asked.

46

Arusha, Tanzania, 2013

Seth left the hospital looking at his watch. It was just after five o'clock. He had been so absorbed in Dr. Jackson's stories about local healers and witch doctors that he hadn't paid attention to the time. The young doctor was a Tanzanian who had gone to medical school in England. He had a special interest in traditional healers in his country and, more recently, he had published a journal article about the witch doctors and widespread beliefs among the people. He had also told Seth a great deal about crime syndicates that engaged in human trafficking of people with albinism.

Seth didn't immediately see Goodluck's Landcruiser outside the main door of the hospital. He walked toward the parking lot while pulling out his cell phone to call Goodluck. One bar flickered and disappeared on his phone. He walked a short distance, still looking for the tan SUV, and then tried the phone again. On the third try, Goodluck picked up.

"I'm on my way, sir," said Goodluck. "So sorry--but I had a bit of trouble. I'll tell you about it when I get there. I'm ten minutes away."

"Ten minutes? Please hurry. I'll be standing near the entrance doors."

Seth was struck by a sudden sense of impending doom as if a cold fog had enveloped him. Alex could be in danger. He shivered despite the heat. He tried calling Alex's cell phone, but it went straight to voice mail.

"Please call me when you get this, Lexy." He paused and then added, "I love you."

He was scrolling through his contacts to find a number for the orphanage when Goodluck pulled up at the curb.

"We've got to hurry, Goodluck. I've got a bad feeling," he said as he climbed in. He looked at the driver, who did not look like his usual calm self. Sweat beads were visible on Goodluck's forehead, his shirt had a streak of dirt on the collar, and he was unsmiling. "You okay, man?"

"I ran into some trouble. Two men--or boys maybe--I saw them, but too late--they let the air out of my back tires when I was at a local shop. I was gone only a few minutes--"

Seth frowned. "You saw them?"

"Running away when I returned."

"You didn't know them?"

"I don't think so. I didn't get a good look--but they looked young--troublemakers I guess."

The sun was close to the horizon now. Seth glanced at his watch again. "Please, we need to go as fast as you can. I think Alex may be in danger."

"Yes, sir. I will get us there quickly."

Goodluck was an experienced and excellent driver, used to driving under all kinds of conditions within the Serengeti Park. He drove the Landcruiser nimbly and faster than Seth would have dared toward the orphanage.

Seth was thinking about how people in this country stared openly at Alex as if she wasn't quite a real person. Dr. Jackson had explained that in the eyes of many people, maiming or killing albinos was justified because they were ghosts to be feared and, besides, one couldn't kill something already dead.

His whole being buzzed now with the thought that Alex could be in danger. He should never have agreed to leave her at St. Cecelia's. He argued with himself to regain his mental focus. He willed himself to be calm. He told himself that his fears were exaggerated because of what he had heard from Dr. Jackson. He reminded himself that he had visited the orphanage, he had inspected their security measures, and he had talked with Boniface about the need for tight security. Sister Angelica was able to call the local police station on a direct line at any time on her landline. There were fences--wooden fences it was true but topped with barbed wire--surrounding the facility. *Everything will be okay. Please, please be okay, Lexy. Please.*

When they reached the place along the road where the path to the orphanage began, his pulse jumped when he saw a large black car with tinted windows parked at the side of the road. Blood pounded in his ears. All that Dr. Jackson had told him about crime syndicates and human trafficking flashed through his mind. They pulled up behind the car. Seth jumped out and started up the path.

"I'm coming with you, boss," Goodluck called out.

"Follow me at a distance, Goodluck. It could be dangerous. Stay out of sight."

Now, he was in the intensely focused zone that he knew well from his army training. He was alert to the direction of the wind and any small movement in his environment. He moved fast and with stealth. Within a few minutes, his ears picked up the sound of male voices and the screeching of angry crows in the trees ahead. He had one focus. *Lexy, where are you, Lexy?*

47

St. Cecelia's Orphanage and School, 2013

Alex stood watching Nico and Lilia, who were waiting for their mother just inside the high wooden gate of the orphanage. Miriam arrived every Friday after work to take them home for the weekend. The children were dancing around wearing their blue New York Yankees caps and sunglasses, which Alex had thought to pack in case they would have the opportunity to visit a school.

Earlier, she had stood in front of the classroom and shown the fascinated children pictures of herself as a child--probably around eight-years-old. She had described Southern California beaches and what it was like to swim in the ocean. The salty waves, she told them, could sometimes be very big and make loud crashing sounds on the shore. Sea birds, called gulls and pelicans, often flew over the water and the sand. She described the magical world where she had happily spent much of her childhood. The students were especially interested in a picture where she was standing on the beach with a boogie board. The ocean waves were behind her, and she was wearing a long-sleeved shirt, a baseball cap, and sunglasses, all to protect her sensitive skin from the sun's rays. She explained that she wore sunscreen every day.

Around 5:00 pm, Sister Angelica walked down to join them at the gate. "I just got a call from Miriam," she said to Alex. "Unfortunately, she had to stay overtime

"

at the clinic today. She sent her apologies and asked if Boniface could walk the children home. She'll meet them there. He's just finishing up a chore, but I've let him know, and he's on his way. I'm so sorry--I know how much you were hoping to talk with Miriam, Alex."

"Well, I'll walk down the path with them and Boniface. Seth should have been here already, so we'll probably meet him on his way up the hill. Then he can drive us all back to town and take the children home. We can wait with them until Miriam returns."

"If you're sure Seth is on his way--"

"Oh, yes. He's coming from an interview at a hospital in Arusha. He is probably walking up the path right now."

Boniface appeared and greeted Alex and Sister Angelica as he watched the children running and tagging each other. "These children are looking very chic--is that the right word?"

Alex laughed. "That's a French word, but we use it in English, too. Yes--a good word to describe them."

Sister Angelica took Alex's hand. "Goodbye again, dear Alex. Thank you again for your generous gifts to the children. We will stay in touch." And then she returned to her office.

Boniface unlocked the padlocks, let them walk through the gate, and locked them up again.

"Boniface," Alex said, reaching into her backpack, "I happen to have one more baseball cap, just for you. Perhaps it will help you study to qualify for the courses you told me about."

He grinned and put the hat on backward. "Like the guys in the American movies, yes?" Then he made a slight bow and said, "I am grateful to the beautiful lady from America."

"I've been thinking," said Nico as they started walking, "about that ocean and the big waves that could knock you over. How did your glasses stay on when you went there?"

"You know, that's a good question, Nico. My glasses were attached to a croakie--hmm, I don't know the word in Swahili. It is like a thin strap--so if my glasses fell, they would just fall around my neck. My regular glasses had a croakie too."

"Where are your glasses now?" Lilia asked.

"Somewhere in my backpack. I don't need them for everything, but when I read or work on my computer, I can't do without them. That's one thing I want to talk to your mother about--having an eye doctor examine your eyes. It would make schoolwork much easier."

They walked in a single file down the path toward the line of eucalyptus trees that someone must have planted years ago to screen St. Cecelia's from the road. Alex admired their graceful shape, but the medicinal smell made her wary--without reason, she told herself.

And then, a smell stronger than the eucalyptus reached her nose, and she stopped dead. "Wait, wait!" she said in a loud whisper. Boniface and the children stopped and looked back at her. It was the acrid smell of male perspiration carried on a slight breeze. She was sure of it. Her muscles became taut, and she was ready to flee, but of course, she couldn't do that. She would protect these children as if they were her own.

A large-bellied man dressed in a gray suit and shiny black shoes stepped out from behind a tree and smiled at the small group. A scar ran down the side of his face. A moment later, another man appeared from among the trees. He was short but well-muscled, his head shaved to a bristly gray. He carried a machete at his side.

"Well, well, well," said the man in the suit. "Look what we have here. It is our old friend Kaj, who disapproved of us and left without even collecting his money. Too good for us, eh, Kaj? It's been a long time."

"And that's the lady we've been following--the one from the airport," said the shorter man.

"Then we are lucky to have a bonus today," said the big man in the suit. "And you, my friend," he said looking at Boniface, you could also be lucky if you do just as I tell you."

The children were clinging to Alex's legs. Alex felt terror in the grip of their small fingers.

Without a word, Boniface reached for a knife he kept sheathed at his waist, and jumped at the large-bellied man, stabbing him in the neck. They fell to the ground together as the man with a machete came toward her and the children, who were screaming.

Alex pushed Nico and Lilia behind her and swung a foot up with all her strength to his groin. He dropped the machete and went down onto his knees, groaning loudly. She looked over at Boniface struggling with the man in the gray suit beneath him, and then she heard a gunshot. Boniface fell backward. The man was bleeding profusely from his neck wound, but he got to his knees and aimed a gun at her and the children.

She ran toward him, ready to fling herself against him. *I will protect these children. Even if I die doing it.*

Another shot rang out as Seth jumped from behind the man in the suit and knocked the gun from his hand. In a blur, Alex watched him punch the man down to the ground, where he lay motionless. Then he went after the short man who was reaching for the machete. Seth locked his arms around the man's neck, pulled them around to his back, and tied them with his belt. He picked up the gun and the machete.

Goodluck emerged from the path and stood horrified as he stared at the scene before him. "Miss Alex, are you okay?"

Alex had pulled the children close to her, one under each arm. She wanted to run, to fly, to escape. But something was wrong, a strange weakness in her limbs, a fog drifting over her. She looked down to see blood dripping from her shoulder onto Nico's cap. A sharp pain pulsed through her. "I have to sit . . . a minute," she said releasing the children and falling to her knees. In a moment, Seth was by her side.

48

St. Cecelia's Orphanage and School, 2013

The loud noise and the children's screams brought Sister Angelica running outside her office toward the gate, her blue gown swirling at her ankles. Sister Bernice appeared at her side a minute later. They peered down the path leading to the road.

"That was the sound of gunshots," said Sister Angelica. "And the screams of Nico and Lilia! Oh, dear God, no, no, no."

She tented her hands and held them up to her lips as she closed her eyes for a few seconds. In a calm voice, she said, "Sister Bernice, go call the police station. They must come immediately, and they must send an ambulance too. And tell Sister Ursula to take all the children into the classroom, lock the door, and keep them quiet. I'm going down the path to look for Nico and Lilia. Lock the gate after me."

"But, Sister," Sister Bernice said. "You could end up getting hurt."

"Then we will just have to depend on Him," Sister Angelica said as she fumbled with her keys at the padlocks.

"Yes, Sister. I'll make the call and talk to Sister Ursula, and then I'll follow you."

Sister Angelica heard no further gunshots, but she could see people at the line of eucalyptus trees. Several crows were making frantic squawking noises from their perch above as if calling for help.

"Nico! Lilia!" Sister Angelica called as she tried to run on the uneven ground. Her heart leaped up when she saw the two little figures running up the path toward her, and she paused to catch her breath.

"Boniface got shot," said Nico breathlessly as he drew closer. "And he's not moving." He began sobbing.

"Oh, thank God, you have been spared," Sister Angelica whispered. Then more loudly, she asked, "Did anyone else get hurt?"

"Yes," said Lilia, who arrived a few minutes behind her older brother. "Alex has a lot of blood on her blouse. She said she had to sit down." The child looked bewildered as she looked toward Sister Angelica.

"And those bad men are lying down on the ground," said Nico through tears. "Seth punched them so they can't hurt us. He has a knife."

Sister Angelica hoisted Lilia into her arms and hugged Nico against her skirts. "God has protected you. Everything will be all right now."

She glanced up toward the orphanage. Sister Bernice was on her way hurrying toward them. "Sister Bernice, please take Nico and Lilia back up to the orphanage. I must go and see if I can help. And I'll wait for the police."

*　*　*

Seth tore a piece of cloth from his own shirt and pressed it against the wound on Lexy's shoulder. Alex seemed stunned as she sat still on the ground looking up at him. "I'm bleeding," she said in a flat voice. Bright red blood was quickly soaking her blouse. "I'm so sleepy."

"You're going to be okay, Lexy. You took a bullet in your shoulder. We just need to stop the bleeding. You're going to be okay." He leaned her back to lie down against her backpack.

Seth looked over at Boniface, who lay unmoving several feet away. Seth heard groans of pain from one of their attackers. The big man lay silent and unmoving in a pool of blood.

Seth had kept his focus and disarmed the thugs, but now his mind was flooded with thoughts of catastrophe, and his hands were shaking as he pressed against Alex's wound.

"Goodluck--you're here! Can you get in touch with the police? And--I'm going to need the Land Rover."

"Yes, yes, of course," said Goodluck pulling out his phone. "Here are the keys."

When Sister Angelica appeared, Seth thought he had never been so grateful. *She must have heard the gunshots and the screams.*

"Sister! Thank God you're here," he said. "Can you see if you can help Boniface? He's been shot in the chest. Alex was shot too. I'm trying to stop the bleeding."

"Boniface!" she cried out, kneeling next to the young man and putting her head to his chest. "He's still breathing." Tearing the scarf from her head, she pressed it against the wound on his chest.

"We need to get them both to the hospital," said Seth. "I'm going to drive them. You won't have any trouble with these guys now, but here is my gun, Goodluck, just in case."

Sister Angelica shook her head. "The police are on their way. Are you okay, Seth? You're not injured?"

"I'm fine, Sister. Stay here with Boniface while I take Alex to the car. Goodluck will be here with you. I'll come back for Boniface."

Seth picked Alex up, carried her down to the road, and placed her in the passenger seat of the Land Rover. She was barely conscious. He knew he had to get her help quickly.

With Goodluck's help, he hoisted an unconscious Boniface on his shoulder and was able to walk down the path and place him in the back seat of the vehicle.

He drove as fast as he could along the rutted road, heading back to the hospital where he had been an hour earlier. He glanced back at Boniface a few times but saw no movement.

Alex seemed to be in and out of consciousness. "The children--Nico and Lilia?" she asked, her eyes half open.

"They're fine, Lexy. They're safe with the Sisters. Keep talking to me, Lexy. I need you to stay awake." *I can't lose you, Lexy. Please hold on.*

"We're almost at the hospital. The doctors will take good care of you," he told her. "Please talk to me. I love you more than anything in the world."

She opened her eyes wide. "You are a good man, Seth Melaku. I love you too." She smiled before losing consciousness again.

49

Arusha, Tanzania, 2013

When Alex awoke lying in a white-sheeted hospital bed, it took her a minute to understand that she had been dreaming about her infancy during the deep haze of anesthesia. The beings she had called "the light people" since her childhood were more solid to her now. Her visit to Charlotte Canfield outside London, and her recent conversation with Dr. Espinoza about her memory had persuaded her to trust those strange visions as actual memories, not figments of her imagination, not hallucinations.

But the dreams she experienced under anesthesia now made sense of everything, and they were vivid in her memory. She recalled those cold hands clutching her as she tried to escape back into the arms of the screaming woman *who must have been her mother*. Alex's heart started pounding in her chest. Charlotte Canfield hadn't been honest with her, she realized now. Charlotte was the woman with the cold hands, and the man with the beard and mustache was her husband. The Canfields must have forcibly taken her from her mother. And they had flown with her on an airplane, though she had no idea of that at the time. But her body remembered, and some part of that experience was buried in her brain as an image. She knew now that it was all true. All of that had happened to her.

Why? And what were the circumstances that allowed the couple to take her from her mother? Where had her father been? She thought about what Sister Angelica had told her about parents who had abandoned children because the parents were sick and couldn't care for them. And she had learned that infants who were born with albinism sometimes just "disappeared" soon after birth, without explanation or investigation. And that it was not uncommon for fathers of such children to reject them as well as their wives, even accusing their wives of having slept with a white man. Is that what happened to her? Did her father reject her? Had her mother been terribly ill?

She thought about their dining room server, Mr. Juma, at the hotel. He had warned them on their very first day of the dangers in this country for people with albinism. She had felt something familiar in him. Even the white columns outside the hotel had given her a sense of déjà vu. Had she been here before? Had Arusha once been her home?

She wanted to stay awake to figure all this out, but she fell back into a light sleep. When she awoke again, a nurse was at her side taking her blood pressure and her temperature.

"Good, you're awake," the nurse said. "Your vital signs are fine. And we are hearing that you are quite a hero." She smiled at Alex. "How are you feeling?"

"I need to see my friend--Seth. I have to get out of this bed."

"Easy now, darling. You've had a bullet removed from your shoulder, and you'll need a little recovery time. I'm bringing you some juice. I believe your friend is waiting outside. You'll see him soon."

In her mind, she relived the moment when Seth had appeared out of nowhere to deal with the attackers. Silent, efficient, and quick like the special forces military officer he had been. Her heart was flooded with warmth as she remembered his look of tender concern and his whispered "I love you" as she was being wheeled into an operating room. Minutes later, she was counting backward from ten with a mask on her face, falling into the oblivion of sleep.

50

Arusha, Tanzania, 2013

When the doctor pronounced Alex well enough to be released from the hospital, she and Seth went to visit Boniface, who was on another floor in the hospital. They had breathed a sigh of relief when they learned that his condition had improved from critical to stable, but he would have to spend a few more days in recovery. They found Sister Angelica at his bedside murmuring prayers and holding her rosary.

Kaj--they learned for the first time that Boniface's given name was Kaj--greeted them with his charming smile. Seth and Alex told him how the police had visited with them and praised the three of them for capturing Mr. M and his thug. The officers had explained that their attackers were part of a human trafficking ring that was involved in kidnapping, maiming, and killing people with albinism in Tanzania, Malawi, and Kenya.

They spent some time reliving the details of the ordeal they had shared. They told each other how each of them experienced those few minutes beneath the eucalyptus trees near St. Cecelia's. All of them remembered the crows cawing madly above them. They wondered at the forces that had brought each of them there at that point in time. They played out some what-ifs. What if Miriam had been able to pick up her children that Friday afternoon as she usually did and was alone on the path with them? What if Seth had arrived five minutes later than he did? What if Alex had not been on the path with Kaj and the children? What if Kaj had not had his knife? What if Alex had not learned self-defense tactics as part of her job training?

The three of them turned to Sister Angelica, who had been listening with a half-smile on her face, as if she were listening to children's chatter. "What did you think of all this, Sister?" Alex asked.

"My heart is full of gratitude and praise to God-- and joy that all of you are here alive and well. Boniface-- Kaj, I am so proud of you for putting yourself in great danger to protect your friends. Greater love hath no man ... I'm so glad it did not cost you your life, dear boy. May He bring you to good health once again."

Kaj smiled and reached out a hand to Sister Angelica.

Alex looked around at their unlikely group in amazement. She doubted anyone could explain how individual life pathways come together, how their paths cross each other at crucial moments. She wondered at the unseen forces that had brought each of them together at that precise moment in time. How could a woman who had been born in Africa but brought up in Southern California cross the path of a man who had been born a black Jew in Ethiopia and made *aliyah* to Israel during the secret airlift that was Operation Solomon? And how had their two pathways intersected with that of a man born in a hut in rural Tanzania, grandson of a traditional healer and witch doctor? Their lives had come together like different colors in a kaleidoscope briefly creating new and beautiful patterns.

51

Arusha, Tanzania, 2013

I am growing old now, my hair more gray than black. But the memory of my lost child burns as brightly as ever. I will rejoice with Miriam and Samuel that my precious grandchildren have been saved from unspeakable horrors--snatched from the jaws of something far worse than a lion. And I will soon welcome the foreigners who were full of courage and compassion, determined to keep my grandbabies safe. Sister Angelica would say that they were sent by the God that the Sisters have taught me about since childhood. But I have long ago given up on that God. I stopped believing in him when he allowed my own treasure, my own tiny perfect daughter, to be stolen right out of my arms and taken to another world where I could not follow.

All these years, even when Miriam was born to us, I have silently blamed that God and longed for my Annika, my beautiful, first-born daughter. Samuel and I survived together only because I finally understood that he was convinced that he was saving her. And who knows? Perhaps he did. Does she live in England now with those cruel people? Is she happier than she would have been with us, her parents? He would say--perhaps not happier, but she has a better chance of being alive. Yes, I have forgiven my husband. But now I am brought to tears again as my sweet Nico and Lilia could have been snatched from me as well. Does God test us with such unthinkable horrors?

Sometimes, I lie in bed with Samuel snoring softly beside me, and I think about my Annika. I can see her beautiful face still. And that gives me hope that she is indeed alive and well somewhere in this world. Sam told me there are over seven billion people living on the Earth, but he couldn't really explain a billion to me. More than we could count, he said. Even if we counted every day for a year. My Annika is out there among the billions, but I will hold on to the memory of her violet-blue eyes and white lashes, her crown of white curls and that one little spot of color on the back of her neck. These memories are all I have. But they are enough for me to feel her again in my arms, to feel again how I first became a mother attached forever to my beloved child.

52

Arusha, Tanzania, 2013

Two days after Alex had been released from the hospital, she and Seth climbed up three flights of stairs and stood at the door of an apartment in Arusha.

Seth gently adjusted the sling on Alex's arm and was about to knock on the door. He squinted at her in the dim light of the hallway. Patches of pink glowed on her cheeks, and her eyes looked glazed. "Are you sure you're feeling okay, Lexy?"

"Seth!" Alex grabbed his arm. "This will sound weird, I know, but I've been here. I'm sure of it. Can you hear the tuk-tuks from the street? I've heard that sound in so many visions, but I never knew what it was. It was always the tuk-tuks!"

Seth looked at her. "I hear them. And it's not weird. After all you've told me, I no longer have any doubts about your memories or your visions."

As the apartment door swung open, they were greeted by two very excited children.

"Alex! Alex!" Lilia lifted her arms toward Alex, while Nico danced around them.

Alex laughed as she knelt and reached out to hug them both with her good arm. "I'm so happy to see you two. You remember Seth--he's our hero!" she said to them. "He doesn't speak much Swahili, but if you want to ask him anything, I can translate for you."

The children smiled shyly and thanked Seth, who was carrying gifts for them--puzzles, some candy, and boxes of crayons. He smiled as he said their names and handed the gifts to them.

"You are both heroes or perhaps angels," a low female spoke behind them, "and I am forever in your debt."

Alex looked up from the children to a dark-skinned woman with kind eyes and a warm smile. Perhaps a couple of years younger than Alex, she was almost as tall. Her black hair was pulled back in an elegant bun. Colorful beaded earrings dangled near her bronze cheeks.

"You must be Miriam," Alex said, standing to greet her. A sensation of something like electricity raced through her veins as she stared at the woman's face. She wasn't one of the light people, but there was something . . . She held Miriam's hand in hers. "I've been wanting so much to meet you--talk to you. I adore your sweet children." *This is what I might look like if I were born with dark skin.*

"The children have told me so much about you and your kindness, Alex. They are especially fascinated to hear about how you swim and ride a boogie board in the great ocean in California!" She laughed lightly and Alex laughed too.

"And here is my father," said Miriam. "I owe it to Dad that you visited St. Cecelia's and met my Nico and Lilia. So he has played a part in protecting them too."

"We are also in his debt," said Seth putting his hand out in greeting. I'm pleased to meet you, Miriam. Good to see you too, Mr. Juma. Thank you for inviting us to your home."

"Please, I hope you will call me Samuel now. We are like family because you put yourselves in mortal danger to protect my grandchildren. I give you my deepest thanks for keeping them safe. But I am also so sorry that you have suffered,' he said looking at Alex's sling.

"I'm fine, really, Mr. Juma--I mean, Samuel. I owe a lot to Seth and Kaj, our real heroes. This sling is just to keep me from moving my arm too much. I'll be fine in a couple of days, and we'll be traveling back to New York."

Sister Angelica, dressed in her usual blue robe, spoke up then. "Dear Alex and Seth!" She placed both hands over her heart. "Seeing you here makes my heart sing with praises to God for bringing all of you through this terrible trial."

"We are so glad to see you again, Sister Angelica," said Alex. "Has Kaj been released from the hospital yet?"

"Not quite, but the doctor said he may come home in a few more days. He's doing well and sends his love to you."

Miriam called to her mother, who was busy in the kitchen. "Mama, leave the cooking for a minute, and come meet Alex and Seth, our heroes."

The children's grandmother was drying her hands on a dish towel when she emerged from the tiny kitchen.

This is my mother," said Miriam, putting her arm around a thin woman with graying hair and a welcoming smile. "Her name is Lily."

"Lily, I'm delighted to--" said Alex. She stopped mid-sentence. In the next moment, she felt wrapped in a brilliant white light, and she thought she might faint. She could still hear the tuk-tuks on the street below, and she was aware of others in the room, but the wheel that had been carrying her through time seemed now to have reversed itself. Suddenly, everything here was familiar. She knew this place, these sounds, these smells. She knew these people.

"Don't let this be a dream," Alex whispered in English. For a moment, she felt unable to move, her body stiff, her heart thumping, and her mind racing to understand what was happening.

"Lexy, are you okay, my dearest?" Seth asked taking her arm.

"We are at the home of Samuel and Lily," she said to him softly in English. "Sam and Lily."

"Yes--the children's grandparents," he said unsure of whether she was making a statement or asking a question.

"Lily. A lily is a flower," Alex said as she gazed at the older woman.

Lily was staring back at Alex with one hand up to her mouth and the other stretched out to the wall to support herself. Her dark eyes were focused on Alex. "You look so much like Miriam . . .I thought for a moment . . ."

Samuel came to stand at his wife's side. "Here, Lily, I think you need to sit down. You don't look so good."

"Lily," whispered Alex. "You are Lily." She put her hand up to her lips and then started talking rapidly. "Mrs. Canfield said your name was a flower. And I have a photo of us--you and Samuel holding me as an infant. In front of a hospital, I think. I've studied that tiny picture--it's you! You are my mother."

She turned to look toward Mr. Juma. "And you are my father--Sam!"

Samuel searched her face, unable to say anything.

Nico and Lilia, who had been examining their new crayons now grew quiet. So did everyone else in the room.

Lily held on to her husband's arm and spoke. "Yes! You are my Annika. My baby. I have longed for you every day of my life, but I never dreamed I would see you again." She spoke softly, tears ran down her bronze cheeks.

The two women, mother and child, fell into each other's arms as everyone watched in awe.

Samuel put his arms around both women as he sobbed. He caught sight then of a tiny heart-shaped bit of color, a birthmark, on the nape of Alex's neck. The spot he had gently kissed in the taxi the day he had said a silent good-bye to her, the day she was taken to England by Dr. Canfield and his wife. This was indeed their Annika.

The wheel of time had not reversed, Alex realized. It had come full circle. She could let go now of the visions and the light people. Those memories, embedded so deeply in her mind, had proven to be important after all, just as she had sensed as a small child. Some primal aspect of her brain had preserved the love of her parents deeply within her pointing the way to this reunion.

There would be time to ask questions and listen to explanations. But right now, nothing mattered but the fact that she had found her mother and father--and a sister, a nephew, and a niece besides. She was filled with a gratitude and a lightness that made her feel she was floating above all of it, observing smiles and tears on all the faces in the room including her own.

I'm only eight, Sam, but one day, we will find them, and then we will understand.

Acknowledgments

Zeru Zeru Girl, although the product of my imagination, also reflects the reality of people who are suffering every day somewhere in the world. The novel also celebrates those who go beyond themselves to be compassionate and to do whatever good they can to help those who suffer. I have gathered information for this book through research, travel, books of both fiction and non-fiction, videos, articles, and the deeply felt experiences of both me and so many people I have encountered along my path. I am grateful for all of these resources, which have allowed me to take a journey with and learn from the characters of *Zeru Zeru Girl.*

The seed of this novel was planted on a trip I took to Tanzania, under the guidance of Overseas Adventure Travel, with remarkable guides, Boniface and Goodluck Godson Kombe. My concern for the mistreatment of people with albinism led me to read about conditions in several African countries, and to the work of various organizations including the United Nations and Under the Same Sun, which are working to educate and change attitudes among the population, while also providing help to victims. The human rights organization in this book, CAPE, is fictional but loosely based on Human Rights Watch, an international organization that continues to investigate and report violations of human rights all over the world. I am deeply grateful to those who put themselves in danger on the chance that their witness to suffering will make a difference.

I wish to thank editors Mark Spencer and Craig Hillsley for their close reading, encouraging words, and suggestions for helping this novel come alive for the reader. I am also grateful to family and friends who have encouraged me during endless hours of writing, especially my beloved Mia Rose Kerr Davis and Lisa Davis. And good friends who have read the entire manuscript, some more than once, with goodwill, kind words, and emotional support--Marty Graner, Coni Marchant, Barry Sommer, Don Rooks, and Chris Knox. Thank you also to Leigh Farrell and Lyn Hardy who read some early excerpts and offered their suggestions.

About the Author

Barbara Kerr is the author of, *Emotional Intelligence for a Compassionate World*, a workbook for adults; *Laughter for Shazpara*, a novel for middle-grade youngsters; *You Can Choose Your Own Life: Stories for Decision Making*, an interactive book about decision making for middle-school kids, written with co-author Barry Sommer. Barbara loves living near the Pacific Ocean in Southern California, and she is grateful for family, friends, her dog, hummingbirds, and the growing family of crows who visit her balcony every day to dine.